THE CHEF, THE BIRD
AND THE BLESSING

THE CHEF, THE BIRD AND THE BLESSING

Andrew Sharp

Matador
9 Priory Business Park,
Wistow Road, Kibworth Beauchamp,
Leicestershire. LE8 0RX
Tel: 0116 279 2299
Email: books@troubador.co.uk
Web: www.troubador.co.uk/matador
Twitter: @matadorbooks

ISBN 978 1800463 929

British Library Cataloguing in Publication Data.
A catalogue record for this book is available from the British Library.

Printed and bound in Great Britain by 4edge Limited
Typeset in 11pt Adobe Garamond Pro by Troubador Publishing Ltd, Leicester, UK

Matador is an imprint of Troubador Publishing Ltd

Not all who ask for the impossible are refused
Swahili proverb

Chapter 1

In the thin soup of the fading night, I almost collided on my bicycle with a grey and absent-minded elephant. It straddled the dirt track, as motionless as a stuffed exhibit in a museum. I smelt its sour and grassy breath and sensed its crushing weight on the gravel. I retreated, quick time, to linger behind a tree, suffering a nervous fidget as I waited for it to vacate the way. I, Chef Mlantushi, head chef —no less— at BOD-W safaris, could not be late for work that morning. There were VIP guests to prepare for, one of whom excited my highest expectation.

The elephant was in no particular hurry, but after I had endured a tiresome ten minutes it broke the silence by relieving itself, pouring like a punctured water tank. Finding its standing place puddled, it moved off into the bush with a dipping gait, coiling its trunk playfully around its ivories as if it had found it amusing to delay me.

Where there is one elephant, there are always more nearby, stealing through the bush as silent as smoke. I wasted no time. I hoofed the pedals, urgent as the creatures of the night —porcupines, civets, servals— which I saw scurrying to their burrows, fearful of being spotlighted by the sun. A sloping hyena appeared ahead on the track to feast its soulless but hungry black eyes on me, and then as quickly vanished, to haunt my passage. Its panting left a fresh meat odour on the track. Every morning I risked my life on my way to my duties. The authorities should have provided street lighting and constructed strong fences beside the way. How could citizens safely go about their business?

As always, I had been first up in the village, setting off at four forty-six hours, leaving my good wife sleeping. The glow of the milky way had guided my passage; a billion bright worlds, like my beckoning dreams of career advancement. I had passed the thick fences of barbed euphorbia which protected the village from roaming predators, and which bottled milky sap to scald the skin of the unsuspecting. Then past the standpipe from where I collected water. Soon, I was away from the fug of village woodsmoke that lingered from the evening and was breathing the so-called fresh air of the bush. But I was not fooled. The air was in no way hygienic but was infested with spores and furtive odours. No, nothing out there was what the innocent tourists believed it to be.

The track twisted like an animal path through the scrub next to the National Park but I sported no cycle light. I had no wish to attract moths to frighten me with their soft but strong flapping if they became trapped inside my shirt. I accidentally cut in two a black serpent of marching ants, crossing the track in a risky search for moisture. The rains should have started but the weather had altered these last seasons, causing creatures to grow restless; to want to escape to a better place.

I arrived at last at five twenty-three hours just as the stars checked out above the east horizon. In the pasty light, my employer's thatched dwelling resembled an abandoned mound of timber and old bricks scruffily haired with hay. No home should have been there, out alone in the wild like that, with only crooked trees and spikey bushes as neighbours. Beyond, the scrub spread in a tangle of perils and mysteries as far as I dared imagine. But soon the sun's fierce light would sear across the bush, stirring the crawlies in the thatch and the ants in the timber. Its heat would dry twigs and leaves to powder.

I parked my transport against the broken wall of the outhouse and started the moody generator by the hazardous operation of a squeaking fuel pump and a sparking together of wires. I coughed out the smoke and entered the house by the back door. A night fowl alarmed its last, the quivering call shivering my spine. I took great comfort to be indoors.

In the kitchen, I shined the sink to Presidential palace standards although I hasten to say that the inside of my employer's abode was little better than the outside and by no means a place of national pride. Conversely, it was a sad disgrace due to his disordered practices and his lack of aspirations. Despite this, I strived to maintain a suitable standard for our illustrious guests. The red cement floors were cracked but I waxed them to a grade so smooth that a person who walked on them in socks —in the way of my employer's English birders— found difficulty in remaining upright. I swept away curling skins of yellowing paint fallen from the ceiling, two lost beetles and a scouting patrol of ants.

Everything sanitised to my specification, I hotted the iron in the kitchen annex, took an apron and pressed it with said iron, utilising a firm hand. I lifted the garment to my eye and exclaimed 'Ha!' to myself. I ran my finger along the so-white fabric to confirm it conquered. I attired myself. What a fine pleasure to feel the apron's warmth against my stomach and smelling like a fresh baked bread. I tied the apron in a two-knot bow behind my back. There is no more shameful sight than a head chef whose apron strings have come undone.

After placing my employer's breakfast on the veranda under a net to protect it from the flies, I prepared the finest alfresco luncheon for our VIP guests Miss Camlyn and Mr Summerberg:

green mealie fritters with tangy avocado cream, carpaccio of smoked ostrich with nasturtiums, pickled bream, cherry and pecan nut cookies. I placed a bottle of my home-made granadilla and mint cordial into the cool box. That cordial was always a big deal with guests. Indeed, I hoped that Miss Camlyn and Mr Summerberg would say (in the fashion of their native tongue) that they were 'blown away', although it was the lady who excited my highest expectation. According to my employer, she was a prosperous notable who owned restaurants in the greatest cities of the world. What an opportunity was arriving for a young chef with noble ambitions, such as myself. She would deliver me from that woeful place and her gracious patronage would undoubtedly lead to fantastical benefits.

Certainly, I reasoned, Miss Camlyn would wish to complete the satisfaction of her diners by placing me in a high-end chef position in her restaurants. It is true that I indulged a harmless fantasy. Before long, famous food pundits would write *Head Chef Mlantushi has excelled himself again with this sumptuous dish of black sesame bavarois dacquoise with fennel and Alpine strawberries.* Yes, top professional realisation was my sure destination.

The only disquiet on my mind as I prepared for our two guests was this: I hoped that they planned to marry. My wife would ask me if this was so. She was a full immersion member of the Divine Prosperity Assembly and so valued purity and piety and did not like to imagine me being exposed to —and so corrupted by— Westerners living sinfully. In bygone days she was not so exacting, I tried to forget.

My devotion was interrupted by Mr Bin, my employer. He stumbled uninvited through the kitchen door whilst I folded a snack of smoked marlin pancakes. With regret, I have to report that he was in shorts and bare feet, like a village boy. A boy who had grown far too tall for his class. His hair was a heap of charcoal having not yet found a comb and his face begged a razor. Some guests titled him The White Tribesman, they finding that he was birthed and reared north of the Zambezi, just like an indigenous. But he was not truly indigenously indigenous, being the child of an expatriate Irish female and a South African male with a work permit for digging copper and gold. But Mr Bin himself was not a fly-in-fly-out expatriate like his mother or a business visitor from way down south like his father, although he had schooled there. But all could see that he was not skinned as an indigenous. I concluded that his was a criss-cross, problematic identity. He no doubt had two passports, just in case.

He finished dressing himself, fumbling his shirt buttons with fingers that had not yet woken up, rubbing the doze from his eyes and huffing and grumbling.

'Jeez Mozzy, why didn't you wake me man? I've got clients to pick up. I'm going to be late.'

His furry little night ape, hearing he was awake, streaked through the door, sprang onto his shoulder and stared at me in a threatening fashion as was its custom. It bobbed up and down whist it held onto Mr Bin's ear with its tight little claw hand and its long tail straggled around Mr Bin's neck. Mr Bin chuckled baby-like and said *hi* to the ape, raising an arm to scratch its neck.

I arranged the pancakes on a porcelain plate delicately decorated with a floral fuss, suitably fine for illustrious guests. 'Mr Bin, you're the gentleman with the difficulties.' I presented to my employer a disappointed countenance although this had not previously been conducive to changing his performance. 'I've politely informed you that I'm the company head chef. Not your carer. Nor your domestic servant. In any case ... I'll not enter your bedroom. It causes me great offence. It's like the rubbish dump of a shanty town. No one should live in such squalor.'

Mr Bin indulged himself in a foolish smile and said, 'Eish! You're on form this morning, Mozzy, and let me remind you ... it's Ben. B E N. Not Mr and not Bin.'

'Then I'd like to respectively remind you,' I said with all tolerance, 'it's Savalamuratichimimozi. Not Mozzy. I'm asking you again to make the minor effort to learn my name. If I learn yours ... you must learn mine. The colonial period is long past —two generations ago. As a point of fact, in a top establishment you'd address me as Chef Mlantushi.' I fashioned napkins for the safari picnic into the form of crowned cranes. 'And furthermore ... kindly stay out of the kitchen. This is my place.'

'Unreal! How can there be anywhere out of bounds to me in my own house Sava ... tichimimozi?' He up-squinted to speak to his ape. 'It's a human right ... don't you agree?' The ape arched its eyebrows and displayed his little teeth at me. He always took Mr Bin's point of view.

'Truth is,' said Mr Bin, 'I'm in a huff. I don't pay you to wake me ... but you could put your dozy head around my door. Check I'm up. It's the friendly thing to do.'

I maintained silence in all dignity. I had work to do. Friendly was not for work. Friendly could lead to sloppy enactment of duties and disturbance of professional etiquette. I witnessed that the ice was ready in its trays in the gas freezer and that I had stocked enough lagers (Export Quality) in case Mr Summerberg was expectant of dousing his throat with alcohol. Myself, I did not imbibe on account of the restraint necessary for an individual in my exacting vocation.

Mr Bin pulled the ape from his head to his chest and rubbed its belly fur, consulting with it again. 'I could find another cook. If that's what he wants. Someone who acts helpful.'

I fetched the hallmarked tea service (bequeathed to Mr Bin by a more respectable ancestor) and the Italian coffee percolator. If he could not see that I was wasting my youth years helping him, then I had nothing more to tell him. In truth it was our guests that I strived to serve rather than Mr Bin. Mr Bin was my duty. Service and duty, I had those principles. Service? A sober joy. Duty? A doctrine and necessity.

'There are hundreds of unemployed cooks pleading for work,' he told his ape. The ape turned its head to fix me with the evil eye although I did not subscribe to such superstitions. 'They'll all be kind enough to knock on my door to check I'm up. And I'm sure he's not the only *oke* who can boil an egg and slap a *sarmie* together.'

'Mr Bin, I've left your breakfast on the table outside … if the monkeys haven't helped themselves. The eggs benedict has certainly cooled because you departed your bed late.'

'I'm also thinking of all the *tickeys* I'll save on his fancy cooking. He's bankrupting me.' The ape had closed its eyes on account of the belly rub.

I noted with further disappointment that Mr Bin's shorts were as creased as the thigh of a dehydrated elephant. The previous day I had taken on myself to iron them to a knife edge like my aprons so that I would not be obliged to apologise to our guests for my employer's unprofessional deportment. I was in no doubt that he had left them on his bedroom floor overnight with a composting heap of shirts, dusty boots, baseball caps and encyclopaedias on the multitudinous configurations and chromates of fowls. There was no ending to disenchantments with Mr Bin.

I consulted my LCD watch. 'Mr Bin, put on your shoes. You must depart immediately to collect our guests. They're new guests and they're prosperous. You'll wish to give a blameless impression.

You can't progress your business on the patient benevolence of your clients. Discipline ... professionalism ... diligence are the proper ways to achieve excellence in business. Indeed, in the passaging of life.'

Mr Bin's cat entered my kitchen. He had named it Caterpillar on account of its fur of orange and black. Something writhed in the cat's mouth, I thought a short snake or perhaps a long worm. It dropped its prey on the floor. The little serpent continued to dance about, spilling spit on the recently polished surface, encouraged by the paws of the cat. Mr Bin crouched down to examine the creature with a close eye, but the ape flew from him, landed on the other side of the doorway and scurried away to hide.

Mr Bin stroked the cold pipe of the snake's skin as if it was a loved one. 'Leptotyphlops nigricans. Slender blind snake. A natural wonder—'

'Kindly move yourselves out! All three of you!' I gestured the direction of the door.

Mr Bin scooped Caterpillar and stood up, open mouthed as if catching flies. He made no effort to shift himself. He delivered a big deal sigh. 'I've had enough. You'll have to go. Just take your bike and *voetsek*!'

'What? Right now?' I said, bored with his whineful complaints and frustrated at this fruitless converse whilst I tried to complete preparations for our guests. I filled a silver bowl with cubes of crystalline sugar.

'Don't be a *domkop*. Wait until Camlyn and ... er ... Summerwhatsit finish their safari this evening.'

When I did not respond further to his provocation, he hugged the cat to his unshaved cheek and said, 'There, there ... it's okay puss. You just brought a pressy for your old man.'

Caterpillar dangled from Mr Bin's arms. Thick blankets of fur fell to the floor as Mr Bin stroked it, perhaps due to a mange, creating further impurities in my kitchen. I did not want a predator's bristles in my dishes.

The wriggly attempted to slither away but was unable, due to the polished floor. Mr Bin squat-kneed and he and the cat inspected the specimen once more. Mr Bin could become absorbed for long hours in zoological study. I took a dustpan and brush from its designated hook in the cupboard. Despite Mr Bin's unreasonable protestations and the displeasure of Caterpillar, I slung the thrashing object out of the window into the wilds where it belonged. I had no doubt that it would have considered itself more comfortable in Mr Bin's bedroom.

Mr Bin remained uncorrected. 'Oh … come now Mozzy. It wasn't doing you any harm! You've no feelings.'

How mistaken of Mr Bin. In actuality, I felt deeply. Too, too, deeply. The happiness of my diners was my heart's desire. For instance, if our guests were merry, I was satisfied, if they were discontented, I was disconcerted. Yes, too deeply. On rare occasions I even came close to an emotional cracking, a fateful fault to avoid for the sake of good order.

I turned to urge Mr Bin, yet again, to get moving and fetch our guests, but he had left the kitchen. I cleansed the floor, dreaming of prospering in a refined locality, away from scurrying vermin, never again to have to endure the maddening tinnitus of flies or the stings of the cunning tsetses. The restaurant of my happiest dream was in a modern metropolis of polished stone, shining metal and glass, hosed pavings, ordered and scheduled transport systems. Far overseas: either the rising East or the progressive West, no matter. As a sublime bonus, when I escaped the wilderness, I would also escape Mr Bin.

Whilst grinding the finest Arabica coffee beans, I allowed

myself a prospect of superlative happiness. I imagined Miss Camlyn finishing her safari picnic, dabbing her expensive lips, and saying, 'Excuse me Mr Mlantushi, may I have a private word with you?'

'It's my pleasure. Of course you may,' I would reply.

'May I compliment you profusely on your culinary skills? Mouth-watering! Little did I know I'd have to travel all the way to the African bush to be served the finest dishes I've ever tasted.'

'Thank you kindly. It's nothing.' I nodded my head in tactful acceptance of her praise. 'I never compromise my gastronomic standards.'

'I should also mention that many foods cause my fiancée Mr Summerberg to swell up like a hippo and his tongue to peel like a banana. But since dining on your splendid fare … well … he's as healthy and content as a baby after its mother's milk.'

I bowed with all humility. 'The ingredients are grown in mother nature's earth, madam.'

'What I'm coming to is this,' said Miss Camlyn, her excitement as irrepressible as the golden bubbles in a Perrier-Jouet champagne. 'I need to appoint a head chef in the new restaurant I'm opening in New York. You're ideal. Or would you prefer Paris or Singapore? We shall, of course, fly in any fresh produce you require from this organic country so you can create your signature dishes in our kitchen.'

I saw myself rubbing my chin to indicate a balanced consideration of her benevolent offer, but my heart leapt like an impala.

'I'd like to mention —just in case it's important to you— that the kitchen has the highest security against intruders and pets. It's crafted from one seamless cube of easy-clean stainless steel. We have a launderer whose sole responsibility is to wash and iron the aprons.'

'Mozzy! Mozzy!' I became aware that Mr Bin was shouting for me. 'The *bakkie* won't start. Come and push, will you?'

For a short while I remained in my kitchen in New York, wearing the finest, whitest, chef's toque and apron and arranging walnuts and dried cherries on a frisée and apple salad. With effortful resolve I landed myself back in the camp-kitchen in the remotest bush. I had duty to fulfil to the best of my abilities. Yes, I had certain principles, certain doctrines and disciplines. Duty was indeed one such principle. Until Miss Camlyn appointed me, I would endeavour to remain diligent in Mr Bin's employ.

'Mozzy! Are you deaf? You'll make me late.'

In truth, such shouting and blaming caused me to question my principle of duty, inclined me to believe that my only obligation, my only loyalty, should be to the path of career advancement. Far away from Mr Bin and his primitive environs.

But I had to help him to bring that future to me. I took off my so-white apron and called out, 'I'm arriving now, Mr Bin.'

CHAPTER 2

It was only five minutes after Mr Bin's departure that I heard a vehicle roll up outside. I feared that Mr Bin had double-booked. It had happened before. Unexpected guests expecting fine cuisine after their fowl spotting, requiring me to up-scale my dishes in record time. But the man standing at the foot of the veranda was no list ticker strapped with optical devices. His black hair glittered and he was tailored in a pastel-blue sports jacket, ivory chinos and stitched leather shoes. His chest hair was barbered in a horizontal line above the open neck of his shirt. No, he would not be inclined to snare his trousers, or bore himself, seeking featheries out in the bush. He was well sculpted. His pastimes were surely the gym, shooting, skiing — snow and water.

'Greetings, good sir. Can I assist you?'

'You the domestic help around here?' An American. A low, unhurried voice.

'No, I'm—'

'Whose property's this? Who lives here?'

'I'm … might I enquire … your name? Your business?'

'All super confidential, little guy.'

Confidential was no business of mine but I did not appreciate his tone, his poor manners, his lack of regard for the head chef. Whatever his tailoring. I stalled.

'Hey! I've asked you a question. Who lives here?'

This could not be called a 'courtesy' call, no. And I did not appreciate his planting himself outside the house with his big black four by four, interrupting my preparations. Mr Bin's place, however dilapidated, was invitation only. Exclusively for our guests.

'An ape ... a cat.'

'Don't try funny with me.' He pushed his thumbs into his belt, settling his arms to wait for however long to have his answer. But he had reminded me: I must not allow offence to compromise good etiquette.

'Only Mr Bin.'

'Mr Bin, huh?' He laughed short. 'Mr *Bin*. That makes sense.'

'It does?'

'Where is he then? Is he in?'

'No, he's ... not here.'

'When will he show?'

We had VIPs that day, one of whom was my destiny. There must be no distractions to disturb their welcome and nothing to compromise the opportunity for my advancement.

'Tomorrow.'

'Tomorrow huh?'

I gave him what I intended to be an inscrutable smile. He studied me with a scorning —perhaps disbelieving— frown. Maybe he judged me as simple, as well as little.

'We'll see. I'll be back.' He short-laughed to himself again. 'Yeah, Mr *Bin*. That figures.' He turned to go.

'I'll inform him.'

He swung back. 'Negative!' He pointed his finger at me. 'You saw no one. You copy me?'

I shifted, uneasy. Was this all not irregular? I grinned wide again, pleasant and obliging, without yielding. He rolled his eyes and strolled over to his vehicle with its tinted privacy windows and big-boy wheel arches. He thumped his door closed, revved the potent engine, and departed.

I found myself somewhat disturbed as I changed into my whites. Apart from guests, that man was the first visitor to have come to Mr Bin's place. I could not surmise his purpose. He was no tourist. A private investigator? A man looking to recover money from Mr Bin? A corporate wishing to take over the place, bulldoze its thatch and bricks into the bush and build a five star? International law enforcement? An Interpol! Could Mr Bin have a felonious past? Was that why he hid out in the wild, using his business as a camouflage? True, he had the obligatory knowledge of the timber, beasts and fowls of the National Park, but cramming taxonomies was insufficient qualification to CEO a tourist corporation. A bona fide manager in hospitality would have a personable, sociable disposition. But Mr Bin craved solitude. He had no friends. He did not court a girl. I rested my case: he was hiding from someone or was hunted by the law.

I would say nothing to Mr Bin. Be discreet, as was my nature. If he was a wanted man, I should not tip him off. He would abscond.

I was soon ready to welcome our VIPs. I stood behind the table on which I had arranged the welcoming beverages, chest puffed out like a goose and wearing my oh-so-white double-breasted jacket and my head chef's toque. A superlative display of red and yellow flowers from Mr Bin's unruly garden edged the table, scented of Seville marmalade and African wild honey.

I could hear Mr Bin's *bakkie* coming burping and squeaking down the road. Our esteemed guests would be visiting our country and, in particular, that way-out-of-town safari location not only to tick their bird lists but also to tread on wild paths of an aboriginal nature. Where our guests came from, Mr Bin had informed me, it was not possible to step on the ground as it was in the beginning. It was not feasible to experience the first soil, the undefiled loam of the Garden of Eden, 'the virgin bed before it was fornicated by rapacious anthropoids' said Mr Bin. Everywhere they trod in their own country had been violated by planners and paving, the soil shot-gunned with plastics and soaked with pesticides, fungicides, insecticides, herbicides, and many other toxic cides that Mr Bin related to me at tiresome length. For the privilege of walking on celibate ground of an organic nature for just one day and of breathing our chaste air, our guests were willing to pay Mr Bin five hundred US dollars per person not including tips, gratuities, tourist taxes, service and community charges. Of course, they also wished to view our picturesque fowl, our giant timber, our impenetrable thorn bushes, and all the kinds of meat before it is snared and eaten. They were welcome.

The *backie* came to a halt with a final squeak. I trembled to think that I was now to meet Miss Camlyn, my destiny. I hoped that my outstanding bearing would incline her to favour me; that her executive self would see my unrealised potential.

But as soon as Miss Camlyn and Mr Summerberg disembarked, I saw that they were not quite the personages that I was suspecting. The intelligence I had received about them from Mr Bin was incorrect. Miss Camlyn was a young lady, skirted and bloused in floating yellows and rippling blues. She was boldly goggled with lemon-yellow sunglasses and had a bright blue braid in her hair. Her hair shone fair and free in the lusty light of the morning. A blue jewel decorated the side of her nose. It flashed in the sun. Her sandals were popped with beads and flowers and she exhibited a coloured thread around one ankle and a small tattoo on the other.

I surmised that she was too young, too immature, and too frivolously presented to be the owner and CEO of international restaurants. Mr Bin had been misinformed or, more likely, had been careless in his attention to detail. Consequently, my posting to New York was in question. Was there to be no escape from Mr Bin and his flies?

Mr Summerberg, in disparity, was exceedingly old. In truth, it was surprising that he was still living. He was ninety years or more, bony inside a black suit and braces, white shirt and polished black shoes. He looked prepared for lying in a coffin rather than adventuring out on a bush trek. But his purest-white hair burst industrious out of his ears and his scalp, and his sinews still heaved and pulled, and I liked his sharp blue eyes. He was not quite ready to be laid out.

I hoped that with the excessive disproportions in years, Miss Camlyn and Mr Summerberg had no intention to marry. On this one occasion, I hoped that my good wife's prayers would be refused.

Miss Camlyn assisted Mr Summerberg down from the vehicle, her hair and skirt swaying as if in flows of water as she turned, but Mr Bin jerked knee forward, then back, like an uncertain giraffe.

'Shall I hold his other arm?' said Mr Bin.

Mr Summerberg replied to Mr Bin himself. His voice was cracked but passioned. 'No, don't hold his other arm, you mug. He needs it to grip his walking stick. El, pass me my stick. If we hadn't had to wait years at the hotel for Ben to collect us … I'd still be young and fit.'

'Grandad, you refused to bring your stick … yeah? Remember? Let me take your arm.'

'We missed the dawn chorus. What a disaster.'

'Oh look! Awesome!' said Miss Camlyn. 'That nice man over there is waiting with refreshments. It all looks to-die-for!' She happy-faced me and gave me a little wave with her free arm.

Mr Bin offered his hands in the manner of holding a net for fishing as if to catch the old gentleman in the circumstance of him falling. I had to abandon my post and go to help.

'Good morning, Mr Summerberg and good morning Miss Camlyn. Welcome to Bird Observation Day-Walk Safaris. My name is Chef Mlantushi. Let me be of assistance to you.'

'At last! Some help,' said Mr Summerberg. 'Hold my arm, will you? I'll soon loosen up and you'll be panting to keep up with me.'

'Listen to Grandad. Don't you love him?' Miss Camlyn handed over supporting duties.

'Very much already,' I replied.

We proceeded with caution towards the veranda. Miss Camlyn ogled the place with her big yellows and I was ashamed that we could not oblige her with a finer residence as a venue for their Reception Drinks. Mr Bin's house was truly an animal's den, a disintegrating hutch. The sun had revealed creeping plants growing without restraint up the beetle-bored wooden posts of the veranda. The scented bushes close to the house had attracted a mob of stinging insects. Even the citizens of our poorest villages took pride in clearing away the bush and sweeping the earth around their houses, but Mr Bin forbade this. I was truly embarrassed that we could not welcome our guests to a modern, ordered domicile.

'Wow! It's amazing here,' said Miss Camlyn. 'Such a pretty house and beautiful garden. Such colours. Listen to all the birds. They're deafening. And so sunny. So warm. I love it!'

Myself, I saw that she was exceedingly polite and that she herself had a sunny and warm personage.

'Oh my god … what's that huge bird in the tree up there?'

We stopped to observe the fowl, but I made sure that Mr Summerberg was firm on my arm as he had a propensity to fall rear-ways when he looked up.

'It's an enormous ostrich,' said Mr Summerberg. 'An ostrich has flown high into the tree.'

'Yeah?' said Miss Camlyn. 'That's awesome. Surely … no, it's not! Grandad, you're such a tease. Ostriches have much longer necks. You do make me laugh.'

'It's a male yellow-billed hornbill,' said Mr Bin, proud no doubt to demonstrate his top-of-class marks at bird school and to engage in the safety and comfort of academic avian discourse. He handed Miss Camlyn his binoculars. 'See its oversized beak? It's a sound box for its booming call.'

'How do I work these?' said Miss Camlyn. 'I've never even held binoculars before. Can you believe it?' She leaned mirthing towards Mr Bin, but Mr Bin was not able to respond in an easy fashion. It was not his way.

'Look through here,' he said. His brow furrowed in full earnest. 'This way round. There. Turn that knob to adjust the focus.'

She took off her yellows and peered screw-eyed through the lenses. After a short period of face-deforming bafflement in which she pointed the binoculars all over the sky, she said, 'Ah!' Then she said, ' — — , it's amazing. It's like watching the telly. It's like a nature program.' (To my esteemed reader: please do not try to imagine what Miss Camlyn said, indicated by the — symbol of discretion. I do not wish to embarrass you, or my good wife or any descendants, should they read this. God bless them richly.) Then she said, 'It's sicking something up. Uerr, totally gross!'

'It's feeding its mate and chicks through that hole in the tree trunk,' said Mr Bin.

'Whoa, he's feeding them sick?'

'Just his gizzard store. He has to, she's sealed in with mud and droppings—'

'He's sealed her in? How does she get out?'

'No, she—'

'What if he has an accident before he lets her out?' She shock-faced. Her eyes saucered. 'What if he forgets? Or ghosts her?'

'No, she—'

'I don't like him,' said Miss Camlyn.

Mr Bin made to speak again, I think to correct a misunderstanding on who had sealed the hole, but Miss Camlyn called up to the hornbill, 'We've clocked you! Don't forget her … you controlling misogynist.'

Mr Bin fired yet again, but then he appeared to give up. Perhaps he thought there was no countering Miss Camlyn's hot opinions with scholastics and pedantics. In any case, the customer should not be contradicted.

'That's the cruel and uncultivated way of nature, madam,' I said. 'Out here … we're in the savage past times. There are no civilising influences.' I knew that my upmarket beverages and cuisine would soon help her to forget such a disgusting scene.

She lost interest in the fowl and turned to Mr Bin. 'I read on TripAdvisor you're ultra-close to nature, Ben. They say you're living wild. Totally unplugged!' She pointed the binoculars towards him as if she herself was studying nature, and she giggled.

Mr Bin grunted, scratched his three-day jaw hair as if to rid himself of an irritation, and turned away. She smiled with a certain mischief at me. I returned the smile, without the mischief of course, but was thinking what to do with the young lady? We had never welcomed such a rainbow exuberant before. Such a lively. Such a breathy, upfrontal personage. It had always been quiet and sober gentlemen in flop-brimmed hats and stiff brown walking boots, tinkering with their spotting scopes and tripods, check lists and stub pencils.

I came to my employer's help. 'He doesn't behave like a hornbill. He has no wife and tots sealed in a mud house.'

Miss Camlyn laughed like cow bells, but I was serious on that.

We were close now to the veranda. I suggested to Mr Bin that he fetch a higher chair for Mr Summerberg from inside the house, to which he was hasty to oblige. Mr Bin had circled about these guests with futile gestures and ineffectual shifts and manoeuvres. He needed my know-how and instruction.

I assisted Mr Summerberg's legs onto the veranda, and we reclined him into the chair.

'Oh look!' said Miss Camlyn, praying her hands. 'A cute little monkey has climbed onto Ben's head!'

The ape should have been asleep at that time, not delaying the guests' enjoyment of my comestibles. It jumped from Mr Bin and in one reckless leap it crash-landed on Miss Camlyn's shoulder. She squealed and tucked her head to her shoulder.

'Stay still! He likes you,' Mr Bin said. 'He's Freddy. He's no monkey, he's a bushbaby. He's very friendly.'

The ape inspected Miss Camlyn's braid, pulling it and sniffing it. Miss Camlyn's eyes and mouth remained far open as the creature nested on her shoulder, holding her braid. When she understood that it would not bite her, she reclined herself with slow delicacy into her chair as if balancing a child's toy.

Her shoulders reclined. 'Freddy, the friendly bushbaby!' The ape's bushy tail lay around her neck and she reached with a cautious hand to stroke it. 'Wow! Wow!' Her eyes spilled wonderment. 'The softest thing. I've never… this is just … just …'

To my distress and confusion, she started to cry. I was unsure of how to reassure her.

'This is the coolest thing that's ever happened to me. Freddy trusts me. Freddy loves me!'

No guest had ever cried on us on safari before. I was bewildered, and I'm sure Mr Bin as well.

'Will he let me take a selfie?'

'Keep still until he gets used to you,' said Mr Bin. I think he was worried for his ape, that Miss Camlyn would do something chancy that would frighten it off into the bush, where it would no doubt be devoured in no time.

But I was worried for Miss Camlyn. The creature was semi-wild and so was prone to out-of-order behaviour. 'If you wish me to shoo away that monkey … I'll be pleased to oblige.'

'This is all so crazy good,' she said. 'Everything since we got here has been way beyond fantastic. I've found the place of my dreams!' She wiped away a tear from her cheek. 'I feel so alive.' Her crying burbled into a half-suppressed laughter. 'I'm going to take you home, Freddy!' Then she sobered. 'But dang —I can't! My mother won't visit me if I do. She loathes anything cute or furry. Even her partner is waxed and bald.' She slid an aside to me. 'Not that she ever troubles herself to drop in anyway.'

I was minded of my father's saying, *Home affairs should not be talked about on the public square*. 'Would you like freshly ground coffee, madam?' My duty was to help her forget the regrets and bothers of her life back home and so to aid her to a merry vacation. 'Finest Arabica, of course … and I can offer Real Dairy Milk.'

'Awesome! Thank you, Mr Mlantushi.'

'And would you like to partake of my pinwheel shortbread creations?'

'I'm sure Grandad would.' She kissed the ape's tail. I had never seen the ape so easy with a client, so drawn towards the guest and so relaxed. It somehow got me thinking that it was trying to tell

Mr Bin something. To direct his attention. Or had its behaviour just pulled the string of a bow in my own head?

I was pleased that Mr Summerberg assented to a pinwheel shortbread and was gratified when he said, 'Very good for a bush biscuit.' I genuflexed in appreciation of his appreciation.

'Now, where's Ben?' he said.

Mr Bin had turned away and was staring out as if searching for a path to the far horizon. An escape route perhaps. Or was he listening out, in fear of being tracked down by someone from his past? Only I knew that he had already been found. That tomorrow he might be taken into custody.

'Are you clear what we're going to do this morning?' said Mr Summerberg, raising his voice.

'Shhh! Ben's communing with nature, Grandad,' said Miss Camlyn in a loud whisper whilst stroking the ape's tail. I hoped that it was not going to relieve itself on her gaudy raiments. 'Wow, Ben's so out there. We mustn't disturb him. We should learn to be soundless like him and listen to the call of nature ... ha, ha, I mean the wild.' She was surely merry now. Even the old gentleman twitched a smile when she tapped his arm for a response.

'Excuse us, Mr Bin,' I said loudly. 'Mr Summerberg has asked you where you are and if you know what his requirement is today.'

Mr Bin turned slowly as if he had indeed been occupying a faraway location. 'Excuse me?'

I repeated.

'He told me in the *bakkie* he'd like to record bird song,' said Mr Bin.

'He would,' said Mr Summerberg.

'Grandad likes collecting weird stuff,' explained Miss Camlyn to myself. 'He's got green beetles ... old globes ... hot chillies ...

antique telephones and … um … turtle shells and now he's a bird song collector. Like some people collect teapots.'

'Teapots! No, this is the rarest thing.' Mr Summerberg pointed a crooked finger to the sky and shook it. 'This isn't any old object. It's …' He appeared to be struggling to find the correct words. 'You have to play it at my funeral. Promise, El.'

'Grandad, please! I don't want to think about that.'

Mr Bin, all of belated attention, said, 'They've the best songs, small birds. Complicated tunes. Hundreds of notes too fast for us to hear. Some sing two notes at once. A duet from one beak. They also have dialects … depending on where they live.'

'What? Some speak swanky and some speak northern?' said Miss Camlyn.

Mr Bin blank-looked her. No, she did not have the vain and haughty discourse of the ornithology gentlemen that comprised our usual clientele. 'I guess,' he said eventually, 'and each has its own voice. I can tell which bird is carolling when I've got to know them.'

'That's so cool,' said Miss Camlyn. 'They sing carols! Like *Do They Know It's Christmas?*'

Mr Bin started a you-are-so-funny smile before thinking better of it, as if he did not know if Miss Camlyn was a magnificent jester, or playing with him, or deeply unschooled. Maybe he thought her daft. But I somehow liked her uncommon talking; her not ashamed of being unscholastic and speaking whatever she found on her tongue.

'Grandad, don't you agree? Ben's got the brains of David Attenborough and the looks of your plumber, Patryk. You know … Patryk's lean but fit physique.'

Mr Bin statued.

'If you say so,' said Mr Summerberg through a perfectly

crumbling pinwheel creation shortbread biscuit. 'Don't embarrass him, El.'

'I'm just, like, complimenting!' She flicked a strand of hair away from her neck and turned her head to present a portrait of herself, perhaps hoping for a reciprocal flattery from Mr Bin. He was not looking. The ape pulled Miss Camlyn's blue braid to reposition her head to its liking.

'Let's remind ourselves why we're here,' said the old gentleman. 'We have to find that bird.'

Miss Camlyn leant towards me. 'It's the brackish akalat,' she whispered, as if this bird's name should not be spoken out loud in case it brought us a misfortune. In truth, I had never heard of this fowl, but the park was infested with many featheries.

'As you can see' —Mr Summerberg stabbed his legs— 'this is likely my last chance to record it.'

'Grandad's going to donate his collection of rare stuff to the Natural History Museum in London,' said Miss Camlyn to myself. She appeared rightly proud and I was appreciative of the information.

Mr Bin tracked a ragged vulture slow-flapping the sky. Mr Summerberg called to him. 'With your alleged reputation for finding rare birds, Ben, I've every confidence we'll succeed. And I'm not interested in anything else apart from the brackish akalat.'

Mr Bin reconnected again to his guests, sucked air and said, 'Jeez, I don't know. Sheppardia eximius. A sweet song I believe but it's as elusive as … as a Jubjub bird and it—'

'What?' said Mr Summerberg. 'El says you list it on your website as a sighting on your guided walks. I hope we've not been misled, young man. I'll want my money back.'

'Thing is—'

'Thing is, what?'

'We'll be lucky to hear it.'

Mr Summerberg inflated the hollow carcass of his chest. 'Never been a rare thing that's escaped me yet and nor will this. Especially this.'

'Do all birds sing?' said Miss Camlyn. 'Perhaps it doesn't actually sing. Is that why we won't hear it, Ben?'

Mr Bin scratched his chin with uneasy fingers. 'It's been heard, but—'

'But what?' said Mr Summerberg.

'It's said that … only certain people can hear it.'

'People who're not hard of hearing, I expect,' said Miss Camlyn. She promoted her fingers as ears above her head. 'Ha, ha, good thing Grandad's brought me along! I can hear worms chewing in apples.'

'There's this story,' said Mr Bin.

I saw Mr Summerberg nod once, privately to himself, as if he thought he knew such a story and was satisfied that Mr Bin was about confirm it.

But I was fearful that Mr Bin might have been influenced by primitive fables and was about to talk nonsense and so embarrass us. I interrupted him to say loudly and slowly, 'Mr Summerberg was asking you whether you truly see it on your walks.'

'Apologies. Once or twice.' Mr Bin stared at Mr Summerberg's trousers which accommodated the skeleton of his legs. 'We've only seen it on our guided *walks*.'

'That's why I've brought young El with me. If I don't make it, then you and El will carry on with my recording equipment until you hear the akalat.'

'I couldn't leave you on your own in the bush, sir,' said Mr Bin. 'There are predators and buffalos.'

'Does it matter? It'll hardly be the premature death of me,

will it? Hear this Ben. I'd rather die tragically young today than too tragically old tomorrow. Too old's the curse of my generation.'

'It's the no-claims bonus on my liability insurance,' said Mr Bin flatly, 'and my reputation for always returning guests alive.'

'I love it, Ben!' said Miss Camlyn, singing out like the birds. 'I love your dry humour! You could sell it in packets ... like those dehumidifying crystals.' The ape leapt off her shoulder and vaulted away into the house. 'Wow, sorry Freddy. Didn't mean to jiggle.' Then she smiled most pleasantly at me. 'I'm sure Mr Mlantushi could stay with Grandad —if Grandad can't go any further— whilst Ben and I go on together to find the bird.'

'— no,' said Mr Bin.

'Yay!' said Miss Camlyn.

'Excuse me,' said Mr Bin. 'What I'm saying is ... unfortunately, Mozzy ... Mr Mlantushi ... has many domestic chores to get on with here today. Today he's going to be working in the house.'

This was news to me. Bad news. Was it to be domestic chores for the head chef? Who was going to serve the guests their sumptuous picnic?

'A sterling suggestion from my granddaughter,' said Mr Summerberg. 'In the almost certain event of my incapacity, your man and I will wait for your return. He'll wait with my body, if necessary.'

'Grandad! Please! You do make me laugh. Why don't we ask Mr Mlantushi himself since he's right beside us?' She turned to me. 'Mr Mlantushi, it would be awesome if you could assist us. Will it upset your plans today if you come with us?'

What could I say? What should I do? My employer was instructing me in contradiction to the petitioning of my VIP guests. I remembered my father's proverb. *The cow that likes two herds is eaten by the lion between them.* His proverb was pertinent.

I had to make a decision this way or that way so as not to be devoured by the lion of vacillation. But which way?

Miss Camlyn had spoken to me by way of her most gracious request, but Mr Bin shot at me through rifle eyes, telling me to stay in the house. I perceived such, but there was also other talk in his eyes. He also saw a lion that he feared. The lion was the impending circumstance of being alone with such a lady as Miss Camlyn should Mr Summerberg and myself need to stay behind on the path. Mr Bin, I had observed, was unable to converse in a comfortable manner with young female personages. He was at ease only when speaking to the cat and the ape or to persons who talked birds. If it was necessary to make civil and everyday chit-chat with a lady —which might indeed be required if he walked alone with Miss Camlyn— then he became as perturbed as a worm on my kitchen floor.

Miss Camlyn turned her ear to me in expectation. To whom was my highest obligation? To my employer or to our guests? I always looked for the top responsibility in such judgments. The superseding obligation. My wife said I would make a fine preacher as I 'accidentally' had spiritual discernment but, in truth, my calling was culinary, not clerical.

I discerned this: there was a higher duty to my employer than he was perceiving for himself. He must be facilitated to speak to the young lady. He needed to acquire pleasantries so that one day, after much social education, he could catch a wife, and so comply with the correct order of things.

In fairness to the true record of my thinking, I also hoped that by staying with the party I would have the opportunity to discover whether Miss Camlyn did indeed own the promised high-end restaurants. Had I been prejudiced against her? Maybe her decorated razzle was just a packaging. The modern world was made by young entrepreneurs who had achieved their money and dreams whilst still living with their parents, promoting their businesses by selfie-dressing and face-painting in their childhood bedroom and posting worldwide for advantageous marketing.

I did not vacillate further. 'It's no problem for myself to accompany your safari party, Miss Camlyn. It'll be an honour to assist Mr Summerberg if it becomes necessary. But I'm certain Mr Summerberg will walk all day like a Maasai.'

'What an obliging and helpful gentleman you are, Mr Mlantushi!' said Mr Summerberg. 'What a lucky man you are, Ben, to have Mr Mlantushi working with you.'

Mr Bin twisted away from us. He held his throat to suppress the emission of a goose-like noise, but I saw that the lion that likes to eat the vacillating cow had turned and slunk away.

CHAPTER 3

'You're right principled. I so have a thing for that,' said Miss Camlyn to Mr Bin. 'And even though you're, like, eco and ethical, you don't bang on about it.'

The guests were roosted on our Luxury Winchester Safari Recliners in a location in the National Park under the shade of one of those timbers, which the guests open-mouthed on account of its plentiful dimensions. They had gorged on the picnic feast I had provided on our Winchester Safari Table. The guests had experienced high-end dining despite the rough locality. With all humility, I venture to propose that any success achieved by Mr Bin's guided safari footing business depended, by the grace of God, on myself, his head chef.

Miss Camlyn had commented that Mr Bin had not partaken of my carpaccio of smoked ostrich with nasturtiums.

Mr Bin said, 'I'm the only vegetarian in Africa.'

'I want to be a vegan,' said Miss Camlyn, 'and some days I actually am.' She squint-lipped me, then she said to Mr Bin. 'Is it because eating meat is literally murder or because it's the cause of global warming?' She gazed eager at him, as if believing him to have superlative wisdom, or perhaps to hear him deliver a parched jest.

Mr Bin appeared confounded by her enquiry, but after stalling he said, 'It's more the way Mozzy here prepares it. He smothers it in curry.' Mr Bin designated spices and garnishes, whether clove, thyme, capers or whatever, to be curry.

Mr Summerberg reposed with his chin on his chest, hardly breathing, but now he stirred himself. 'What are you talking about, Ben? That was one of the best luncheons I've had in a long time. Frankly … it's been the only pleasure of the day.'

I bowed in appreciation of his appreciation.

'*Curry!* Ben's just joking, Grandad. He thinks Mr Mlantushi's dishes are totally delish. We all do. Ben doesn't want to boast about his eco-friendly lifestyle.'

Mr Summerberg choked. I assisted him in reaching for his glass of iced water with parfum of elderflower. 'If we'd heard the bird this morning … I'd be in a better mood for humour. If that's what it was.'

In the paradigm of seeking out the singing beak, it had indeed been a disappointing morning. Mr Bin had led the eager safari party with due deference to Mr Summerberg's slow passage. I had offered to carry his black jacket, but he had insisted on wearing it despite the heat, saying that wearing a suit was all an old man had left of dignity. His only concession to the heat was to be tieless. We struggled on an un-swept path splattered with animal excrement and encroached by tick-laden grass until we reached a forested area, which Mr Bin deemed would give us the opportunity for success. We heard every noise of the bush, reminding me of creaky hinges and unhappy babies. Sudden raucous guinea fowl gave me fright. All discordant sounds, for sure. Raw manure and beast-sweat stinks passaged our nostrils. Timbers leant over their shadows, a premonition of their graves. But Mr Bin fascinated Miss Camlyn, due no doubt to his problematic identity and unsociable manner. Occasionally he indicated varieties of fowl by sound or sight and Miss Camlyn said such as, 'Unbelievable', 'You're kidding', or 'Never seen anything so gorgeous'. A very polite lady.

The quarry remained elusive. I portered the sound recording apparatus for Mr Summerberg. Every time a bird sang, I pointed the microphone boom in its direction, but every time Mr Bin shook his head and said, 'Wrong akalat', 'A cricket', 'A bursting seed pod', and such like. The brackish akalat, I concluded, would sound like nothing else but itself. I could appreciate how its voice would be a most singular loss if it became extinct.

Of course, I was not personally vexed to fail to hear the bird, only for our guests. The bird had caused us a tiring and purposeless morning. And all the time, I had been asking myself what the well-tailored American wanted and if he was about to crash call our luncheon, uninvited, to arrest or to confront Mr Bin. Could I hear the threatening throb of a potent engine on a nearby track? Always, everything, concerning Mr Bin distracted me from perfect service to our guests.

After dining we all inclined to be quiet. Miss Camlyn leant back in her recliner, permitting the sunlight to pet her face through the leaves. She smiled with polite contentment at no one.

'I never ever want to leave this place,' she said lazily. 'I think I said that before. Did I Grandad? It's so luxuriously warm and bright. Everything's perfection. I'm floating like … weightless in wonderland.' Mr Summerberg had lapsed into coma, so did not respond. 'Do you ever feel like you're living in the wrong place Mozzy? That you're not really where you're meant to be … and you've got to do something about it?'

How could she know my thoughts? Yes, she had a certain wisdom. She was not as daft as Mr Bin might believe.

Mr Bin stood on his own, away from the table, listening to the distant honks and screams of the bush. We had no choice but to do the same. It would have been more in keeping with the price of the safari if Mr Bin had provided our guests with a radio to entertain them with an upmarket experience whilst they ate. Perhaps opera or, at the least, a choir. Instead, we were pressed about by intimations of menace. A breeze from nowhere, carrying the dry smell of bones and suggestive of the witchcraft in which I did not believe, disturbed the crispy leaves of the heavy tree, under whose old and unpruned branches —waiting to drop on the unsuspecting— the guests had collapsed. A mournful dove lamented its circumstances. Furthermore, the ice was melting in the Kilimanjaro Spring Water and a fly had stealthily insinuated itself underneath the Brussels Lace Net that protected the plate of green mealie fritters with tangy avocado cream. I could not swing my fly swat as I did not wish to disturb the guests and Mr Bin forbade me killing any creatures in the park. 'This is their place, Mozzy, not yours,' he would say, as if my grandfather had won independence from colonial rule only to give the country over to flies.

Miss Camlyn sighed. 'It's such a shame that my mother's so, so, busy she couldn't come with us. Shame in some ways, anyway.' I thought she raised a conspirating eyebrow at me as if we had a secret between us —although she alone knew what it was. 'She needs to get a perspective on life. She's so, so, driven. So grasping. She should sell all her restaurants.'

I spilled the Real Dairy Milk. A grasshopper of hope leapt in my heart. Mr Bin had misinformed me. It was her good mother who owned the top restaurants in the greatest cities of the world. My dreams of prodigious opportunity had not been a fancy. I would be bold at a discrete moment to ask our guest for an introduction to her mother. It would put me on the fast-track to my future. They had commended my cuisine over and over. Had not Mr Summerberg said that he had never partaken of a better luncheon in all his ninety years? I was, of course, seeking a firm offer of employment as my wife had insisted that only a guaranteed position would persuade her to leave her Divine Prosperity Assembly and our village. This would now surely come. I had to self-deny my imagination from entering that New York kitchen again. I awaited an opportune moment to make my request.

Mr Summerberg stirred himself at last and said in a voice that was weakened by the proximity of his no doubt impending demise, 'We're wasting the day. We can't afford to sit about like beach bums. I'm ready to march out again.' But he made no attempt to leave his recliner. In truth, Mr Summerberg was like an old bird that does not understand that its wing is broken. I feared that he would not last if he walked under that ruthless sun once more, stumbling on that stony ground.

'Poor, poor Grandad,' said Miss Camlyn, and leant across to put her hand on his arm. Then she turned to me and spoke quietly. 'Did I tell you, Mr Mlantushi? It's been like literally his one ambition this year. He's got to record the bracky bird. Grandad really wants it.'

I could understand this. A man must be stubborn and relentless in his quest for achievement.

'Now it's all come to nothing. It's really sad.' Her words brought a teary shine to her eyes. I bowed my head to be alongside her in her sorrow. 'Grandad'll never be in the Natural History Museum with the dinosaurs.' She addressed Mr Bin. 'Can't you do something? Anything?'

'He can't whistle for it, El,' said Mr Summerberg. 'It's rare. It may have snuffed it … it may have beaten me to it. Let's hope our fortune turns. Didn't help that we missed the dawn chorus.'

Miss Camlyn stood up and went to Mr Bin, grasping hold of his bearded arm whilst pressing into him with advanced familiarity. 'I know you *can* do something, Ben. Yeah?' Her bluish gaze combed his charcoal hair.

Mr Bin found it imperative to take a cloth from his pocket and hard-rub the glass of his binoculars. Then he stared out into the lonely wilderness that encircled us.

'My life coach says we have to act on even our wildest dreams. That's the only way they'll happen.' She cocked her head at him. I could not tell if she was expecting a dismissal of her coach's conjecture or was seeking his endorsement.

Mr Bin chewed the side of his lip.

She turned to me. 'What do you think, Mozzy?'

'Of course, madam,' I concurred, cognisant of my own soon-to-be-fulfilled dreams, 'but my father used to say, *To walk is not necessarily to arrive.*'

She released Mr Bin. 'To walk is not necessarily to arrive,' she said to herself. She turned to me. 'Your father said that? Your own father? Awesome! It's sort of, yeah, meaningful. Was your father totally ethnic? Like, it would be amazing if he was all traditional … like wore claw anklets and leopard skins. Painted his face with clay and went into trances.'

I corrected her. 'He wore a city suit. He rose to the position of assistant bank clerk and his only religion was football.'

'Oh, of course. No offence intended … but disappointing in a way. You see … we've got this ginormous coffee table book at home of … I expect he heard it from his ancestors.'

And her book must have been inherited from her ancestors — as if I had a picture book of her cave-dwelling parents in deer skins hunting in a forest in the UK.

She turned to Mr Bin again. 'Whatever, Ben, we're totally depending on you. You're our Moses leading us to the Holy Grail … or whatever he did.'

Mr Bin scuffed the toe of his boot on the ground. He stared out into the wilds and then talked strong. 'I'm going to scout out that way for a couple of minutes.'

'Yay, Ben,' said Miss Camlyn, springing up and down on her toes. 'I knew you'd work something out. I just knew it! I'm coming with you. I'll carry Grandad's contraptions.' She made a hasty arrangement of her hair and picked up her hat from the back of her recliner.

'I'm actually just going … behind a bush,' said Mr Bin.

Miss Camlyn replaced her hat. 'Ha, ha, silly me! And it's literally a bush out here! You're so, so, grounded Ben and so … real-world!'

I stepped forward to top up her glass of home-made granadilla and mint cordial. In that heat, lips cracked and throats became dry river beds pleading for a flood

When I turned, I saw Mr Bin beckoning. I excused myself and followed Mr Bin, but with half an eye on our guests. It was not advisable to leave guests exposed to mortal danger in such a wild place with no fencing, although Mr Bin had his rifle, always over his shoulder. He was never without it in those dangerous locations.

I followed Mr Bin, but he passed the Safari Comfort Station tent with courtesy Kudu Horn Tissue Dispenser, which we had erected earlier for our VIP guests. Then he stopped dead as if he had walked into an invisible timber and turned towards me. 'What am I going to do, Mozzy?'

'My father used to say—' I started.

'I don't want to hear your old man's lousy sayings. What should I do? I'm asking you as a confidant. I'm actually asking for your advice.'

'I'm a chef, not a bird spotter.'

'Is she a complete airhead? Or is she taking the mick out of me?'

'Do you mean Miss Camlyn?' I was shaken by this perplexing turn of events.

'She's hectic. She wants me to magic up the bird. She's spouting half-witted things. She asked me how big hippo eggs are and why the mummy doesn't break them when she sits on them. There was no chance of hearing an akalat because she was jawing so loudly.'

'Please, Mr Bin! Be forgiving. Miss Camlyn is kind and polite. She's also fragrant and comely, unlike our regular guests.'

Mr Bin looked to be inspecting my words as if I had opened his vision to something previously curtained. 'I prefer Merops Nubicoides or Coracius Caudatus.'

At that time, I thought that he was referring to Greek and Italian actresses but a later knowledge revealed that he spoke the Latin names of colourful fowl.

'She's in admiration of you,' I said, 'and look at the concordance between you. She loves nature, and you love nature.'

'Loves nature!' Mr Bin fake laughed. 'She loves the idea … the notion … the cute Instagram image. And she likes that she can buy it —or her grandfather can. But, damn it, that's beside the point. She asked me about my dreams for the future. I don't have any …' He looked away. 'I guess I used to.' He shrugged. 'But now I'm living in the moment. We're on a birding walk, not in therapy. I want to be quiet in the bush. Preferably with like-minded ornithologists.' He nodded slowly to himself in the absence of the ape to concur with. 'Alone in the bush … even better. Ja, most days I like being on my own.'

I wondered again why this was so. Why he preferred to be on his own. Why he had no friends and no desire for such. Why he was not pleased at the adulation of Miss Camlyn. Surely a vexation in Mr Bin's past impacted on his present in a negative fashion. What was afflicting him? Of course, I did not pry by asking. It was necessary to keep a professional relationship where personal issues and failings were put aside for the benefit of the guests. In the year that I had worked in Mr Bin's employ, I had always maintained a proper respect for his privacy, discouraging inappropriate familiarity. But why was that sportsman looking for him?

I said, 'Is that your problem right now, Mr Bin? How to endure Miss Camlyn?' I asked this in a stern tone to bring him to the chief requirement of the guests for which they had paid five hundred US dollars each notwithstanding supplemental costs. 'Is that really your problem?'

'Ja, totally.'

I became a little distracted. I could hear a vehicle. It was somewhere out there on a track. Circling in towards us?

'The old *toppie* can't trek any further,' said Mr Bin. 'She'll want you to stay with him. Then she'll want to come looking for the akalat again with me. There'll be loud psychobabble and *domkop* questions. Or is she revving me?'

Still with an ear on the vehicle, I said with all forbearance, 'What about recording the dull bird? It's why we're out here suffering this forsaken location. That's what our guests are crying about.'

'Damn it Mozzy! I don't want to be on my own with her.'

I saw then that he was begging my opinion, even advice and guidance as if I was a brother instead of his employee. And what if Mr Bin upset our VIPs, making Miss Camlyn ill-disposed to my request for employment in New York?

'For the sake of your business ... for the five stars on TripAdvisor ... you should be personable towards her. But most importantly, for her happiness. It only requires your civility for a few more hours.' I recalled then my father saying when he worked at the bank, *The truth is not like money to be tied up and hidden.* To speak the truth, I said, 'It shouldn't be difficult. She admires you with blind respect.'

'Did you say blind? What do you mean … blind?' Mr Bin turned his thoughts, no doubt, to Miss Camlyn's healthy eyes. Mr Bin had no understanding of expressions of a symbolic nature.

I remembered the ape, how its friendly manner towards Miss Camlyn had pulled a bow in my head. I found myself releasing the arrow. 'Forget that blind business. What I'm saying is this. Take this opportunity!' He looked at me straight and I saw that he attended to my words. 'Our guests are most times decrepit. True? You don't meet eligible persons. Yes? But now … here's a young lady! Correct? She admires you. Exactly. She sees you're in cahoots with nature. She sees you have few words but you know many things. She's come to find the brackish fowl. Instead … she's found you!' I nearly teared at my moving discourse. Yes, I felt too deeply.

'What are you saying?'

I spoke plain. 'Court her with a view to matrimony!'

Mr Bin's skitting eyes suggested that he thought I spoke as a village crazy.

'Be calm! Here's the best of it. You don't need to talk dreams to her. Your disposition is interpreted by her as philosophic … scholastic … intriguing. You don't need to say anything to keep her admiration. Let her continue to believe you have righteous convictions and concealed fortes. At all costs, don't show her your true character. Don't cause her terrible disappointment.'

'Cause her terrible disappointment? How would I do that? You think—'

'Yes, most definitely,' I said with solemnity and in a spirit of benevolence.

'I've heard enough. I'm not listening to your … impossible suggestion. You don't know how impossible.' He waved away my hands.

Impossible? No, just a lack of imagination on his part, an absence of dreams. Or maybe he did not want advice from his 'cook'.

'I don't need this,' he said. 'I'm glad I gave you the *voetsek* this morning.' He nodded agreement to himself. 'You'll take your bike and go … this evening.' Then he spoke to his ape although it was not present. 'Why did I think I could get advice from my domestic help as if he were a *broe*? Instead, he hits me with insults.'

'I'm the company head chef,' I reminded him. It was not for the first time that I had given instruction to Mr Bin and he had responded with abuse and invective.

'I've only spoken at your own request.'

Mr Bin was turning towards our guests, but I wanted to make my proposal compelling. I said after him, 'If you marry Miss Camlyn, I'll hand over my duties to her. I'll leave for a higher posting. She'll no doubt charm your guests. And, what's more,' I said, succumbing —I am ashamed to report— to the pain of a crack in the delicate shell of my feeling heart, 'I'm sure she can boil an egg as well as I can.'

I do not believe he heard me as, just as I spoke, two things happened. I heard again the potent engine, but much nearer. And then Miss Camlyn cried out.

Chapter 4

Mr Bin swung his rifle off his shoulder and streaked like a cheetah towards Miss Camlyn. He could get himself together when necessity demanded. I hastened after him. In a place like that, every possibility was probable. She had certainly been bitten by a venomous snake or was faced by a merciless predator. I could not keep up with the long-strided Mr Bin, but I too was ready to defend our client to the death. A necessary and expected customer service.

When Mr Bin reached our guests, I saw him stop and lean his gun against the tree. A disturbing thought came to me that Mr Summerberg had passed away. RIP, at last. For the very first time Mr Bin would not be returning all his guests alive. It would be a regret and would impact his no-claims bonus.

'Ow! Ow!' I heard Miss Camlyn say. 'I trod on a thorn.' She had capitulated into her recliner. Her sandals lay discarded and she examined the sole of her foot, pain-faced. 'The ground's a bit sandy. I thought I'd go bare foot, like, to feel Africa between my toes … like you can feel Ibiza when you dance on the beach there.'

'Fetch the first aid kit, Mozzy,' said Mr Bin.

I noted that, during this crisis, Mr Summerberg was asleep, or in a mortal coma.

'I'm already moving.' I hurried to fetch the Safari First Aid box from the vehicle, following the procedure that I had had to devise for myself for such emergencies. Again, I heard a vehicle engine, teasing me, but it was fading as if it had been on the wrong track to reach us. We would not need to manage two troublesome events at the same instance.

When I returned, I found Mr Bin standing silently by the injured guest with an insufficient bedside manner.

Miss Camlyn was crying. 'Oh Ben, I'm sorry. I'm a dork. You must think I'm dumb.'

'It certainly settles it,' said Mr Bin in a tone that leant more towards unmannered than jest.

'He means the numbing cream in here will settle your pain,' I said with haste. I passed Mr Bin the First Aid box.

Mr Bin took a needle and I brought a canvass stool to him so that he could sit beside Miss Camlyn to perform the necessary act of mercy.

'I expect it's deep,' said Miss Camlyn. 'It's probably gone right through my foot. Is there a helicopter ambulance? My mother will pay. I hope.'

Mr Bin held Miss Camlyn's creamy-white foot in his sun-brûléed hand and studied closely.

'It looks tiny.'

'For a man of Mr Bin's experience to deal with,' I said.

'Ahh Ben, your hands are very soothing. Mmm.' Miss Camlyn closed her eyes and succumbed to the comfort of her recliner, as if she had forgotten that she was deeply stabbed. She smiled vacantly as if entering a pleasant dream, which she had no wish to wake from. I thought Mr Bin was distracted for a moment by the grace of her legs, making me expectant that he could be charmed into a change of heart.

Most fortunately the thorn was just visible to the naked eye. Miss Camlyn was exceedingly brave, although she fainted —or pretended to— when Mr Bin flicked it out. I took over customer service, bringing her a glass of iced water with elderflower parfum, and then I fanned her face with a freshly laundered and ironed tea towel.

'Ben was so amazing. I hardly felt a thing,' she said. Did she wink me?

Mr Bin stood back and looked out again into the bush where he would have no doubt preferred to be, on his own. He turned and addressed Miss Camlyn. 'With a potentially septic puncture wound you should rest your foot. I'm taking you both straight back to your hotel.'

Miss Camlyn lost her secret smile. 'You're kidding.'

'The bacteria are the most dangerous creatures in the park. And there are billions of them. They're far more dangerous than the buffalos.'

'You're having me on!'

'Fulminating septicaemia … gas gangrene … tetanic paralysis … pustular putrefaction … necrotising fasciitis. You name it.'

'You have. Oh my gosh!'

Mr Bin stood unyielding. He was certainly exercising maximum caution. Too much caution, and he had also become a determined man of unflinching decisions. I suspected his motives. I had to conclude that the day was ending in a car wreck. These were the facts: my employer had failed to court Miss Camlyn, Miss Camlyn had sustained an injury, Mr Summerberg had failed to record the bird and, even at that moment, was passed away or, at the least, was soon to pass, and the opportunity for my dream posting had died. I remembered my father's proverb, *A patient man will eat ripe fruit.* But how much patience can a man suffer?

'It's all my fault. I've let Grandad down.' Miss Camlyn touched her eye with the back of her hand.

'Nonsense!' shouted Mr Summerberg, jumping us from the ground. He stood up from his recliner as if resurrected as a young man. 'Thanks to Mr Mlantushi's refreshments and my siesta, I'm fully revived. Mr Mlantushi will wait here with El whilst Ben and I make one last do-or-die expedition to record the brackish akalat. I refuse to peck defeat from the beak of victory.'

Miss Camlyn clapped her hands. 'Yay! No way am I not coming too. It's do and die!'

Mr Bin raised a hand to discourage Miss Camlyn from standing.

'Mozzy, sit in the *bakkie* with Miss Camlyn and wait for Mr Summerberg and me to come back.'

Miss Camlyn dropped her hands into her lap. 'How's Grandad going to manage without me?'

Mr Summerberg stood with no support, although swaying somewhat, with his jaw out towards the horizon like a colonist explorer. Mr Bin picked up a broken branch from close by and with his penknife cut off protruding twigs and thorns, even smoothing the bent end to make a suitable handle. He gave it to Mr Summerberg to use as a walking stick. Mr Summerberg swung the stick and poked it out, as if spearing an attacking beast. Then he had to plant it firmly as he was in danger of toppling. Mr Bin picked up the recording equipment and his rifle and then, with not a further word, he assisted Mr Summerberg into the wilderness again.

I turned my attention to Miss Camlyn's comfort, craving an opportunity to ask her for a commendation to her mother. To such purpose, I wished that I had cooked even finer dishes for our guests that day. For example, my Roast Eland with Gooseberry Sauce followed by Banoffee and Amarula Sundae. Such dishes required a special import of ingredients by clandestine or expensive traders, which Mr Bin was not always disposed towards. But I hoped that my cuisine had already spoken for me. Mr Summerberg had eaten four cherry and pecan nut cookies. I was of the opinion that these had medicinal properties —he had fresh elastic in his sinews.

'Let's sit here ... not in the vehicle. I feel closer to Ben's world out here,' said Miss Camlyn, resting her head back in the Winchester.

I was mindful of our exposed situation in the bush and Mr Bin's instruction, but I could not be officious with our VIP guest by insisting we sit in the stuffy car. She was also under a contemplative disposition and we were on our own. The time was ripening to request my ticket to New York. It was now most urgent to do so, in case of Mr Bin's arrest or other commotions relating to the American.

'I'm gutted I'm not with Ben and Grandad,' said Miss Camlyn.

'Mr Bin's only concerned for the safety and the health of his guests.'

'What's worse ... Ben didn't want me to come with him. I know it. All that bacteria baloney.' She coiled a strand of her hair in her fingers and frowned at it. The soufflé of her happiness had surely collapsed. 'What's up with him?'

'I wouldn't know. He's just my employer.'

'He's got issues, hasn't he?' She was quiet for a few seconds, then said, 'Mr Mlantushi, can I confide in you? Despite that ... I think I'm catching the feels for him. Does it show? He had me when he picked us up. He gave us an awesome smile and said *howzit?* I forgave him right there for turning up late. But he doesn't like me. I admit I've been sort of tipsy today.'

'The mint and granadilla cordial's alcohol free, I assure you,' I said.

'I mean I've become drunk on nature. On this place. It's made me loopy… I've become childish … starry eyed. Everything's so beautiful here. Even the grass is stunning. It's long and lazy and … luminous and misty. Wow! See! It's made me into a fricking poet.'

I clapped her softly, pleased to hear her little recital.

'Ben thinks I'm stupid, yeah? I bet it started when I asked him who put the hay in the trees for the giraffes. How was I to know that they were birds' nests? I've never seen nests as big as hay bales before. I'm from — Dagenham.'

'It was an innocent question.' I rolled forward on my feet. 'But if I might ask—'

'Perhaps Ben could find himself conflicted. In love with me, even if … in some ways … he's not sure about me.'

'I have a—'

'What do you think, Mr Mlantushi? Can I call you Mozzy?

'Please call me by any name you wish, certainly.'

'He liked my legs. It's a start. We could work up from there. Not literally, of course. Has Ben got someone else?'

'I can assure you there's no one at all in Mr Bin's life. He's not dating. Here, we're too far from city lights. Here, it's only fowl and vermin.'

'He's only in love with nature, isn't he?' said Miss Camlyn. 'I'm probably not wild enough for him. I should be more natural. Mess up my hair and make a fire … eat with my fingers and pick my teeth with a twig.'

I subsided back on my heels but was cognisant of the delicate nature of this conversation with a client concerning my employer. Furthermore, my future might depend on the outcome. I hoped for discernment.

'He's dedicated to nature, true, and so are you,' I said. 'That's undeniable. There's a perfect concordance between you.'

She served me a doubting glance.

'Furthermore … he both loves you and likes you when you're appreciating the silence that travels with him. Be like … a bat.'

'A bat?'

'As silent as a bat.'

She weighed my words. 'I'm more like an excited parrot, aren't I?'

I offered her my finest Arabica coffee or another glass of homemade granadilla and mint cordial, which was always a big deal with the guests, but she declined, and I could see that she wished to practice being soundless. I stood discretely in the background ready to be of service to her any request. Even though I sorely needed to ask about her mother, I restrained, waiting for a more receptive moment.

After approaching ten seconds she said, 'Who does Ben's marketing?'

'Marketing?'

'His website, for example.'

'I'm not a party to that information. He handles every aspect of the business himself except the cuisine and … the customer service.'

'It's rubbish!' said Miss Camlyn.

'The customer service?'

'Oh no, that's awesome —in a kooky sort of way. It's his marketing. His website looks like it's been thrown together by a self-employed tarmac layer. The links go nowhere. The design's hideous! As for the ultra-bad name of your safari company. BOD hyphen W! Bird Observation Day … I can't even bear to say it. If the brackish akalat hadn't been on his bird sightings list, we wouldn't have come. He's not even on social media. I know about these things. I'm in marketing.'

I drew breath to speak. But she started divulging again.

'But I loathe my job. I'm a tiny ball in the marketing division of a bearing-distribution company. So boring. I want something more. Do you ever feel that, Mozzy? Something more … and I want someone more. Someone like Ben, I guess! Hah … Ben's just the sort of man my mother would despise. May be that's what I love about him. That, and his rare smile.'

'I believed you worked with your mother … in her restaurant business.'

'Oh my god no, she doesn't need *silly little Chantella*.'

I put my face in neutral gear and declined to comment on my future employer's reported opinion of her daughter. A misunderstanding, surely.

'My mother's got her marketing all buttoned up and I'd be a danger in the kitchens. I can't even boil an egg.'

I would have to conceal this information from Mr Bin, concerning Miss Camlyn's lack of skill in boiling an egg, but I was building to decorously enquire if her mother might need. A chef who could create a first-class dish of creamed scrambled egg with truffle and sage. I would even, I admitted to myself, have been exultant to take employment with her mother as just a sous chef, not yet as head chef. Not in the first instance.

'Now, if you don't mind, Mozzy, I'm going to read my book.'

She reached inside her bag and pulled out a heavy book titled *Purple Hornbill* and extoled on the jacket as *Conrad meets Naipaul. Serious and disturbing.*

At all times I respected my guests' wishes, so was silent. This was not yet to be the auspicious hour of the first step on my path out of the wilderness. *A patient man will eat ripe fruit.* I so wished it. I tidied the lunch accoutrements into the Safari Hamper.

I did not disturb Miss Camlyn, but I only hoped that Mr Summerberg was still living and that they had heard the fowl. In my opinion they should have found a way to trap it, or flush it out by throwing stones, but Mr Bin would never have considered such a pragmatic solution, forgetting that the needs of the guests should come first before the amenity of the fowl. If I was in Mr Bin's *veldskoen*, I would have made it sing.

Miss Camlyn, I saw, was easily distracted from her book to close her eyes or to stare up at the tree. She seemed to read the same page three times. Then all sudden she turned to the last page, read some and then dropped *Purple Hornbill* back into her bag and pulled out another fable, thinner, titled *Into the Red Sunset*. The jacket featured the eye of a weeping elephant, a politician with a greedy eye and an expatriate girl with a seducing eye. *Can conservationist, Kylie Strong, save the last elephant family?*

A fantasy fable indeed.

The afternoon passed in a lazy hum of insects and wafting bush miasmas whilst Miss Camlyn read. Still Mr Bin and Mr Summerberg did not return.

'Wow … just look at the sunset,' said Miss Camlyn towards late afternoon. 'It's like the thousands in my book.' She sat up. 'It's getting late! Where are Grandad and Ben?'

'It's five forty-six hours … very late. The sun goes down at six zero-five.' In that geographical location the sun falls off the horizon as sudden as a tomato rolling off a table. Presently, we would be blind.

'Do you think they're lost?'

'Mr Bin's never lost in the bush. It's his habitat. He'd like to be a beast and sleep under a bush. We'll just have to wait. We can only conclude that they've found the bird and are occupied in recording it.'

The sky behind the trees caught fire for a minute before flaring out, leaving only the dark plum cloak of the dusk.

'Have they taken a torch?'

'I'm sure so, but we'd better retire to the safety of the car. We're now in the sights of night predators.'

Surely there would be another chance in the car to enquire of an introduction to her mother.

'Let's sound the horn so they know we're worried about them.'

'No, no, Mr Bin would be most dismayed if we disturbed the night. He only permits the sounds of nature.'

'Of course, silly me. Even so … I'm really scared about Grandad. Hasn't Ben got a phone? He must have a mobile.'

'There's little signal here. We're on our own, far beyond help. That's the way Mr Bin likes it. He plays at being stone-age man.' I did not confess to her that Mr Bin did not own a phone. He was the only person on the continent without a mobile phone. He did everything to make it difficult to connect with the human race.

Miss Camlyn peered into the foreboding shades and shapes of the night. 'We can't just do nothing. What if something's happened to Grandad … like he's fallen …. broken his hip and Ben's hoping we'll come and help? We should go and find them.' She put on her sandals and then her hat, even though the dark plum of the dusk had become the black gravy of the night.

This presented me with a situation of a delicate nature. Miss Camlyn was willing to bravely put herself in gravest danger to find her adored grandfather, but I had a responsibility to protect her from the scorpions of the night. I did not have to ponder this dilemma for long. We heard a loud and terrible scream out in the darkness. It was like the scream of a lost soul; a lost soul falling into a bottomless abyss.

When the scream ceased, the bush fell as soundless and still as the dark side of the moon.

For a moment, Miss Camlyn was also silent, and then she hissed, 'Oh my gosh! Oh my gosh!' She ran behind me.

The scream repeated. Miss Camlyn clung to me. I could feel the goosey bumps on the skin of her arm.

'What was that?' she said, crying. 'Something's out there. Something horrible's happening. Someone's being eaten! What if it's Grandad?'

'We should shift to the sanctuary of the car,' I suggested.

'Quickly!' She clung to me. 'I'll stay close to you, Mozzy. I'm scared witless.' She hunched over. 'Ben was right, I should've waited in the truck. We need to get help. We should never have come here.'

I neglected to inform her that said scream was the call of a bird. Mr Bin had instructed me on a former occasion that it was the call of a giant owl named Pel's fishing owl, which occasioned a water hole. It makes a scream like the scream of a lost soul falling into a bottomless abyss. The sounds are so alike that if you heard a lost soul falling into a bottomless abyss, then you would erroneously conclude that it was a Pel's fishing owl and continue about your business without concern and without offering aid to such a soul.

When we reached the vehicle, Miss Camlyn dared to look back. She released me. 'Oh yay! Look! They're safe!'

It was indeed Mr Summerberg and Mr Bin. Mr Summerberg was carried in Mr Bin's arms like firewood. I hastened to his assistance.

'Let me down now,' said Mr Summerberg, struggling feebly, but Mr Bin passed him to myself. He weighed hardly more than a chicken.

Whilst Miss Camlyn held his hand, I carried him towards the vehicle. 'Did you hear the brackish akalat?' I enquired with polite formality, as if it was a regular service to carry our guests around whilst discussing the sounds and sightings of the day.

'Don't ask,' said Mr Summerberg with much groaning. 'We only saw it … we think. Just a glimpse. But maybe we didn't. Put me down, will you?' I lowered him to the ground, but he could not bear his chicken weight, so I put his arm around my shoulder and transported him like a sack, his white hair bursting out like cotton bolls. Mr Summerberg groaned again, but said, 'We thought we saw it … then nothing. Like a ghost. We sat around until dusk. Never glimpsed it again. Never heard it. Here's a thing, I'm not even sure we knew what we were listening for.'

'Only certain people can hear it,' said Miss Camlyn. 'But which people, Ben? Who? We need to know.'

'Did you hear the Pel's fishing owl?' said Mr Bin. 'It makes a call like the scream of a lost soul falling into a bottomless abyss.'

'It was just an owl? I nearly wet myself. I thought something had died.'

'It had, it had,' said Mr Summerberg. 'All hope died out there today. They'll be no farewell message from me at my funeral.'

Miss Camlyn puzzle-faced me, then said, 'Oh Grandad, how sad. At least you tried. A lot of people your age wouldn't even bother. They'd just be shuffling into the sitting room to doze off in front of the telly.'

In the vehicle I served Mr Summerberg a glass of Kilimanjaro Spring Water. Miss Camlyn said that I should not trouble with the ice as Mr Summerberg needed resuscitation and rehydration rather than 'silver service pampering'.

So it was in silence and in a sombre mood that we returned our guests to their hotel, but both alive, thank the heavens. Miss Camlyn was attentive to her grandfather and said not a word to Mr Bin. Mr Bin, of course, said not a word to any of us.

The brightly lit hotel was well away from the scrappy village and had its own driveway, and a weed-suppressed, block-paved forecourt lined by a trimmed hedge. Its sharply-plastered white walls and polished black stone steps leading up to a mahogany double door with long gold handles was all in the style of a civilised residence. Everything was tidy and straight under its tiled roof. It was of a suitable standard for our guests to step into, unlike Mr Bin's primitive dwelling.

A concierge in a scarlet jacket hurried to open the vehicle door, delivering a face-splitting smile and verbose expressions of overwhelming delight at welcoming the guests back to the hotel.

Mr Summerberg leant forward and in a feeble voice said, 'Ben, do you have any guests tomorrow?'

'Ja.'

'No, Mr Bin, you forget,' I said. 'We've no one. It seems that bookings are poor.'

'El,' said Mr Summerberg, strengthening somewhat, 'as soon as we're in the hotel, email our agent and say we're rearranging. Ben will pick you up tomorrow morning at six and you'll return to where Ben and I thought we saw the bird. As Ben says, if it sings, it'll do so at dawn. It'll be the last chance. I'm relying on you El.'

'Yikes! But yes, I'll do it Grandad.'

'I can't,' said Mr Bin.

'I'll pay you double, Ben. It'll save on inheritance tax.'

'Tomorrow's out because—'

'Ben, tomorrow,' said Miss Camlyn, 'I'll only be interested in knowing about the birds. The difference between a brackish akalat and a not so brackish one. I want to know their Latvian names —ha, Latin names.'

Mr Bin did not reply.

She corrected her expression to thoughtful and prudent, as

if regretting her silly word conjure. 'And when you're not telling me everything about birds … I'll be as quiet as a bat. No dumb questions. No silly-ha-ha.'

'Miss Camlyn is born again, converted to orni … theology,' I said.

My Bin's gaze slid up to the roof, but his fists no longer gripped the steering wheel as tight as a man hanging from a branch above an abyss.

The concierge assisted Mr Summerberg out of the vehicle with precise consideration. Mr Summerberg turned, leaning on the concierge, and said to Mr Bin, 'Six o'clock!' He pointed the makeshift walking stick at him, pinning him to the commitment.

Miss Camlyn deported herself modestly and smiled pleasantly at Mr Bin although he was not looking. 'Six am! See you tomorrow. Can't wait!'

Mr Bin thumbed his chin, but he did not contradict her. Maybe he was becoming conflicted, as Miss Camlyn had hoped.

Our VIP guests turned to go. What a fantastical emolliation. I became light of heart. We had swerved at the last moment and so had avoided the car wreck. Miss Camlyn had learned fast how to soothe Mr Bin. Mr Bin had accepted to go with Miss Camlyn. Surely the bird would sing on such a romantic occasion and, after, I would have another opportunity to ask for an introduction to Miss Camlyn's mother. The fruit of my labours had ripened. Tomorrow I would eat.

That's what I concluded, but the fruit was soon to foul. Mr Bin had only just lifted his hand to acknowledge our guests' departure when a woman appeared at the top of the steps of the hotel. She had dark cigarette-thin trousers and a most fashion-fitting blouse of a black satin nature. Her hair gleamed like a wet puma. She stayed a moment in the light of the portico like a pointy-bosomed manikin in the window of a high-end departmental outlet, an imperious hand poised on the arch of her hip. She bore a glossy crocodile-skin satchel from her shoulder, embossed in an upmarket font of silver calligraphy. I much admired her modern look. She no doubt flew in fast jets and dined in top restaurants. She strode towards us, her knee-high boots spanking the paving.

'Ag shame! I've tracked you down at last, Robert Benjamin Du Plessis!' I looked around to see who she was addressing so forthrightly without so much as a greeting. 'You thought you could hide, did you? Out in the *gammadoelas* with your twitchers. With all the other losers. But I was never going to give up, was I?'

Miss Camlyn and Mr Summerberg stopped to bug-eye this handsome but discourteous woman who was, perhaps, in a tiffle with a boyfriend. There were only four men in the proximity. Who was this Robert? It was not me, of course, and not Mr Summerberg, certainly not. It was not the concierge; the woman was not fixing at him. It could not be Mr Bin. He had no one. In any case, I saw that the lady must have been perhaps ten years older than Mr Bin.

I leant out of the window and said, 'It's a case of mistaken identity, good madam.'

'I know where you hide. My fiancé found your ... hovel ... this morning and he's been driving around looking for you.'

'Please, Jemima, cool it. I'm with guests!' Mr Bin spoke without looking at her, holding the steering wheel to his chest as if it was a shield.

She stopped only a hand away from Mr Bin's window and said too loudly, as if Mr Bin was deaf, 'You're a useless unproductive *domkop*! You're an ambitionless ... spineless ... indecisive ... timid ... aimless yellow jelly. But I told you that a million times before.'

Mr Bin could only remain dead still with unblinking eyes, like a chameleon that has fallen under the shadow of a hawk.

'All you've got to do is sign!'

The woman who Mr Bin had called Jemima reached into her crocodile-skin satchel —by Gucci, I noted with further respect for the lady— and presented a bundle of papers to the window.

Mr Bin actuated himself and fired the vehicle. I impacted the back of my seat as we spin-wheeled away as if escaping said puma, determined to claw him.

'Stop!' I heard the woman scream without restraint. We did not. Her papers scattered like a flock of panicked white fowl.

We arrowed along the track, Mr Bin and I, flying deeply into the dark, which promised to hide us from the discourteous woman. I was perturbed by this unexpected state of affairs.

For a long time we were silent together until Mr Bin slowed down, allowing me to release the handgrip. He said to me, 'Do you want to know who that was, Mozzy?'

'Only if you wish to say so.' I had no wish to intrude on a private matter but there was no escaping from the catastrophic chaos of Mr Bin's life, the runaway sixteen-wheeler truck of his failings.

'I guess I've got to admit it to myself. To face it again. I have a wife.'

CHAPTER 5

We arrived at Mr Bin's residence with no more words. He told me to stay in the vehicle whilst he collected my bicycle and my backpack and dropped them into the load area. He said that he was taking me home. I wondered then whether, for the very last and final time, Mr Bin was enacting my sacking. Surely, he no longer required my services. The impediment in his personal life was not conducive to attending to his business any longer. It would be essential for him to return to the civilised world to attend to his wife's request and to apologise to her for his behaviour. To seek her forgiveness.

Of course, I wanted to escape Mr Bin and his backwards and primitive habitat. In every respect except the fiscal one, I wished to quit in order to pursue my career. Furthermore, my estimation of Mr Bin's personal character had fallen still further. I would be even more uncomfortable in his employ. Jemima was his legal wife. He had made vows. He was subject to a wed lock. He should not have been hiding from her. For myself, I found it important to respect my employer. I could respect Miss Camlyn's mother for her achievements in creating the finest restaurants in the world, but Mr Bin had no redeeming accomplishments. I could only think of this: he had been disloyal to his wife and run away from her. I thought again of my father, how he was never disloyal to his wife, my mother, despite worst circumstances. Mrs Bin seemed to me a most respectable woman even if understandably upset and concerned by her husband's running. So, yes, I would be glad to move on and upwards. But it would be a convenience to quit at a time of my choosing, when I had received an alternative posting.

'Shall I tell you about my wife, Mozzy?'

'No need.'

'She's my wife of two years. The first year? Ended horribly. Shall I tell you about it? I suddenly feel a need to blab.'

'No, no, please don't.'

'The second then? But you know about that. Out here. Evading her.' He glanced in his mirror as if she could be pursuing us down the road in her spanking boots, sleek hair and puma eyes burning red in the night. I saw that he was cavern-eyed and pale.

'Ja ... sorry ... gonna tell you anyway. I made a mistake, Mozzy. I got carried along. I should have said no when she told me to marry her. She make-believed I had some sort of potential ... my first-class degree and a Masters. She thought I'd become a banker or an entrepreneur. Make a load of dosh. For Piet's sake ... my Masters was in avian ecology!' He frowned. 'I think I wanted her to be someone else as well. Not sure what. We both ended up disappointed. Ja, I was ... despondent but she was ... spitting. No. She was more than that. She was ... apoplectic.' He blew out his lips. 'You heard her ... tuning me like that in front of guests.'

We drove on for three minutes, both quiet, and myself ill at ease. *Home affairs should not be talked about on the public square.*

Then he said, 'Spineless.' Then, 'Unproductive.' Presently he added, 'Ambitionless ... indecisive ... timid.' He furrow-browed. 'Oh yes, a yellow jelly. What the — does that mean? Can you think of anything else she said about me, Mozzy?'

I was happy to have the opportunity to help with that. 'You're useless, as well.'

'I guess so,' he said.

But I thought how Miss Camlyn did not think that this was the case. She had seen the worst of Mr Bin and yet she did not hold negations against him. On the contrary, Miss Camlyn had expressed love. It was a tragedy that she had been misled by Mr Bin. He had many opportunities to inform her that he was already married, but he had never had the courtesy to do so. I thought of her now, how she would be sitting on her hotel bed, bent over with her hands in her distraught hair, weeping from her pretty but wounded heart. She would be oblivious to the eases of civilisation that surrounded her: the memory foam mattress, the embroidered pillow cases of Egyptian cotton, the bedside lamp by Tiffany, the soft white bathrobe and slippers, the silent-running ceiling fan, the dressing table spread with body lotions and scents of highest expectations. My heart was bruised for her.

I was also in pained cognisance of the negative outcome of my proposed application for a head chef position.

'She's with Tarquin Wallington-Williams Junior and she wants to marry him,' said Mr Bin. 'He's a proper businessman. He's got the MBA from Harvard or somewhere important. Like his Daddy. He's got the connections ... the stocks. And he's got the spine. She wants me to sign the divorce papers. Then she can fly away to Florida.'

I coughed.

'Thanks for hearing me out, Mozzy. Thing is, I'd agree to a settlement if she agreed to share a few coins. A little pocket money, crumbs of her geld. She won't notice it. They cosy up in larney hotels, do their shopping in Joeys. It's the principle. It would help me to pay for your cookery, damn it.'

'Am I dismissed from your service?' I said.

Mr Bin continued to fish in the dismal waters of his thoughts but after we had travelled further, he said, 'Why would I ever dismiss you, Mozzy?'

'You already dismissed this morning and this afternoon, and on many previous occasions,' I reminded him.

'Heat of the moment, Mozzy. Believe it or not, you're my only *broe* out here in the bush —after Freddy and Caterpillar, of course. I don't care for your cooking, but I'll say this ... you're reliable. And you suck up spectacularly to the guests. But the strangest thing is this. I like you. I really don't know why. We could almost be friends.'

That did it. I had to go. I had to dismiss him. He had crossed a line. I could not let Mr Bin distract me from my career path by sentimental leanings, by breaking the proper positions of professional relations, by this 'could be friends' nonsense. It would lead to disaster and deep regret. That I knew from experience.

He slowed to negotiate a deep ravine across the road, the headlights making hazardous dark valleys of the ruts. I always had to step off my bicycle for this dangerous perturbation on my way to and from work.

'Jemima just wants me to sign.' He crunched the gear as I gripped the handrail again. 'Thing is, I'm not *that* spineless.' He nodded to himself as if this reassured him that he was not as useless as all believed.

We turned onto a side-track on the untidy edge of the village, past the standpipe from where I collected water and then past the barbed euphorbia until we arrived at my gate, which my good wife had made with a latticework of branches. Our small house was overlooked by the moon of a small satellite dish on a makeshift scaffold and a looping wire which brought power from six to ten evening from an entrepreneur with a generator. I saw how it was like a jail on account of its breeze block walls and window bars, but these ensured security against the elephants and other night poachers, which strayed out of the close-by National Park. A cull of the animals was truly overdue.

I thanked Mr Bin for the transportation home and exited with my bicycle, then I leant to his window.

'Mr Bin, I thank you for your employment.'

'Huh?'

'I'm needing to step up, to take higher employment in another location. It's been satisfactory gaining experience in your employ, and I'm grateful to you of course, but now I need to select a higher gear.'

'Is it the money?'

'No, you've paid me well. I thank you.'

Mr Bin looked away. 'That's it then?'

'I wish you success. As you said, there are hundreds of cooks looking for work. I'm sure you'll find it easy to replace me. It's simple to boil an egg.'

Mr Bin did not respond.

'I thank you again,' I said.

'I guess it's for the best. I can't go back to the hotel in case Jemima's waiting for me. It means tomorrow's off. In any case ... there's no way our clients will want anything more to do with me. Not after that shameful scene. Bookings are thin. I'll have to downsize.'

I felt I needed to say more. This dismissal of my employer was not as easy as I expected. Mr Bin and I had worked in close proximity for a whole year, I noted in belation. Sun up, sun down, through rains and drought, clients in, clients out, we were close at hand. 'We've made guests happy,' I said to concede some positive and because —it was true— we had indeed achieved for guests.

'Um, Mozzy?

'Yes, Mr Bin.'

But he put into gear and said so quiet that I could hardly hear him, '*Totsiens* Mozzy.' He revved and departed.

I stood there in a muddled mingle of thought, seeing the red light from the single working bulb at the back of his vehicle become as small and faint as the glow of an ember in the night. The ember died. Mr Bin was out of all sight. He had disappeared into the infinite weave and tangle of the bush. He had fled to where no one else lived, where he would not be troubled by personal matters. I surmised that he would like it that way. Now he could be truly on his own. He would not have to converse with guests. He could freely enter my kitchen with cats, apes and snakes. He would no longer have to eat 'curries'. When day came, he could trek out where the beasts roamed, binoculars in hand, an easy giraffe gait, his footprints cavorting with the hooves of the beasts, clouds of insects rising as he passed, to flutter whitely in the sunlight. He would have the freedom to listen all day to birds carolling and to search for the brackish fowl without distracting and probing talkative company. Truly, I did not understand Mr Bin, his lack of a dream for his future. His wife had spoken honestly when she said that he had no ambition. He was indeed an unfitting individual to be the proprietor of a safari business and my father spoke truly when he said, *The heart of another is a hidden place that we can never know.*

CHAPTER 6

My dear wife, Dorothea, was watching TV in our principal room when I opened our front door. She was attired in the plain colours and shapeless, spiritless vestments of the Divine Prosperity Assembly, namely a purple headscarf with a white headband and a leg-concealing purple dress under a white pinafore. I was momentarily nostalgic for those days when she outfitted in hoop earrings, a gold blouse, pepper-red skirt and sheer tights. She had tuned the TV to the Sanctified Success channel, as was her recent custom. A preacher orated with a mighty voice, pouring the sweat of forceful sincerity. He called on the unsanctified to come forward to receive said sanctification and so, as a sure consequence, blessings, harmony and prosperity. Personally speaking, I preferred watching a cooking competition named *MasterChef*.

'Ah! My beloved husband's home,' Dorothea said. She turned off the TV and skipped to me to peck the air next to both my cheeks as was her delightful custom. No holy outfit could suppress her light, dancing movements or her glittering eyes.

'My dear wife, thank you as ever for your unfading greeting.' I was so sorry that it was necessary to break what would be uncomfortable news to her concerning my employment. Whilst readying myself, I asked, 'How was the Assembly?'

'We were blessed, truly blessed!' She clapped her hands. 'Pastor Cain preached with overwhelming power. With such authority! And look, see, he's bestowed on us a precious gift. I'm so excited.'

She gestured the wood table with a throw of her hand. On the table was a tower of promotional leaflets for Pastor Cain's More Blessings Campaign, which she energetically distributed in the village. In the centre of the table was the trumpet-like vase, which we had received as a wedding gift. This was most fittingly made of unbreakable glass. A purple and white flower, of a durable plastic variety, bloomed from the vase as symbolic of Dorothea's late piety. There was also a brick, a russet brick squatting on silver-starred wrapping paper and a purple ribbon of the high gloss synthetic kind that is machined in China. The said brick was burnt at its edges and I recognised it as typical of the bricks that were fired at the small kiln outside the village.

'Where is the most precious gift?' I asked.

'Open your eyes!' She held a reverential hand above the brick and spread her fingers as if to catch invisible rays. 'This is the gift of course. Look, it came beautifully wrapped.'

I came closer to inspect said gift. I took it and lifted it with a studious disposition to see if I was missing a concealed compartment underneath, but no, it was solid through and through, and heavy. Indeed, each of its six sides presented a brick-like face. I lowered it again with care as Dorothea had tensed in case I dropped it.

'But surely, this is a common brick,' I said to my dear wife.

'Oh, ye man of little faith! That's not a brick. It's been consecrated by Pastor Cain. It's an ordained stone. A spirit-fired rock from the clay of the earth.'

'My mistake,' I conceded. 'To me it looked like a brick.'

'We'll lay it in the wall of our new house. It'll be the founding stone.'

'What new house, dear wife?'

'Dear husband!' She threw her arms in the air to have to hear her slow-witted husband. 'Pastor Cain's prophesied that we'll be blessed with a new house now we've received this sanctified stone. The timing's perfect. We're ready right now for new blessings. See how our sofa's far too large for this small room.'

My wife spoke with veracity. We could not pass our table and our two simple wooden chairs without impacting our knees on the pink leather sofa. That sofa was much admired by Dorothea's friends in the village. It stretched the length of the wall and sported polished wood detailing on the frontage of each arm and large pink buttons on the back of the seat. Some said that it was like a buffed limousine, smooth and shining, even opulent and progressive. Some said that the arms were like the sunburnt thighs of a heavy tourist: fleshy, curved and soft. It depended on the light of the time of day. Whatever, it was splendid and sumptuous. Furthermore, the seat was truly voluminous. Even the obese village policeman, Mr Bambatiwe, looked diminished when he occupied the sofa on those occasions when we were obliged to entertain him and feed him cake. The villagers concluded that the pink sofa was a sure sign of spiritual blessings on my wife. Indeed, the proof and the fulfilment. They aspired to the same. For myself, I was content that it brought a modern comfort to our small house, but I also concluded that without my salary from Mr Bin, we could not have purchased such an amenity. This point of fact was on my mind as I examined again the brick on the table. It would make only a solitary and, in truth, negligible contribution to the walls of a new house.

'My beloved wife … that was most kind of the pastor. Is he gifting us a house?'

'My beloved husband! It's a symbol. Please understand! A denotation. He's gifting us blessings! They'll pour on us from on high. We'll build the house. The brick is the promise of blessings. The hope of the future. The sure sign of grace already given.'

'And did he gift us the brick?

'Of no faith! Of course! He gifted this baked loaf of blessing.'

'A most generous man,' I concurred.

Dorothea took a yellow duster and wiped the burnt edge of the brick as if she could increase the promised blessing with such attention. 'Of course, I signed up to give the suggested love offering.'

'Pastor Cain suggested? How much was the suggestion?'

'Just one thousand.'

I weakened and sunk down into our soft pink sofa. Had anyone in all world history, I asked myself, from the Tower of Babel to the Dubai Burj, paid so much for one brick? I stared again at the brick, trying to utilise the eye of faith. Despite my scrutinising eye, I saw that the brick was not glowing in a golden ray, or fluctuating in the rainbow colours of paradise, or undergoing miraculous multiplication. No, of course not, it was a russet brick —plain brown even— from the smoky brick kiln outside the village.

'Dear husband, be reassured, Pastor Cain promised that we'll receive a hundred-fold ... maybe a thousand-fold. That's one million. This holy brick is a small investment for such a blessing. We can't fly unless we first jump off the false safety of the branch. That's what Pastor Cain so truly said.'

'How will we pay for this beatified brick?' I was on the tip of divulging my dismissal of Mr Bin as my employer, but Dorothea was quick to state her case.

'You're asking how we'll afford the love offering? My blind husband, how could you ask such a foolish question? Don't you know? Love is priceless, but it costs next to nothing. Pastor Cain graciously accepted a commitment from us to gift in instalments.'

I may have then nodded to politely acknowledge the benevolence of Pastor Cain. 'We always, by heaven's grace, have change left over from your salary. You're blessed with employment. It's promised that if we give back a blessing ... then we'll receive even more blessing. Pastor Cain says that we'll climb a pyramid of gold.' I may then have grunted to acknowledge my wife's holy beliefs. 'A thousand-fold! Jezek eight. Verse nine. Line two.'

I may have replied, 'Jezek eight.'

'Dear husband, please! What bank account would offer such a high rate of interest? See how Pastor Cain himself has been showered with blessings. His new palace has an electrified perimeter wall three metres high. It's secured by a topping of broken glass from champagne bottles. And it's painted holy-gloss-purple and bright-angel white.' She looked at me and maybe thought that I needed more convincing. 'He has his own borehole and generator. An Italian marble jacuzzi! His reception room has lilac and cream reclining chairs ... a French chandelier and pouf upholstery. That, husband, is the pouf ... proof ... of blessing.'

I may have been silent in response.

'Oh, faithless one! So much to learn!' She shook her head and turned to busy herself. 'Now, let's be thankful that we're also to receive such blessings and let's eat.'

I could not eat. I was cognisant of my father's saying, *Beautiful words do not put money in your bank account.* As an assistant bank clerk, he had the expertise to know such. I was suffering a stomach-ache and was fatigued. I had lost the strength to tell my good wife that this was an inopportune time to pay 'love offerings'. I excused myself and departed for bed early. I needed to rest and to organise my thinking. Dorothea pecked me forgivingly near my cheek and offered her prayers for my hasty recovery, but mostly that my faith would materialise.

As I washed and prepared myself for bed, I heard her singing with abundant cheer. She was blessed most, I realised, with no cares for the future. Blessings were assured. In her thoughts she had already partaken of Pastor Cain's blessing, had already received it, was already living in a palace with a vault ceiling reception room that would make our pink sofa look like a child's seat, was already bathing in sparkling spring water imported from the high lands of Scotland. Such must be the true reward of faith, to have a guaranteed prospect. No wonder she passaged life singing and dancing. In truth, her joying charmed me, even to endure and forgive her religious indulgences. In this way, we lived in harmony.

Later, it was pleasing that Dorothea slept soundly beside me, but I did not. I thought that even now, so soon after sacking my employer, I had an urgent need to cook superlative dishes for guests once more. Had I made a hot moment mistake? Would anyone ever say to me again, 'Mr Mlantushi, your cuisine is divine'? It passed my mind that if I did not find a high-end chef posting in double-quick time, I would indeed be a lost soul falling into a bottomless abyss. I did not accompany this thought with the vocal expression of such a soul out of a respect for the peace of Dorothea's sleep.

Such a soul would have a propensity to self-pity as it plummeted without hope. To distract my thoughts to a healthier comportment I remembered my boyhood. Ah, those happy days. I had no cares in that little town, even though the streets were littered and dusted, even though the sidewalks were cracked and crazy, even though wires hung in loose knots from poles or drooped low between the houses like vines. Lying there in the dark, I took myself back. I smelt again the odours of that faraway place: roasting corn, cattle pats, the smoke of burning grass from the surrounding fields. I heard the scratching of the crows' feet on the tin roofs of the houses and I heard the popping of the joists in the hot sun. There again were the shouts of my friends. My feet kicked a football once more with those boys, our limbs smacking into each other's like staves. Where were they now, those friends? I had many.

I remembered helping mother when she was in a peaceful state of mind to feed the brown hen in the yard and I remembered collecting the warm egg each morning. How proud I was to take it without dropping and breaking it to the kitchen. My father took care of everything else. He took my mother to the clinic, got her out of bed in the mornings when she did not wish, cooked for both of us and brought her back from the bar if she'd been out drinking and spending. He fetched her from the street at night if she'd gone out naked in a disturbed state of thinking. Her life was indeed commotional, but my father looked after her and succeeded in maintaining order while I played. Yes, in those days I had no strivings to contend with.

I wished to allow my remembrance to float there in that contented time, and then I would drift to sleep, but I could not. Once a consternation is recalled in the dark ocean of the night, it sucks thought into a whirlpool from which it cannot swim free. I remembered that I was thirteen years when my father lost his capacity. He suffered a brain stroke. My mother, she lost control of her mind; my father, he lost control of his body. He could not speak and his limbs were both stiff and limp. I do not know which is more unfortunate: to be crippled in the mind or the body.

Mother left us soon after my father's stroke. She went away with a friend of my father. I always remembered that it was a friend of my father who took mother away. Yes, a friend. A man he trusted. A man he talked and laughed with. What then, is friendship?

Mother left a chaos in the house: broken plates in the sink, glass on the floor, dirty clothes, a bare pantry and a dead hen. But I missed her.

I had to step out of class to care for my father. My play days were over, my strivings had begun. To spoon edible food into my father's mouth, I learnt how to cook. To please my father and maintain his example, I took on myself to sustain an orderly house and kitchen and I washed and ironed his clothes. I dressed him in his suit every day as if he was going in to work at the bank. I had experienced from my mother what befalls if there is a lack of dignity, if there no self-mastery, if there is loss of control. Duty, discipline, decorum and diligence. Those were the four Ds of necessity. Otherwise there was destruction, disgrace, dirt and disorder.

I told my father that although he could no longer speak to voice his sayings, his wisdom was in my heart. I do not know if he understood me.

After one year I returned to class, but I also took employment in the kitchen of the finest hotel in town to pay the school fees and for living. My father's disability pension paid only the rent. I became specific in my habits. Without such I could not have accomplished the timetabling of my father's care, my schoolwork, my household duties and my position at the hotel. There was no more footballing in the street. No more hanging about with the boys. That was the time, in truth, when my friends quit coming around.

The hotel chef resided under the kitchen table under the influence of alcohol and so I graduated in record time from dish washer, to vegetable chopper, to stew stirrer, to cook. There I found my talent and my calling. When I served my dishes, the truck drivers who stayed overnight in the hotel, complimented me. 'You were taught by my grandmother, yes? Fetch me another serving.'

True, my grades at school became compromised after my mother's departure and my father's infirmity. My no-nonsense (and so, to my liking) English language teacher, Miss Nyanda —who had herself been drilled in correct English by an old missionary lady— wrote 'outstanding diction, if a little archaic' in her school reports but in other subjects and endeavours, only my stews had top marks.

Dorothea turned in bed which helped me skip-thought past the direful occasion when I neglected the four Ds. I thought instead of my good fortune in meeting Dorothea. To court a woman was problematic whilst also looking after my father on account of his overall dependency on my assistance, but after my father passed I had eyes on the gold-bloused, pepper-red-skirted, sheer-tighted receptionist to the hotel proprietor. A very modern lady and of a joying disposition to balance my temperate comportment. I presented myself to Dorothea's father and he accepted that I was a suitable groom on account of my steadfast income, my illustrious but sober personality and as a favour for some favour given to him by my father relating to fiscal matters at the bank. Dorothea had no objection. She was tired of being jilted by sugar daddies. Whilst a honeyed sentiment is claimed to be necessary for marriage success, I was satisfied that she testified that I was a kind man and a man of principles. From the first, we lived in wedded contentment. There is no greater satisfaction … and convenience.

I studied my profession to advance myself, enduring a bus to the capital to spend ten-hour shifts in the National School of Catering library, and volunteering in the restaurants. I mastered cuisines from all over. Idiyappam, friggitelli with tomatoes, beef wellington, egusi, kuku paka. From Keralan to Kenyan and more. To exceed the expectations of the truck drivers, I experimented with every combination of flavours: pineapple and cinnamon, banana and anise, mango and coriander, bacon and eggs. I souffléd, grilled, steamed, basted, sautéed, marinated and smoked. I plated out on leadwood, soapstone, catalpa leaves, scalloped shells and —on one celebrated occasion— hubcaps. The truck drivers cheered on that one. I experimented with high-end presentation: dusting, drizzling, sprinkling, fluting, grating and blanching. Out of the muck and disorder of earth-soiled vegetables, crushed-up peppers, fragmented flakes of cinnamon and snapped twigs of cloves, I crafted creative order presented to please the eye. To be a chef is like being a Doctor of Medicine. Fine food is like good health, conducive and necessary to a satisfying and productive life. The promoters and creators of good food and good health are to be lauded in equal measure.

The hotel guests surely benefitted. I upped my game, month on month. A person must be stubborn and relentless in their quest for advancement.

Dorothea often said, 'Your cooking is an obsession.'

I thanked her for her praise.

Yes, I bolted myself to duty, to order, to control in living. All to achieve excellence.

Then one timely day the hotel manager said to me, 'The truck drivers must have traditional food. They've tried your carrot marmalade on crumpets but now they want to go back to cassava and chicken stew with *chibwabwa* relish. They'd like fried rice and smoked fish. They'd like *nshima* and *kapenta*. They're dismayed by your vol-au-vents with porcini mushrooms and I'm dismayed by the costs of your ingredients. We're not the Ritz or the Park Hyatt. We're the Tom Mbolo Overnight Stay Motel (Cash Only). I can't afford your excesses. Curb them, or I'll curb you.'

I had experienced, in truth, that the drivers had recently expressed a preference for their food on a tin dinner plate, served with a ladle from a big pot rather than, I am quoting, 'a thin smear of rainbow colours on a fancy china side plate with a dwarf leaf on the edge'.

Mr Tom Mbolo's remonstration served a predestined purpose. That's where I should be: at a Ritz or a Park Hyatt or equivalent high end. I now dreamt big for my career and suggested to Dorothea that we should journey to the capital to pursue such. I needed discerning customers. I needed sophisticates. I needed clients with up-to-date tastes and refined palates. I had also become displeased with the noisy disorder in the town; the dust and litter in the streets; the cow pats, which dirtied shoes; the grass fires from the nearby fields, which garnished my dishes with ash; the children kicking their footballs; the men sitting idly on plastic chairs in the streets or loafing in the bars. I wanted to be in a place of highest order, endeavour, and strict regulations. In short, an advanced city.

'I don't want to leave my friends,' said Dorothea.

Myself, I did not suffer that constraint.

I opened the *National Reporter* and pointed out an article.

The President announced yesterday that Mpili village, in Northern Province, has been designated as a Growth Point. 'This remote area needs a fiscal kick,' said the President. 'For too long it has not benefitted from economic empowerment. We will found a new regional city there. Mpili will be renamed Romaji.'

Below His Excellency's words was an artist's impression of the proposed city showing taxis and buses on a wide street and many skyscrapers behind a large mall busy with consuming consumers.

A spokesperson for the Ministry of Economic Advancement said, 'A tarred road will be laid to the existing village to increase market access. Tenders are invited for the procurement of land for the building of a petrol station, a clinic and a supermarket.'

With a sharpened pencil, I drew another building next to the mall and drew a large sign above the door. *Mlantushi Kitchen.*

'The President is correct,' I said to Dorothea, 'Rome started from a few mud huts. A great city will surely develop from the Growth Point. The population will have the aspirations of city people. This will be the place where I can develop my career as a top chef. Look, there's our restaurant.'

'Your ambition knows no limit, but it needs a sign,' said Dorothea.

'Look, it has a sign!'

'No, a sign from heaven that this venture will be blessed. And look here.' She pointed to the further text in the article.

An objection has been raised by conservation organisations. A spokesperson, who did not wish to be named, said, 'The Growth Point is too close to the National Park. This haven for wildlife will come under threat from population growth.'

'Ah, but the authorities have already anticipated such objections,' I countered.

A government spokesperson said that the needs of wildlife would be accommodated and compromised [sic] in the Growth Plan. 'In any case,' said the spokesperson, 'economic empowerment for remote regions are our priority over all else.'

Dorothea remained resistant, but at that time she became baptised in the Angelic Miracle Mission. She received a prophecy, a sign, that Romaji would, in some as yet unbeknown way, be a place of miracles and blessings. Dorothea had little belief in sciences or political authorities, in worldly explanatories and logics, preferring to rely on unseen mystical influences and supernatural causalities.

It was a two-day journey to Romaji (a Holy Pilgrimage, said Dorothea), taking the weekly bus for the last day of the journey. Two hours short of Romaji all benefits of civilisation ended. The promised tar had not yet been laid. We slid on gravel patches, threatening to roll, jolting and swerving through thorn bush that stretched monotonous to the horizon. There were no masts, no enclosures, no domestications to reassure. On the horizon the scrub ghosted in and out of a thin haze of heat. The road dipped us into gullies gouged out by floods from infrequent but bad-tempered rains. Buffalo droppings occasioned our route and once an elephant trumpeted beside us, loud as the horn of an articulated sixteen-wheeler, and then bashed off into the wastes. The road gave no intimation that it would have a purposeful ending.

We arrived at the terminus with our suitcase and ears coated in talc-dry dust, but with the wettest of thighs from sitting long on seats with plastic covers, and somewhat queasy from the sliding and bumping. I say we arrived, but it was hardly possible to realise that this was our destination. The village comprised thatched dwellings of the simple two-room variety, dotted about without care. The potential city had no petrol station, no clinic and no retail outlet. In place of a downtown skyscraper at the central point of the village, there was a three-metre-high anthill, its skin baked hard by the torturous sun; but I noted that the ants were more industrious than the villagers who squatted away the time of day, observing the passage of shadows, as lazy as the lifeless air. Chickens and children picked around in the shade of the trees that had not yet been harvested for firewood and bare paths wandered aimlessly across the hard and bouldered earth. Nothing from the modernised world had reached Romaji, not even litter. Dorothea and I footed to and fro, catching latrine-like smells, pondering how high-end dining could be fulfilled in such a place, this outpost beyond, where the ghosts of scrub signed the edge of the world.

Dorothea was soon to point down a track to the house of the local chief which was constructed of brick and sported a shining roof of corrugated metal, which scorched the eye. Deployed outside was a saloon car, admittedly of a faded matt paint and needing the inflation of its tyres to move. It was a promising start to the Growth Point, said Dorothea. The chief's prospective wealth would surely leak down. Furthermore, we noted a sign to the *Divine Prosperity Assembly, Ordained Leader: Pastor Cain.* Looking to the end of the track, we saw an open-walled assembly building with a new tin roof and behind that a house, its walls the only white surface in the village and its doors and window frames a deep gloss purple. It was hatted by an enormous, gleaming satellite dish. Dorothea said she would waste no time in becoming baptised in the Divine Prosperity Assembly.

With our savings from my working at Tom Mbolo Overnight Motel (Cash Only), and the cash Dorothea raised from selling the fake-stone jewellery given to her by her sugar daddies of previous mention, I rented the only other brick building in the village and opened *Mlantushi Kitchen. The City's First Restaurant.* I dreamt that one day, in the not-too-far future, tourists might come to the great city of Romaji and be taken by tour guides to see the original city restaurant, admittedly small and quaint amongst the skyscrapers.

I served city cuisine, of course, notwithstanding the difficulty of purchasing and transporting in fresh high-end produce, Dorothea took care of the accounts and served although she was soon to discover that this was not a full-time occupation.

'Is this what Madonna eats?' asked the villagers. 'How does this compare with a feast at a MacDonald's?' 'Please translate for me. What is the meaning of this spiced blackened poussin with aubergine raita and whole-wheat puffs?'

Ready cash was short in the village and there was no bank, so the villagers paid me in local-grown —but starving— sweet potatoes, thin-muscled chickens and with labouring services to build our small house.

So we lived thus but our financial ends did not meet and the villagers' palates were not attuned to such fine food. They came once only to test my menu, maybe just a starter of, say, sesame-crusted tuna with horseradish mousse before quitting to buy a roasted maize cob or smoked mice on sticks, or roasted caterpillars from a vendor with a brazier on the side of the road.

This did not crack me, of course. I noted that safari vehicles sped through the village on their way to the National Park. The tourists shot pictures of the village and us, its resident herd, as they passed, sitting high above us on the rear seat of their open cruisers in their safari outfittings, the ladies wearing hats by Tilly and sun glasses by Dolce & Gabbana, the men in Hemmingway safari suits with many pockets for wallets and smart devices. Sometimes they halted to purchase a giraffe carved from firewood or to finger a weaved basket of perishable straw before hastening away from the jostling, shouting vendors.

In high hopes of attracting new custom, I constructed a new board by the road saying *Mlantushi Kitchen, Finest International Cuisine*. I posted a blackboard advertising such menu items as, *Guinea fowl (legal) with a ballotine of leg, madeira jus, baby leeks, creamed mashed potato, and summer truffle*. But the tourists never stopped to book in, preferring their safari venues where they were not surrounded by thatched huts, pooping chickens and staring children.

This was a problematic interval on my path to success which tested Dorothea's faith and my fortitude although there were auspicious indications of the birth of the city. The ants still occupied their skyscraper in the centre of the village but a billboard, big as a cloud but a lime-green, was erected over it, advertising Zapp mobile phones. Creamy-skinned lovers on the billboard conversed with each other with glad smiles. The Home of Concrete hardware store promised to kick-start the very foundations of the city. A bar opened, benefitting from Outsized Stereo Speakers. There was no clinic as yet, but a healer sold remedies such as Congo Dust and Tyson Manhood Enlarger from a room behind the bar. A lender materialised to oil the wheels of business. Trust Me Loan Holdings, No Loan Too Small. Although there was still no fuel station for the two cars in the village (the chief's and Pastor Cain's), a deep hole was dug in the ground in expectation of a fuel tank and a sign reassured the villagers: Fuel station! Coming soon!! Do not despair!!!

I cognised that I needed more appreciative clients than the villagers and should move myself into the correct environment. I wanted clients with perceptive palates. I sent for a reference from Mr Mbolo. He was kind enough to write, 'Mr Mlantushi was a hard worker and he can cook expatriate-style food.'

With such a first-class testimonial, I applied for a chef's position in the safari hotels around the National Park. They all declared, 'Sorry, there are hundreds of kitchen cooks looking for work.'

Our savings leaked and my career was stalled. A bold letter appeared in the *National Reporter* calling into question where the development money had gone for the growth of the city. I concluded that to fulfil my noble vocation we must leave Romaji and move to an established metropolis. The village would not modernise in my lifetime. We could not wait so long.

'Patience, dear husband,' said Dorothea, 'don't you see? The chief has new tyres on his car. Pastor Cain is staking out a perimeter wall for his new house. He's even planning electric gates. It's a sign.' She would not consent to move from Romaji until she had received a prophecy at the Assembly.

We terminated our rent of *Mlantushi Kitchen* and became farmers, waiting for the President's promised city to take root.

We grew and vended sweet potatoes, tomatoes and groundnuts. Then, on an unfortunate night, elephants from the National Park raided our smallholding and feasted greedily on our crop. We had grown too tasty a menu for them. When I remonstrated with the National Parks officers at their charges' behaviour, they were unsympathetic, disputing my suggestion that they enact a humane cull, citing the requirement for tourist revenue.

One evening Dorothea returned from the Assembly in beatific excitement. 'We're blessed! I've received a word … no, a prophecy! You'll be offered a chef position shortly. We just have to have faith.'

The very next day I saw a tall visitor in the village leaning into the open bonnet of his grazed and cratered vehicle. Steam fumed from the engine whilst he attempted a repair with a screwdriver and a spanner. He had a three-day stubble, his shorts were netted with creases and he wore derelict flip-flops. I felt sorry for him, for his poverty.

'Excuse me, would you like help?' I asked.

He dropped the bonnet and threw the tools through the window of the vehicle. The smouldering engine had fixed itself. He wiped his hands on a cloth and turned to me. 'Help? Sure … do you know any *oke* who can sweep and … um … prepare snacks?'

'In what profession are you working?'

'I'm going to run bird watching safaris.' He told me had rented an ex-game warden's house from the colonial era on the edge of the National Park. 'I need domestic assistance. Are you available?'

'Sorry, I can't help. I'm in actuality a chef, but I could enquire in the village for you.'

'A chef? I don't mind. You can start straight away.'

Thus, I joined Mr Bin as his head chef, serving his guests international cuisine of the highest standard, making their safaris most memorable and worthwhile.

Dorothea said to me, 'See, prophecy is fulfilled and faith is rewarded.' I had noticed that, on unpredictable and sometimes fortuitous occasions, this was indeed the case. I did not complain.

Chapter 7

Dorothea stirred again beside me, no doubt dreaming of fancy porticos and decorative cornices. I consulted my LCD. It indicated five hours. Perhaps I had slept. Then in the quiet, I heard my father say, *If you have not yet arrived at your destination, keep walking, the destination is still ahead.*

So true, there was no benefit in slothful ruminations, I needed to keep footing. The destination was still ahead. It was a new day, a day of opportunity. My stomach was rested. I departed our marital bed in a clandestine manner so as not to wake Dorothea and attired myself in my wedding suit. I found my suit had somehow grown from the occasion of our wedding, becoming spacious. It would perhaps make me appear a man with a potentiality. My wedding shoes remained well polished of course to the extent of gleaming in the dark. As I exited the house, I passed the blessed brick on the table but did not nod to it. It remained in a dull and unitary state.

My bicycle carried me away, but not down the elephant-infested road and across the perilous ravine towards Mr Bin's residence. Those days were now to be only a bad memory. I cycled to the hotel of our late guests, arriving at five thirty-three hours as the new auspicious day declared itself. I concealed my bicycle behind a bush. The guests at the hotel would not wish to be reminded that such common transportation existed, preferring to think only of their life of safari cruisers and fast jets.

I could hear the cooks preparing the breakfast for the guests and so I knocked on the kitchen door at the side of the hotel and asked to see the head chef, Mr Makata. I was advised to wait outside his office. Mr Makata arrived seven minutes later than the promised five, but this gave me time to anticipate my interview, practicing the recitation of my strengths and refuting weaknesses, of course. I had endeavoured to slay any feeble tendencies in myself after my father's death.

Mr Makata was face down, thumbing his smartphone, shuffling along in sandals and wearing an open-neck topaz and blue shirt with bright yellow buttons. He had cool-guy sunglasses pushed up onto his head.

'Excuse me,' I said.

'Ugh, the signal's poor. Ugh!' He glanced up to see me standing to the side of his door. 'Ah, Mr Mlantushi. Blessings on your day and your wife.'

'May those blessings be your blessings,' I replied, to custom.

His phone vibrated. 'GOAL!' he shouted, high-fiving the air. 'Powers have scored against Tobago.' He went to push open his door, his eyes fixated to the screen.

'Excuse me,' I said.

'Did you wish to see me? As you can tell, I'm fully occupied, but come into my office.'

'I'd be indebted.'

I took the chair in front of his desk beneath the framed icon of the President, but Mr Makata tunnelled under his side of the desk and then I heard his computer whir up. He appeared again with a spider web on his hair and sunglasses like a religious cap. 'It takes a long time to boot, so I can spare you this booting-time.'

'I'll therefore not procrastinate. Thank you for offering to interview me. I'll deliver my CV as soon as required.'

Mr Makata rapped a finger on his phone.

'I'd like to apply—'

Mr Makata's phone vibrated again. 'ANOTHER GOAL! This is unbelievable! We'll make the semi-finals, for sure.'

'I'd like to apply for a position as a chef in your kitchen.'

He laughed as loud as a hooting goose, still eyelashed to his phone. 'My daughter's sent a text to ask if I know that Powers have scored two goals in two minutes. Of course I do!' He looked at me. 'Uh? What? A position as a chef? Why would that be? You work for that Ben safari guide … do you not? If I was you, I'd stay with him.' He inputted on his phone. 'He must pay you well. You have a fine sofa. The guests tell me they're happy with your picnics. They cancel their dinner here in the hotel after they've gorged themselves on your snacks. Have you seen this video?'

He lifted his phone and I saw a footballer shooting a goal. 'That was Macheke last year. He's the one who's just scored for Powers.'

'I've left him for a higher post, such as in your esteemed kitchen.'

'Look at this,' he said. 'This is the best. The goal keeper's so upset afterwards. He's weeping! Look, he's holding his head so it won't shake off from his sobbing. So funny. Uh? You must have been fired. Did you steal from him?'

Mr Makata had shown himself to be infected with colonial thinking. In such thinking, every domestic employee steals from his employer. I did not wish to encourage gossip against Mr Bin by exposing his personal life to third parties. Courtesy should not have a sell-by-date. I held my head up in remonstration and said, 'Someone was fired, but it was not me.'

'Beautiful, beautiful. My daughter's daughter.' Mr Makata held up his phone to show a picture of an ordinary baby. 'Life's as hard as bricks, is it not? You are not disrespected in the village … even if you stole from him. Even if your wife is not yet with children. But we have no vacancy here. Not even for a picnic sandwich cutter. Don't you know that there are hundreds of domestic cooks looking for employment?'

I nodded that this information was well known to me. I sat in hope that he would reconsider, but he was not a cousin of mine or from my clan and so no doubt felt no rightful family responsibility towards me.

'Now, as you can see, I'm rushed off my feet. The computer's fully booted and today I need to print off the menus for the next three days. We always repeat the same as no guests stay for longer than this trinity of time on account of their safari schedules.' His phone demanded his attention again, but he said, 'If a vacancy arises in the kitchen then I'll inform you. At certain times a potato scrubber's needed.'

I thanked him kindly and stood to leave.

Mr Makata held up his hand, restraining my departure. 'I suggest you sell your sofa to make ends meet. How much do you want for it? It's no longer new. The whole village has bounced on it. The price should reflect that.'

I promised to remember his honestly spoken request and left his office. I transited through the kitchen and noted that the floor required polish, the draining boards were stained with dishwater, ants ran up a worktop leg and the aprons of the cooks were spoiled. Tea towels straggled from their shoulders. What was more, their apron strings were loose and dangling. There were no true chefs in that kitchen.

I crossed the forecourt of the hotel to the bush, which had hidden my bicycle, thinking I had to keep footing, if not cycling. But VIP Miss Camlyn herself was present in front of the hotel sitting on the steps. She was outfitted in green and yellow and wore a black bean necklace. Maybe she was attempting the colours of the bush to be more natural, more animal, for Mr Bin, but it was no camouflage, the green too bright lime and vivid, the yellow too stand-out canary.

'Miss Camlyn, why are you on those hard steps? I'm sure the hotel has padded chairs for guests.'

'I'm waiting for Ben. He agreed. He's over half an hour late.' She hugged her knees. 'But Mozzy, what are you doing here?'

'I have … business.'

'So where's Ben this morning?'

'He has a personal matter to attend to.'

'You mean that woman last night?'

I indicated affirmative.

She grin-faced me. 'I told Personal Matter and her dandy to — off and they did. They checked out.'

'I see … I'm sorry that Mr Bin has dropped his appointment with you. He was not expecting you to be here after … Personal Matter showed herself.'

'I don't see why. He promised.' Her lips somewhat rubber-ducked. 'What did I say to you yesterday? I wanted something more?' She threw a resigned up-glance. 'Wishful thinking. A silly dream.'

'I'm so sorry, Miss Camlyn. I wished you only the best.'

She sniffed, although in a mild way, then she stiffened herself and said, 'Anyway … Grandad's not that well this morning. I'm taking him home. Even so … Ben should've come.' She frowned and twisted a strand of her hair. 'I think I like him a little less.'

'I hope Mr Summerberg resurrects.'

'Trouble is, Grandad says Ben knows a humongous amount. If there was any chance of finding the aky-birdy then Ben's the only one to do it. Now it's too late. Although … thing is … I'm sort of pleased we've got to go, because Grandad won't have anything to live for anymore if we'd recorded it. He says he can't die until he's done it. He's never been like this on any of his other quests.'

'My father used to say, *Only the man in the coffin is free from need.*'

'Wow, I wish I'd met your father. Even though his only religion was football. But what did Ben mean when he said that the bird can only be heard by some people? It's making me desperate to hear it. And there's something Grandad knows about its song … but he won't tell me.'

'At times Mr Bin has backward ideas. Stone-age-like people used to live in the park … hunting and living a primitive life without fine dining and television. They made up all manner of stuff.'

'What sort of stuff?'

'I don't have that interest, only Mr Bin. He doesn't appreciate contemporary life. He has no lustings for jacuzzis and leaf blowers.'

Miss Camlyn sighed. 'Ben's so different. If only …'

'I would of course be happy to let Mr Bin know of your circumstance,' I said, 'of you waiting here in vain for him like a Juliet, but it's not situationally feasible. I'm no longer in Mr Bin's employ. I'm here this morning to seek employment in the hotel.'

'You're kidding! What happened? You're the one who keeps it all together for him.'

I had no wish to bad-mouth Mr Bin by telling her that I had dismissed him for his reprehensible conduct. 'There's a lack of customers for Mr Bin.'

'I'm not surprised if he no-shows like this.' She rubber-lipped again.

We were now on the edge of separation. Miss Camlyn was not aware that for a short time the fulfilment of our dreams had been, in certain respects, dependent on each other's. Now we were both waking to discover our hope was a false vision. We had reached for it eagerly, but when we opened our hands we found there was nothing in our palms.

Miss Camlyn stood up. I saw then, almost too late, that she was no longer a client of my employer as I no longer had an employer, so I felt a certain freedom to ask her the question that I had not been so free to ask when she was a guest.

'Miss Camlyn, may I be so forward and audacious as to ask you a favour.'

She laughed. 'Mozzy, you're too proper, too toadying! Just ask away.'

'Would you mention me to your mother? I'm looking to apply for a chef's position in your mother's top-flight restaurants.'

'Top flight? Huh! Mozzy, you're too good for her. Far too good for her.'

'Thank you kindly but —even if that's the case— I'd like the opportunity to prove that I'm far too good for her.'

'I don't ...' She saw my imploring look. 'Of course, Mozzy, if you really want me to. I'll try to speak to her as soon as I get back. *Try* is the word. She's usually too busy to listen to *silly little Chantella*.'

'You're most kind.' No impala leapt in my heart at her commitment, maybe a small rabbit, but as my father used to say, *Not all who ask for the impossible are refused.*

'I better get back to Grandad now. Then its ball bearings, here I come! See ya sometime Mozzy. Awesome day yesterday. I'll never forget it.' Her countenance became becomingly grieved again. 'If you see Ben, tell him I waited and waited.' She stepped away into the hotel, but just before she disappeared she turned and said, 'If you see Freddy, say bye for me. I love him.'

CHAPTER 8

When I arrived back at our abode, I was somewhat relieved to find that Dorothea was out on charitable work with her sisters from the Assembly. I reposed on our pink sofa and studied the brick on the table. Maybe if I could believe just a little. Maybe if the brick proved itself first with a small miracle such as a local chef position, then I would nod to it. But then, with such evidence, it would not be a testing of faith. And if not tested, how could it be called faith? There seemed no exit to such a conundrum. But I was of the opinion that Dorothea's belief was not a question of degree of strength, of conviction on a scale somewhere between a wriggling tadpole and a charging bull elephant; it was either present or not. It was not set about with maybes and misgivings. But, in truth, if the brick were to gift a major blessing, I did not care for a palace in the village close to the untillable wilderness and its crawlies, far away from a big city.

I saw that I had become somewhat weak in my thinking, dallying with speculations on the brick's supernatural powers. I was only trying to understand my good wife, to make an attempt on her point of view.

I was of course avoiding a dependence on Miss Camlyn fulfilling her promise of presenting me to her mother. In my experience, when our guests returned to their home nation, they slipped us from their memory. They soon forgot our hopes and privations. Their tears fell freely whilst saying goodbye, they promised a letter of commendation, or —most perplexing— to send a goat to Africa, or to email a photograph of our happy time together. But no, they only remembered the birds and the little ape, and showed their friends the portraits of such. They ate my food but forgot my name.

When Dorothea came home, she was surprised to see me there instead of at my duties. I had never missed a day of work before. I declared to her the termination of my employment although spared her its voluntary nature.

'It must be ordained,' she said.

'Mr Bin's personal and business life is in disorder,' I said, as a matter of fact.

'I'll pray for him. What he needs are friends. Better still, why doesn't he find a wife in the village? There are many good girls at the assembly.' She pulled a ripe mango from her shopping basket. 'Look, hallelujah! We've fruit for breakfast. Let's enjoy.' She went to cut it in the kitchen.

'Dear wife,' I called to her, 'whilst I have a temporary gap in my employment, we'll not be able to pay for the brick ... the love offering.'

She sing-songed back to me, 'Dear husband, do not, do not, do not fear. This is a true test of faith. I expected it. It's to prove our faith. It's only when we lose all hope, when we have nothing more to give, that we become open to the full blessing. Pastor Cain preaches that it's first necessary to reach rock bottom.'

I was of the opinion that in this respect he aided his followers to reach the basement department by clearing out their savings, but of course I refrained from any disrespectful vocalisation.

Dorothea came back from the kitchen, wiping her juiced fingers on a towel. 'How about this? Why don't you forget about being a head chef far away?'

Did I hear right? Forget my destination? My destiny?

'Think differently.' She returned to the kitchen.

My heart tumbled heavily into my stomach. Dorothea had never questioned my vocation before. I did not cook for amusement, as if it were a trifling hobby decorating the necessary feeding of mouths. It was a feat, an enterprise, a high-minded commission. My calling to chef, surely, was a duty and a noble endeavour as sacred as her gospel.

Dorothea came back, the cut mango on plates. 'Be realistic,' she said. 'Don't live a fantasy. There are no prospects in cooking. In any case, mana is given from heaven, not cooked up in a kitchen. Your aspirations are too narrow. You're too inflexible. Heaven's planning something else for you.'

If Dorothea, my good wife, did not support me in my grand objective, what would become of us? Would we not lose the wedded bliss? I did not question in any manifest way her unfailing belief in prophesy and blessings and had always expected her to do likewise for my pragmatic ambition and reasoned career path.

'Dear husband, the village is growing. Have you seen the new bank? Look for something else. There are many opportunities.' She eyed me with playful and affectionate indications and said, 'What about the dance troupe that displays for the tourists at the hotel? You could learn to dance in a crested crane costume.'

Despite Dorothea's attempted jocularity, I considered this an unfortunate suggestion. I could not speak.

She came and tendered my shoulders with her warm hands. 'I'm teasing you! There are better jobs. Worthwhile jobs. You should relax. Have my prayers ever failed? And we have the solid foundation of the brick of faith.' She turned to admire it, to gain satisfaction from its steadfast six-faced presence.

In the past I had been presumptuous of Dorothea's support. Indeed, she had assisted me when I had opened *Mlantushi Kitchen, The City's First Restaurant*. I saw how dependent I had been on the taciful sufferance of my wife. Whilst she had been in unity of hope with me, I could live in fantastical expectation. I could be bravo. She had never opposed my ambition. Now, I feared, she had lost understanding of all that made her husband himself. She had lost the knowledge that I was born to be a head chef, no man more, no man less. If I was not a head chef, I would be someone else, I would no longer be Savalamuratichimimozi Mlantushi, or even Sava. She would have a second husband; she would be widowed from the first. She would not know Sava anymore. I had no idea who I would be and if I could live as that unknown individual.

I joined Dorothea at the table in a troubled disposition to partake of the mango, but Dorothea was in merry spirits, fast-speaking of the thousand-fold blessings coming our way, of the hopeful new members at the Assembly, of the success of the More Blessings Campaign, of Pastor Cain's splendid silver Mercedes with cruise and climate controls, even Lane Keeping Assist, which waited for a tar road with marked lanes.

'With the promised Blessings we should start a family now, no?'

She had caught me by surprise. I dabbed my lips of mango juice. Of course, we both wanted a child, but I had always wished to wait until I was secure in my career, to have achieved further, to be certain of raising our progeny in a desirable postal with top schools so that they could comport in blazers and school-crested ties. They would then follow their father into success in their respective professions having limitless ambitions such as to play for Man U, become international diplomats at the UN, or MD heart specialists. They would better myself.

'Certainly, it's a matter for careful consideration.'

'But Sava, we don't have to carefully consider. What's there even to carelessly consider? Even before we're gifted the promised Blessing, we have a house, you'll find a job, I have the time to look after a baby. If we don't hurry up, they'll be praying at the assembly for my fertility. The most sanctified members will be saying I'm barren because of hidden sin … or even demon possession. They'll blame me, not you, the man.'

'Let me find a new posting first,' I said, without enthusing.

Dorothea took that as an imminent certainty and talked of commissioning the village carpenter to build a cot of ironwood with rocking feet and talked of knitting soft blankets and tiny baby boots.

After Dorothea had joyed out on her charitable work, I washed the dishes and tidied. Dorothea had little interest in household chores herself, they being merely 'of this sinful world' and not directly furthering the gospel of the Assembly. I turned on the TV and switched from *Sanctified Success* to *MasterChef*. The hotshot judges declared that they were looking for 'an exceptional chef', they were looking for 'an inspirational master of the art'. They were looking for myself! But I was far away, up a long dirt track in a far continent. The contestants boasted of their passion, they were going to 'cook their hearts out', they would be 'gutted' if they lost. Quite so. The judges commended, 'That's buttery and almondy, and it's got that subtle hint of green tea', 'Your langoustines are tender, but they still have a bounce to them,' and such. I could only imagine what they would say about my Roast Eland with Gooseberry Sauce. 'A subtle and genius fusion of African and European flavours. Mouth-wateringly delicious.'

Indeed, I saw that there was nothing the contestants had prepared that I had not exceeded for my guests. Admittedly the squid ink black pasta tagliatelle with a prosecco and crab sauce topped with calamari would have challenged Mr Bin's financial resource and supply chain reach, but not in any way my facility. No, I could not deviate in my ethic, whatever my good wife's proposition. I would not dance for tourists.

I stood, rising to my full one-decimal-six-eight metres, and checked that I appeared presentable for interview. I picked a grass seed off my trousers —the wild was even trying to infest my special longs. I would purpose into the village. The idle life was not in my nature. I needed to put myself out and about. Maybe I would meet another Mr Bin of a more professional type looking for a head chef. Nothing would progress if I stayed on the pink sofa waiting for the extortionate brick to bless us.

CHAPTER 9

The village, I saw with a certain wonderment, had advanced since I had last cared to take a look. The main track through the village was basted with tar and specialist vendors had set up thatched stalls along the road, hanging their goods like butcher's meat from rails: pink, brown, white and red trousers of varietal length on the rail of one, handbags of the lustrous kind on another, then shoes suspended from their laces. Maybe pre-utilised in the USA, but clean, and tempting for their branding, at the least. Indeed, certain similarities had developed between the village and my childhood town. Plentiful litter and dust, for example. I even experienced boys playing football in the side-tracks, their limbs smacking against one another. A crow's feet scratched a metal roof, which had replaced thatch. The large timber that the chickens and children used to peck and play under had been cut down to tidy and beautify the village and the tall anthill, which had monumented the centre of the village, was now just a grass-haired stub. The ants and their mud skyscraper were extinct. The aboriginal condition of the village was vanishing. It was, in point of fact, heartening to see such progress. Perhaps there would indeed be chef opportunities forthcoming.

I passed the street vendors and patrolled further, noting the mix of modern and primitive retailers. Be Bold Investments, General Stores – Authorised Super Dealer, sacks of charcoal, Splendid Beauty Salon, Bicycle Repairs – Any Damage and the previous location of Mlantushi Kitchen, now Shocker Auto Parts (proposed premise). I passed Infestation Control (termites, bats and rats) and Everyone has Problems Gentlemen Outfitters, and then a side road signed to the Full Prosperity Hall and to the Divine Health Mission. I was soon on the other outskirt of the village. Beyond, was the high purple and white wall of Pastor Cain's palace topped by glass shards, behind that a satellite dish as big as the ear of God, listening in to the manias of the world.

At the end of the tar, I stopped footing. There had been no offered chef opportunity. I had exposed myself to opportunity, even surreptitiously allowed myself a small leeway over type of employment that I would temporarily accept, but to no avail. I would not be so discourteous as to say so to Dorothea, but if the holy brick was to gift blessings it had bungled its chance to prove it.

What to do? A bus tipped out dusty but wet-thighed passengers and revved its sooty engine to prevent stalling. I would journey on the bus again and find chef work in the capital. It was a dauntless place of rampaging growth, thick, hooting traffic and aspirational energy even if it was not quite the coveted and progressive West or the audacious cities of metal and glass of the rising East. I would admit to such a transit post on my path to the summit. I could commute monthly or Dorothea could join me after a suitable prophecy and there would surely be another Divine Prosperity Assembly or equivalent to join in a city swarming with thousands of hopefuls.

I determined to buy a ticket for the next day's passage, but I had not enough cash for purchase and so I entered the bank to draw from our account. It was the only state-of-the-art location in that place, dropped like a new-minted coin in the dust of the village and backed by an expensively quiet generator. What a foretaste of life success. In the bank I could even imagine myself as in the centre of a fine city. The sounds inside were of hushed refinement: the clicks of polished, leather-soled shoes on the flecked tile floor and the tip-taps of varnished fingernails on computer keyboards. Chilled and filtered air cooled and soothed my brow. A hint of ladies' perfume suggested aspiring clientele. Moulded electric-blue chairs perimetered the room and the customers were ordered into line by matching blue tapes on posts of chromium. A sign requested customers to respect the privacy of other customers at the glass windows of the counters. No sharing in the public sphere of what should be private. It was much to my liking. The cashiers displayed white and blue badges announcing their names: Monica, Sylvestina, Goodyear and such.

Cashier number one, Sylvestina, gave me a black ball pen and directed me to an application form to withdraw cash, which I duly completed in seven-minutes-thirty in capitals, as requested. I returned to her. After entering the pertinent details in a computer, she stamped it and returned it to myself to take to cashier two at the next window, who gave me a form to confirm the exacting verification of my identity —my wife's mother's place of birth— and authorisation for the bank to store additional credentials. I annotated all with infinite diligence and then took said form to cashier three, named Monica, at the last window, whose accent informed that she was proudly from the capital city. Her hair was braided in a cornrow style, just as Dorothea used to, and she wore big hoop gold earrings and precisely applied lipstick of a pomegranate colour. Yes, city ladies were bringing fashion to the village. She transported said properly completed paperworks to cashier four at the back of the room. Cashier four entered my particulars on his computer. It was pleasing to see attention to correct procedures. Cashier three asked me to repose on a blue seat and to wait. I complied with pleasure. I could see how my father had taken pride in his employment at the bank. It was a profession of integrity and exactitude, of service to customers. The moto of the bank was 'Happy to Help'. Exactly my own sentiments towards customer service, although I would append 'Exceedingly' before 'Happy', or even 'Deeply'.

I waited respectfully for three-minutes-ten by the punctual electronic clock on the wall and then cashier Monica called me from her window.

'Mr Mlantushi?'

'That is myself.' I reached Monica's window.

'The bank can't let you withdraw cash.'

'Ah, I must have errored on the paperwork. I can repeat. It's my wife who normally transacts. I'm a little out of practice in the withdrawal methodology.'

'Your paperwork's correct. There's no money in your account. It's overdrawn by nearly three hundred. You're incurring interest.'

I leant forward towards the glass screen that separated our respective places. I said discretely so as not to embarrass her, 'Are you looking at the correct account? If so, may I respectfully suggest that my money's been stolen?'

'This is the National Bank,' announced Monica loudly, as if I was causing offence. The queue at cashier one turned my way. Monica smiled at me in a side manner as if I was an uneducated domestic servant. 'Your money's secure with us. With respect … with great respect, Mr Mlantushi … your expenses must have exceeded your income.'

I was pleased to correct her mistake. 'That's not possible.' I was aware of the attention of the gentlemen and ladies in the queue, so I announced for all to hear, 'As the son of a late assistant bank clerk, I'm cognisant of financial discipline and fiscal rules.' The queue smiled at Monica's error.

Monica returned to cashier four, passing on this indication of my credentials. Cashier four did not even look at his screen, he just spoke to Monica who then returned to the window.

'Your account's definitely cleared out. You're heavily overdrawn. There's been many transfers to the Divine Prosperity Assembly. There's also a new standing order to them and you're paying interest on the overdraft as well as an unarranged overdraft fee. Do you want to apply for credit? There's a form by the door. Give it to cashier one.' She side-mannered me. 'She'll help you fill it in if you have difficulty.' She looked past me. 'Next customer please.'

I heard two men in the queue exchange about me. 'Better for his type to barter goats.' I turned and fixed-eyed the floor as I shame-tailed out of the bank.

Outside, a safari jeep passed by. A tourist was taking pictures of the village with myself in view. Pictures from an up-and-coming town 'in Africa'. In that moment I saw myself in his photo: a small man in an oversized suit, true, but outside a fine new bank in a busy growing village. He was perhaps engaged in a new commercial enterprise; was a symbol, surely, of Africa Rising, of The Coming Continent. But the picture would not tell of the perturbation in the little man's heart, the cash-flow compromise, the not-yet-achieved objective that was always expected, but forever awaited.

I jumped at a hand thumped on my shoulder. Compelled to twist around, I found myself facing a bank guard in his black jackboots and cocoa-brown uniform, with *Security* loudly designated in white above his shirt pocket.

'Yes?' Was I arrested for going overdrawn?

'You've stolen a bank pen.'

He jiggled on his feet like a boxer, as if preparing to catch me if I ran away. Passers-by stopped, hoping for an incident, the more injurious the better, to relate it on to all.

'You're mistaken sir. I merely forgot. I'm an upright man. I've experienced a distraction consequenting to an absence of mind.' I hot-potatoed the black ball pen to him.

'Don't try that again.' He gave me a Monica side look and turned away; stolen goods recovered.

The passers-by murmured in disappointment. I bent my head and took a side-track off the tar and wandered without aim. My feet disturbed the litter, and my shoes took on dust, but I did not resist. There was nowhere to go but home but how was I to 'dear wife' Dorothea now that I knew she had bankrupted us, had rock-bottomed us? I could not even afford to buy a bus ticket out of that dirty end-of-the-road village to find work. In truth, my trust in Dorothea had been shaken in one instance. I had shrugged about the brick and Dorothea's persuasion, but now it was no shrugging matter. How distressing that I could not rely on others to exercise the same personal discipline in all matters as myself. Not even Dorothea.

A football punched me in the back. I took no notice but it caused me to remember that previously, a long time ago, I had my school friends to speak to, to divulge to, to go to for assistance or for distraction. Where were they now? Far away, they no longer knew me. Where was anyone in the village to plead aid and seek advice from? My exacting duties had left me no time to sit with the men on plastic chairs under a last tree in the village or to gossip in the road. *You seek wisdom when you run out of money,* but where were those to speak that wisdom to me?

I was magnetised towards the bar with its outsized stereo speakers. The blasting of sound might nullify the unwanted accusatory voice in my head against my lawful wife. A purchase of alcohol was excusable, even necessary. I had no exacting professional duties anymore. Nothing that required abstinence.

But I found the coins that I had in my pocket too lonely to pay for any other than a small soft drink named Fruit Flavoured Pop-ade. I brooded in the corner of the bar in a half-light away from a window under the benevolent but watching eyes of the President, the founder of the prospective city. I sipped sparingly at both my Pop-ade and my thoughts.

I delayed returning home. I did not wish to extinguish our wedded delight by informing Dorothea of our poverty and its reason. I would certainly have to verbalise my genuine disquiets on the wisdom of the purchase of the bankrupting brick, symbol of unlikely blessings to come. She would be disturbed that by saying such, I would demonstrate a lack of faith, so enacting a self-fulfilling negation of those blessings. The fulfilment of blessings required the full maintenance of faith. Unbelief would block the blessing. Dorothea's faith was unearthly and without logics, but it was as uncompromising in its demands on her as any of my previous employment duties on myself.

A man shadowed over me and then sat himself opposite. I lifted my eyes to see Mr Makata, the hotel chef, sunglasses parked on his forehead. His shirt shouted out a bold orange and green pattern and he was rotating a gold watch on his wrist as if he liked to feel its splendid weight.

I stood to leave.

'Thanks for your respect,' said Mr Makata, 'but please ... sit down again.'

I sat, resignedly.

'How are your job applications going?'

He had surely come to mock. 'There are few.'

'As I told you.' He signalled the barmaid.

I started to excuse myself, but he said, 'Sit and relax. Don't fret. You're in luck. I've an opportunity for you.'

I was silent, still minded on our destitution, on Dorothea's part in it.

'I'm not merely the head chef at the hotel, I also run a profitable business, in fact an international business.' He paused proudly. 'Believe me. Transcontinental. Global.'

He signalled the barmaid again who hurried her bottom to come over with a large beer and a pink cocktail with a green straw and floating cubes of melon. I thought he was to offer one of these to me, but no.

He placed his phone on the table and said, 'I have to keep a watch for overseas calls, you'll understand.' Then he leant forward. 'I happen to be looking for an additional part-time worker.'

'As a chef?'

'You were a chef. Now you're an unemployed man requiring cash. Believe me, there's no more chef work.'

'Exactly what sort of worker would this worker be?' Would I have to dance for tourists?

'Before I give away privileged business information, I need to know that you're discrete.'

'Discrete is one of my core qualities. I've no wish to know anything apart from what's required to do my job. It was the principle under which I worked for Mr Bin.'

'Absolutely correct and reassuring.'

'But you said part-time. With respect, I need full time.'

'If you proved a reliable and long-lasting employee then you could move to full time. The bonuses are good —if you moved to full time.' He leant forward further and spoke softly, causing me to lean forward as well. I could not help hoping that we would not raise suspicions with the President, looking down on us, watching. 'I'm in export. It's a growth market. China, Vietnam, Cambodia. We even have European partners and intermediaries. To serve our customers we have channels … routes … dispatches … transits… relays.' He nodded proudly. 'We have bearers … consignments … carriers—'

'May I ask what you export?'

'and mules.'

'Mules? They are in demand in the East?'

'What?'

'I was asking what you export?'

Mr Makata waved a nonchalant hand. 'Produce.'

'What sort of produce, if I might enquire?'

He lifted a finger at me. 'Mr Mlantushi, you've just said that you're discrete! That you're not a nosy man. Now you're asking me what sort of produce we export!' He looked up and saw that we were alone … apart from the President. 'But I see I can trust you. We harvest natural products from hereabouts. We're organic produce exporters. We also side-line souvenirs for free-minded tourists. The nation … the people … must benefit from our natural resources. Otherwise the National Park is just a useless wasteland. Don't you agree?'

I delivered him a concurring nod. 'What then would be my position?'

'I see you in the transport division. Two wheels in our logistics empire.'

He had not mentioned dancing. Logistics? It sounded mathematically inclined and somewhat specialised. My grades in maths were never good after my father died. Transport? 'I cannot drive.'

'But you can cycle. Does anyone know that you're no longer employed by the Ben guide?'

'Not as yet. Only Mr Bin and my wife.'

'Let it go no further. Listen here. I'm going to rely on your discretion —which you've promised me. Yes? I can see you're a man of principles. In my business we also have our principles.

If you're a man of principles, then you'll fit in well. The most important principle is confidentiality.'

'Another of my core qualities.'

'Here's the job description. When requested, you'll cycle along the track towards the Ben guide's house. As if going to work. At a designated point along the way, you'll stop and collect the produce. It'll be in a box under a bush off the track. You strap the box to the carrier on the back of your bicycle. You return along the road. You drop it at a house in the village. Very simple logistics. No paperwork needed! In fact, we don't do any paperwork due to our principle of confidentiality … and to comply one hundred percent with government regulations regarding data protection, privacy … blah blah.'

'This box. What does it contain?'

He picked out a melon cube from his cocktail and sucked it. 'The produce. I've already told you. The organic produce. Don't fret —you'll not be carrying anything dangerous.' He chortled. 'Far from it.'

'But what if I'm stopped and asked what's in the box?'

'Have you ever been stopped before?'

'No. Only by elephants.'

'Then why would you be stopped? You have a legitimate reason to be cycling down the track.'

I thought of the negative bank balance, of the brick to be paid for, of the lack of chef positions out here in the sticks.

'You'll be paid discretely. Cash in an envelope. You can decide if any tax is due. The company of course has no wish to cheat the state. We have our principles. It'll be up to you.'

He leant back, picked up his cocktail and squinted down the straw and sucked. 'Ahh! So chilled and soothing. Easy to afford when you're in international logistics.'

I put upon myself to consider an extreme and almost implausible hypothesis: that Dorothea was correct to question the road that I had taken in my life. Maybe she spoke truth. Her suggestion of a substitute career concurred with one of my father's sayings, *Do not let what you cannot do tear from your hands what you can.* Surely this was my exact situation. I should not designate myself as a one career runner. Perhaps I could excel in another vocation, which I had no imagination for at that particular time. Logistics was no doubt an up and coming field. It was surely profitable; the proof was Mr Makata sitting easy, sucking on his iced cocktail like a spoilt but happy kid. Was Dorothea not to be adulated for her nimble thinking? A praiseworthy wife indeed.

Then I recalled the sweat that I had sweated in my training to be a chef, the study and experimentation, the exacting work schedule, the employers I had had to put up with. Mr Makata had offered employment whose only skill was to be able to pedal a bicycle. Bicycle logistics. I would not be creating dishes for the happiness of diners. I would be riding into the wilderness again with its merciless predators and irritable beasts. I would not have escaped or succeeded.

Then I heard my father say again, *If you have not yet arrived at your destination, keep walking, the destination is still ahead.*

'I'm grateful for your kind offer of employment in logistics, but I'm devoted to the pursuit of a career as a chef. I shall therefore decline.'

Mr Makata thumped down his glass, slopping the gloop-green drink onto the table. He stared at me. His lips twisted. 'Come now, Mr Mlantushi! Is there something wrong with you? You're wedded to a make-believe you'll find kitchen work. My job offer's unbeatable. The cash is mountainous … on produce delivery.' He put his finger under his watch bracelet and sprung it.

'I'm eternally and solely committed to the culinary arts.'

'You're half-witted!'

I shook my head.

He surveyed me as if he was looking at a blindfolded man attempting to ride a bicycle along a rough and twisty path. Trying to understand such a phenomenon. 'Let me try to help you. Here in this country … everyone has their dreams and everyone is optimistic, no? Everyone believes that good times are coming as early as tomorrow. We all dress to show our faith in this, no?' He indicated his self. 'But you … in your clerk-in-the-office outfit … you'll never achieve. Why? Because you don't let the dream find you. You think you know the dream. But I'm telling you that we only know what that dream is when it arrives. When we hit lucky. Today, you've hit lucky. Your dream has arrived!'

I stayed comported.

'Very well.' He made a dismissing gesture with his hand. 'You'll have to multi-occupation like everyone else. Smallholding … agent for sim cards … small loans. Bicycle taxi service. Barber on Saturdays. By the way, my offer's still on the table for your pink sofa. Now you'll certainly need to sell.'

I left him and footed home, pride strengthening my steps. I had stayed loyal to my calling despite the greatest temptation under the most urgent circumstance. My resolve was as strong and obstinate as Dorothea's faith. I would not give up. But as I approached our house, my congratulatory thinking ended. How was I to indicate to my wife the necessity for monetary discipline without breaking our married bliss?

I rehearsed my style of approach.

'Dorothea, dearest wife, truest companion, joy of my eyes, balm of my soul, I nevertheless have to raise with you a small but most distressing matter. We have no cash in our bank account. We are cleared out and cannot—'

'Dearest husband, where is your faith? Did I not tell you? Rock bottom first, then a thousand-fold.'

Or I could try: 'Wife, there's no excuse in earth or, for that matter, in the holiest heaven to gamble all our money away on maybes and—'

'Husband! Gambling is of the devil, giving is of God. What are you implying and where is your faith?'

Or maybe: 'Let's go humbly to Pastor Cain and explain my temporarily altered employment position, which is consequenting our fiscal health. I'm sure he'll be happy to take back the brick … complete with gloss paper and ribbon. Still reusable. He'll excuse us from giving him this impoverishing type of love.'

'Certainly not! Love should never be withdrawn! In any case, Pastor Cain will rightly say, where is your faith?'

I slow-opened the door to our little house in expectation of personal difficulties. The unbreakable vase of our married bliss was to be tested. Would it shatter or bounce? I was bodeful. Maybe it was wisest to say nothing and keep the peace. I hoped that my father was in error when he said, *In marriage each has a buried flint and each has a buried stone. Do not dig them up and strike them together. It will start a fire.*

Chapter 10

I had no time to speak, Dorothea came to me in an excited condition. She had my mobile phone in her hand. She pressed it on me and then her eyes rolled to the ceiling and she lifted her hands to the ceiling and supplicated in another tongue.

'Hello?' I said, putting the phone absently to my ear whilst fixated on Dorothea's unexpected conduct. My voice, I heard, was disinterested and faint. True, I had the other matter on my mind.

'Mr Tushi?'

Dorothea's babbling ascended the melodic scale. I could not hear the speaker. Could she not see that I needed to attend to the call? I had to quit the phone and calm her, stop her jabbering. Such behaviour was for the Assembly and should not be brought home; its rightful place was amongst other ululaters and wailers, incited by a bellowing preacher. I had to bring a stern and dignified peace to our private room and I needed to prioritise. First to snap Dorothea from living her life in the blessings of tomorrow, then to make plain to her the overdraft of today. And I would not take the 'dearest wife' approach of previous practice. I would take the 'there is no excuse' line to demonstrate that I, for one, was not spineless in such matters. Only then could I attend to the caller who was perhaps wishing to sell me a loan, my financial status having been sold on by the bank.

I said to the caller, 'Please ring later.'

Dorothea quit babbling immediately, her eyes stopped rolling and she looked straight at me. 'No, no, speak to her! You must speak to her!'

I heard the person shout down the line, 'For — sake, talk to me, will you?'

Dorothea nodded vigorously.

'Yes, hello, I'm here, Mr Mlantushi.'

'At last! I'm Chantella's mother, Mrs Zeto Camlyn.'

Surely, a wise-cracker in bad taste. Dorothea started up again, but then uttered a high-pitched scream and fell, raptured, slain, as was her habit at the Assembly. I was about to press the red terminate-call icon but, most fortunately, she fell into the pink sofa and was mute.

'What was that? Sounds like some creature just pegged in agony.'

'Everything's in order,' I said.

'If you say so. Look, you're just the fella I've been looking for. If —big *if*— Chantella's to be believed.' She spoke with speed. 'We'll need to wangle you through immigration, but I'll leave that to my company minders. They'll take care of all that malarkey.'

I made no sound. Dorothea was still unconscious. Only a bird alarmed outside.

'Are you there, Mr Tushi?'

'You are Miss Camlyn's mother?'

'Biologically, yes.'

My heart started kicking like a zebra, but I held the phone firm. I had to keep a sober head. What if Mrs Camlyn believed that I was not truly ambitious?

'I'm seeking the head chef's position—'

'You'll have a key position, believe me. We'll even pay your air ticket and accommodation. Now look, my man Tushi, I'm stopping you right there because you need to attend to your domestic emergency —was that a cat?— and because I've got to fly. My chauffeur —sometimes known as my fella if he's performing well— is dangling the Aston's keys. I'm opening a fab outlet in Boston. I've set everything in train for you. My PA'll contact you soon. Taraa.' She was gone.

She had not given me the chance to pretend to indicate a balanced consideration of her benevolent offer.

I dropped myself onto the fulsome thigh of our pink sofa beside Dorothea. Like her, I had been knocked down by the wonderous call from Mrs Zeto Camlyn; she so decisive, so crisp, so business-like, so praiseworthy. Yes, my father was correct. *A patient man will eat ripe fruit.* What of Mrs Camlyn's daughter, Miss Camlyn? I had misjudged her. She was not like previous guests. She had remembered my name. She had done as she had promised. I could not breathe for restrained excitement. I had a diversionary thought as I came to full belief in the authenticity of the phone call, that the pink sofa would now remain in our own possession.

I then became aware of the russet brick on our table. Had I not received a major blessing? Was it not a miracle? I did not believe in such superstitions, but I found myself offering the brick a little nod just in case it was implicated in some way in this blessing. It would have been impolite not to.

Cautiously at first, and then throwing circumspection away without restraint, I allowed my fancy to clothe me in the finest, whitest chef's toque and apron. Miss Camlyn's mother would need a head chef for the new restaurant in Boston. She had already offered me the key position. I arranged walnuts and dried cherries on a frisée and apple salad. I embellished the salad with blue starflowers. My hard work and self-mastery had been rewarded and my ambition justified. I ringed the plate of frisée and apple salad with a decorative sprinkling of crispy kale.

Dorothea resurrected from her holy collapse. I confirmed to her the satisfactory news. She powered to her feet, clapped her hands and ululated. 'Pastor Cain be praised! What a great leader! I'm not at all surprised! It was prophesied to me in so many words last Sunday at the Assembly.'

She flew to the brick, knelt on the floor and bowed her head. Then she upped and came with open arms to embrace me.

'We are truly blessed, dear husband. You'll send me your remunerations and I'll find a plot of land for our new house.' She released me to dance. 'We'll have electric gates … silent ones. A drive paved with Italian marble. Our sofa will have the space it deserves. Oh husband, the whole village will see how we're blessed. We'll be an inspiration to them. Did I not tell you? A thousand-fold!'

How could I mention the matter of our empty bank account to my dear wife under such transformational circumstances? Why rub flint against stone? In any case, it was of no consequence now. My dollar remunerations would soon reverse matters. Dorothea's belief in blessings had been rewarded, so she would not be persuaded against the down payments she had made. Ditto, my belief in the benefits of holding firm to my progressive ambition. We would remain in harmonic marital, both strong in our respective convictions, both rejoicing in the success of the other.

Dorothea came back to me and pecked me on my lips and said, 'Now, Sava, we'll have a baby. You always said that when you'd achieved your goal, we'd have children.'

Too fast, too fast for me. 'We should certainly give it consideration,' I said.

She pulled back. 'Not now, surely? Not again? What is there to consider, dear husband?'

I could not speak out exactly what was to be considered.

Dorothea was correct in reminding me of my previous promissory words, but a hook tethered me, prevented me from enthusing for babies just yet. Maybe the hook was a fear of a distraction whilst pursuing my noble dream of high service to diners, or maybe a fear for Dorothea's mortal life if illness befell her in the gestational. I could not verbalise these as Dorothea would rightly laugh them away, and I could indeed dismiss such excuses myself, but sometimes a brain hook snags firm even though it does not have a name or a logic.

I had to say some words of sense to my patient and hopeful wife. 'I should be here when we have a baby, to help look after it. *One knee doesn't bring up a child.* What if I'm in Boston? How will you manage on your own?'

'What a modern man you suddenly are, Sava! No other man in the village would be volunteering for baby care. All would be pleased to be on another continent.'

'Maybe we try at my first vacation.'

We left the issue hanging there or rather I should say that it was Dorothea that let it hang as it was her normal habit to conclude, enthuse, and then joy on, but from that evening I was cognisant that she might be displeased with her husband's position in the procreational department of our marriage. True, she joyed over the prosperity, which would soon be ours, but she danced less around me and did not full eye me. Was a little fire smouldering between us? Had I accidentally rubbed flint against stone?

I proudly arranged an overdraft at the bank. Cashier number three, Monica, was wide-eyed and I think deeply jealous to hear of my appointment. She might be in the glass and chrome palace of the bank with its cooled air and haughty clerks, but just outside the door there remained the stub of the anthill, stalls constructed of chicken wire, sacks and iron sheeting, and young boys still sold mice roasted on sticks. Tails, feet and all. I told her of the shining kitchens and sophisticated diners in the black-tie-and-tails-only gala restaurants of the megacities. My clientele, I told her, would know their pate en croute from their gratin dauphinoise. I could tell that she herself did not.

At the lime-green Zapp mobile phone kiosk in the village I bought credit in order to study new recipes on the Google and acquaint myself with the particular likes and etiquettes of Americans such as whether they preferred grain or grass-fed beef, their favourite whisky and even which hand they utilised for their table forks. A chef must read widely around their craft.

Dorothea was delighted to be held up by Pastor Cain in the Assembly as an example of the fruits of great faith.

'Our sister here is a true disciple. And what is her reward? Overwhelming blessings! She had nothing: a lowly cook for a husband, little money, a cramped and simple house with no space for her furniture, but now, dear sisters, dear brethren, her faith has brought her divine wealth.'

Many people stampeded forward to the front of the Assembly to pledge love offerings and so to receive consecrated bricks. There were injuries in the crush, but nothing mutilating. Dorothea was like a testimonial witness on *Sanctified Success*. No one refused her More Blessings Campaign leaflets.

Myself, I was most grateful to Miss Camlyn and her mother rather than to the village brick, but I was discrete in this opinion, especially to the brick, which I raised a discrete hand to when I passed. Why risk upsetting it?

Whilst studying for my climactic employment, I heard a knock on the door and found Mr Makata standing forwardly there in a kitenge-style loose yellow shirt, boldly patterned around the neck and sleeves. He welcomed himself in and dropped a large cloth bag at my feet.

'Greetings, Mr Mlantushi, I've come to inspect the goods.'

'What goods?'

'The pink sofa. I'm ready to reaffirm my offer.' He passed me and stood in front of said sofa. 'Hmm, it's smaller than I remembered.' He sat down on it. 'Shame, I believe a spring is broken. The policeman who visits you for your cakes is heavy, no?' He close-eyed the leather. 'There are imperfections in the piping and it's a brighter shade of pink than I'd like.' He sorrowed. 'It's not as promised.'

When I did not reply, he said, 'So I can't offer much but … for a man of your unemployed status … it'll be gratefully received. He stroked the sofa with a covert hand and then stood and tried to lift an end.

'I thank you for your interest, but I'm not selling. I do not need—'

'Hmm … I'll need some strong men to carry it away.'

'I'm not selling.' I indicated that I was about to usher him to the door. 'I have a—'

'Very well … you drive a hard bargain. I can reluctantly offer you a little more than it's worth.' Mr Makata saw my eyes were on the cloth bag that he had dropped in the doorway. 'That's from a client of your ex-employer. The granddaughter of an old, old man. She wanted it delivered to the guide. There's a note inside.'

I inspected the contents and found Mr Summerberg's recording equipment, the very ones I had carried for him. Mr Summerberg was enacting a desperado attempt on the akalat.

I read the note.

Dear Ben, Me and Grandad would appreciate it if you could record the bird for us when you next hear it. Grandad can't stop going on about it. Ella x

PS I waited for you!

'As you know, I'm no longer in Mr Bin's employment,' I said. 'I do not pedal myself there anymore.'

'As you can see, I'm rushed off my feet,' said Mr Makata, 'it's time to print new menus. I'm sure you'll find a way.' He turned to covet the pink sofa again. 'I'll leave you to think on my offer. My time-limited offer. Call me without delay.'

He came and lifted my hand to shake it, pressed his sunglasses to his eyes, and then strut-legged off.

Mr Makata had left me under an obligation in no way of my choosing, but I had always fulfilled my obligations. I would have to venture out once more to Mr Bin's residence. In a way, I was happy that this onus was upon me so that I could see Mr Bin just once more. I should inform Mr Bin of my fantastical news and hope that he would share the pleasure. I hoped that he would see that he had been unknowingly instrumental in my success. I would never have met Miss Camlyn if I had not been working in Mr Bin's business. It was only a shame that there had never been any chance of tying their love knot.

CHAPTER 11

I had misplaced the memory of how far over that stony ground I had to pedal in order to reach Mr Bin's residence. Every rut I negotiated, and the grey shapes behind the bushes, caused me to be thankful that I was soon to be out of there. I arrived at eleven fifty-nine hours and saw Mr Bin's vehicle under its tree, indicating that he might be present on his property. I expected him to be asleep in his bedchamber, given that I was no longer available to wake him.

The front door was open and I called out politely. After waiting a courteous time, I entered the house and knocked with propriety on his bedroom door. No answer. I called out again with a raised but well-mannered voice in keeping with my status as an uninvited guest in his house. Passing the kitchen door on my return to the veranda, I took the opportunity to inspect my previous place of employment. A sad sight indeed. The Caterpillar cat was consuming oats spilt on the preparation surfaces. It plunged through the open window on seeing me. A drift of dirt from paws and boots eddied the red floor. It no longer gleamed. I was further affronted by an unwashed bowl and spoon on the draining board. An apron had been used as a drying cloth and discarded in a crumple. I stood in mournful silence. Within days of my departure from Mr Bin's employment all the advancement that I had introduced to his residence had been cast aside. Truly, it was as if I had never worked there. I had wasted all that time:

the scrubbing down after him, ironing his shorts, chasing his pets from the kitchen. Mr Bin would not change. I remembered the embarrassment I felt for guests concerning his decrepit premises. I comforted myself: my new kitchen in Boston, USA, could never have such a sorrowful end.

I perimetered the house, calling Mr Bin's name to no effect. It would be impertinent to sit down on a guest chair on the veranda without an invitation from Mr Bin, so I positioned myself on a small wooden bench in the garden with my back resting on the trunk of a timber and waited in quietude. I speculated that Mr Bin had walked out into the bush and would not return. He feared that his wife would find him, even at his remote residence. Had he been consumed by a predator and so had successfully concluded his quest for solitude by passing himself from all company? But such theories could not be dwelt upon with any benefits, so I closed my eyes and turned my thoughts to the dishes that I had served there. Parmesan and black mustard seed wafers; pork bafat with okra pachadi and rice bread; salmon en papillote with braised fennel and creamy caper sauce. I remembered the contented faces of the guests as they hungrily ate under the branches of the big timber. I saw the ablation of their disappointment if they had not found the fowl that they sought. So many satisfied diners.

I believe I slumbered because when I opened my eyes again, I found Mr Bin standing over me. I jumped to my feet. 'Good afternoon, Mr Bin. How relieving to see you. I've been waiting most patiently for your return.'

'Never caught you dossing before, Mozzy!' He grinned. The ape came bounce-footing from under the roof of the veranda and leapt, landing on Mr Bin's head. Mr Bin straggled its tail around his neck. 'Seeing you again is making me nostalgic. What brings you?'

'The reason I've journeyed to your residence again,' I explained, 'is that I've brought Mr Summerberg's recording equipment and a missive from the Miss Camlyn.' I indicated the cloth bag. 'I believe that he left it so that you can record the bird for him. Before he passes.'

'The akalat or Mr Summerberg? I've been out looking for the akalat today. Walked and walked. Nothing.' Mr Bin stroked the ape's tail and did not bend to read the note from Miss Camlyn.

'I'm pleased you weren't predated. You should be careful.'

'I found nets put up by poachers to catch birds, the —.' The ape ducked down behind his head.

I somehow straight away thought of Mr Makata's business. Poachers or organic produce harvesters? Should I tell Mr Bin about Mr Makata? I could see that from Mr Bin's point of view the loss of the birds that laid the tourist eggs would be regrettable although I think he cried more for the birds than the tourists. But I had assured Mr Makata of my diligence on the principle of confidentiality.

'Um … Mozzy, there's no chance of you coming back to work with me again, is there?'

I had not in all my contemplations anticipated such. I had dismissed him as my employer, but he appeared to be without shame, boldly asking for his position back.

I comported myself and answered diplomatically. 'I'm of course listening to your petition. Might I ask you why you ask me now … when you have no guests?'

'A heap of booking requests. More than ever before.' He puzzle-faced.

Even if he had been a most respected employer, I would not have reconsidered. I had received my dream posting. No one would refuse such an opportunity to leave the bush and embrace a high-status role with accompanying professional benefits. Ever since my father died, I had worked all hours for this destiny. It was the uttermost accomplishment of my ambitions and would lead to sensational fulfilment. I wanted an efficient and exacting employer such as Miss Camlyn's mother under whose service I would thrive. In any case, Mr Bin could easily find another employee to satisfy his lowest standards. As everyone indicated, there were hundreds of domestic cooks looking for work. In no time he would believe himself to have replaced me.

'I thank you kindly,' I said, 'but I've taken an important opportunity. I'm going to Boston, USA.'

When I announced such, I could hardly trust my own words, that it was truly true. I visioned skyscrapers copper-glowing in a bright sunrise. I saw sidewalks sparkling with mica, laid by professionals with setsquares and spirit levels on ground that had no swells and ruts. I saw traffic lights synchronised to schedule, everything disciplined to a pleasing degree. I saw determined people walking fast, achieving much, like myself; even placing their litter in designated bins. Custard-yellow taxis purposed by, taking VIP customers to restaurants serving international cuisines.

Mr Bin stared out at the thorns, thickets and stones of the dry badlands. 'I'm disappointed of course, but glad you're pleased with your new job. I guess it's all for the best.'

With a bold urge, I asked, 'Aren't you going to leave this decayed house and tend to your personal matters?'

'Personal matters? I've escaped them.'

I could not resist a negative inclination of my brow.

'Thing is, Mozzy, the bush asks nothing impossible of me. I don't have to try to be someone I'm not. It doesn't judge me.'

He stroked the ape's tail. The tail of his only friend.

'I don't walk into the bush to find myself ... like some would say. The opposite. I go out there to lose myself. To forget Robert Benjamin Du Plessis. To forget all that yellow jelly stuff.' Mr Bin spoke as if his only audience was himself. That he was neither speaking to his ape or myself. 'When I'm out there …' He had a searching look in his eyes as if trying to find expression for some soul-deep feeling. Then he shrugged. 'Birds and buck don't dwell on the past. Don't blub about it.' He saw me again. 'Forget all that stuff about mindfulness, psychoanalysis, meditation, matins … whatever. Try the wild. Every *oke* should get into it.'

While Mr Bin was eulogising the wasteland and philosophising his life, I was thinking on how to assist my ex-employer. I was a decent man.

'What about looking for opportunities to improve yourself? Perhaps you could teach birds in a high education establishment to do something for the advance of civilisation.'

'Civilisation!' He snorted. 'I don't care a monkey's for civilisation.'

If the ape had been human, I would have believed it to have given me the eye of apprehension, even alarm, at Mr Bin's misinformed persuasion. Mr Bin did not wish for success. I despaired for his unhappy wife and I found myself feeling sorry for the ape, which I believed was becoming insightful of Mr Bin's errors. We stood mutely. I concluded that Mr Bin and I were perplexed by each other.

The ape, I noted, had shown no aggression towards me on my return to see Mr Bin and in point of fact it was big-eyeing me, unblinking, but without malice. I had an imagining that the ape had somehow missed me, had missed a certain familiarity in its life. I was surprised to experience a certain tolerance towards the little creature. It was, after all, a living, sharing day to day life with Mr Bin and previously, however meddlesome, with myself.

I surmised that all living beings are in a relationship with other livings, whether happy, accepting, or conflicting. Without such two-way relationing, they are not living. Without such they are just rocks or clouds. I could therefore understand the Freddy ape being sentimental on this occasion of my brief return. On the contrary, I did not understand Mr Bin.

'Hey Mozzy.' Mr Bin held out an open hand. 'If you're so worried about me walking on my own, why don't you come out with me before you leave for your new job. Let's try to find an akalat together.'

'With regret, I cannot run around for you again.' I did not want to be Mr Bin's porter. I had my dignity.

'That's not what I'm ...' He dropped his hand. 'It doesn't matter *broe*.'

We were soon to lose light and so I excused myself. I had fulfilled my final obligation to Mr Bin in delivering Mr Summerberg's recording equipment. I wished him well of course, albeit without informing him that running from his lawful wife was truly recreant. I looked back once and saw him standing in his quiet pool of idleness, watching me leave him there in the sticks, he and the Freddy ape on his shoulder, with his hand stroking its tail.

Despite all, as I weaved down the road, I asked myself whether as a considerate man, I should turn back even now and agree to go with Mr Bin to find the bird. My father used to say, *The locust may fly away, but he leaves hardship behind*. Was it a locust-like desertion to leave Mr Bin standing there without help to fulfil the old gentleman's wish?

But what was I thinking? How could I so easily forget? He had run away from a prosperous and ambitious future with his wife. An indisputable and regrettable fact. *If you borrow the legs of a running man, you'll go where he directs you.* No, I should not follow Mr Bin's legs along the paths that only vanished into the ghosting bush. I must utilise my own legs. When I was young, I had experienced what can befall if I let even so-called friends distract me from the path I had chosen.

I reached the ravine and stepped off my transport because the road was as trenched as a ploughed field. At the lowest point of the ravine, I heard the sound of escaping steam. I recognised such as having emanated from the nostrils of a heavy beast. I rubber-necked in haste and saw a buffalo close by, armoured in mud from a nearby mudhole, hot saliva hanging from its jaw hair. The dim light and my meditative thoughts had made me blind to hazard. I had forgotten that I was close to nature that had not yet been tamed, the greatest impediment to mankind's progress and the greatest danger. The buffalo was a lone male, the most disagreeable kind of personality. A toxic masculine, for sure. The surprise between us was exactly mutual. It stomped its heavy hooves and snorted. I mounted my bicycle and attempted to ride out of the ravine, but it was so steep that I could not retain my balance. I crick-necked back. The buffalo lowered its horned skull and started towards me. I turned my bicycle to face it and sent it on its way, spinning it down towards the buffalo steam-training towards me. I turned with due speed and sprinted up the road. When I looked again at the top, my breath somewhat hard to find, I saw the buffalo throw my bicycle into the air and then stamp on it, without regard to its utility. The wheels cockeyed and the frame snapped like a poppadum. The bell hooked on the buffalo's horn and rang with desperation when the buffalo shook its head at me. My bicycle, I surmised, would not be repairable in the village, even in the Bicycle Repairs – Any Damage workshop.

I wasted no time to fast-pace along the unfenced and unlit

road. I was being ejected without dignity from the wilderness, chased out, just as I had myself chased crawlies from my kitchen at Mr Bin's. Fair enough. Each should keep to their place: beasts in their wilds, humankind in their cities. This was no place for me. The National Park had tried to kill me. I pined to see the kerosene lights of the village, to know that I was surrounded again by even a feeble orange glow of civility, to leave the perils of the tangled forests behind me. I desired more than ever to participate in humanity's technological and civilising achievements. Boston, USA, would be such a place.

The annihilation of my bicycle, which had grieved me earlier, could not, in all seriousness, be mourned. My bicycle belonged to a transitional phase of my life, a developmental phase. No one should accept a life without modern transport. To ride a bicycle when cars were existent was like bare-footing when branded trainers were available. Truly primitive.

Mr Bin and I had embarked on roads of opposing directions. He to the stone age past, myself to the enterprising future. I wished to be a full-immersion member of the Anthropocene; the tidy, plastic-convenient, planned, sanitised, electrified epoch which Mr Bin decried. The lights of the village beaconed, a safe sanctuary ahead, and I left my futile dutiful burden for Mr Bin's correction behind me. At last I had as good as a privileged passport. I was not like those who had to foot north and passage a sea to reach their aspiration. My dream had been served me and I was on my way.

CHAPTER 12

In arrivals, London Heathrow, I advanced along the rank of chauffeurs holding up the names of inflowing executives and professionals such as myself. 'Mr Avalon', 'Amanda Kenny', 'Jack' and more. I nodded in greeting to all in turn and shook hands with one, causing provisional confusion, as I was not his named. My courtesy was misapprehended. At the end of the line I saw the designation *Mr Man Tushi,* held up by a chauffeur who was discordantly dressed-down in a brown fake-leather jacket, jeans and pointed tan shoes with scuffed tips. It was, I conceded, excusable that he was not in uniform, it being evening and therefore out-of-hours.

'I believe that I'm he whom you're seeking,' I said to my chauffeur.

'Say?' He turned his ear down my way. 'Ah, got it. Learn your English from Mr Shakespeare, did you?'

'We're not acquainted. At school I had Miss Nyanda.'

He heavy-blinked. 'I'm Jordan. Can I call you Man?'

'Of course. Call me any name you please.'

'Is this your only bag?'

'I'm carrying only my dreams. They're packed in here.' I tapped my head. 'They weigh much.'

He portered my compactful case and I followed him through the sparkling concourse past high shining metal columns (just as expected) towards the automatic glass doors of the exit, approving the vendors of car hires and moneys all professionally attired in navy, white and black and most able in customer service. If only Dorothea could have seen me. In actuality in London, part way on my journey of destiny to Boston, USA. I took humble pleasure to think of the distance that I had travelled from that day when Dorothea and I, dusty but wet thighed, had stumbled off the bus when we arrived in Romaji. Back then there was no one to salute us with our names. We were uncelebrated immigrants to Romaji. In London, on the contrary, I was awaited and my name known. Even if it was not strictly my own.

Chauffeur Jordon was a man of private opinions who had no need to jaw to passage the journey. In the car he listened to the hectic shout-chatting of London Radio whilst I reposed back in VIP comfort and valued the ride. What a ride! Bright and prismatic lights illuminated the great city, even causing the milky orb of sky above us to glow benevolently. Colours of a firework nature fizzed in the rain. The headlights and taillights of the transportation numbered in the thousands. Dazzling red, orange and green traffic signals enforced a stop and go along our route according, no doubt, to a disciplined system. Every road had a tent of street lighting for our safety and visibility. It was so beautiful a sight, even exceeding my expectations.

We passed a park highwayed by smooth tar paths, shining in the gentle wet of that March month. Timber had been planted at exact spaces along said paths and the paths themselves were street-lighted. No one would surprise-encounter danger as they traversed along such a route on their way to work with their thoughts on important business. I noted the signs instructing the tidying away of dog poops and the designated litter bins. No one was hacking firewood off the trees with axes or suffering stones and pricks under their feet. The cities founding anthill had surely been wiped many years before. In truth, everything met my approval, everything had been designed to ease the lives of persons.

My transit hotel, named Lochview Guesthouse, was presented in the fine and historical style of the thousands of London houses that we had passed on the way. It close-fronted the Grand Circular Road which perimeters the city and a low brick wall separated it from the pavement. There was no need of course for breeze block or euphorbia protection from hungry or fiendish creatures. Someone had placed a sofa with flower patterning on said pavement, perhaps for observational purposes on the unending migration of people about their business. There was a little litter for sure, but it was of a superior and upmarket kind, such as cups from an international cafe chain and plastic bags from exclusive outlets. No doubt.

Chauffeur Jordan said, 'Get a night's kip. I'll be back at ten in the morning to take you to the office.' He tipped his forehead at me, a sign of respect in the native culture.

The lady receptionist, of senior years, was dimly dressed in a skirt of brownish wool and a dark-green tartan-pattern jacket in the style of the papered walls. Her face was somewhat squeezed and pale and was purged of sycophantic expression to the guest, nor did she waste time on nosy questions.

'Let me be understood, Mr Tooshy. No smoking, no music, no dogs, no cats, no cooking, no women overnight. Any breaking of the rules and yer'll be oen yer bike. Stolen linen or sink plugs will be charged. The basin in yer room is not a urinal. Sleep under the duvet, not in it. A toilet and a shower are off the landing. There's a meter if yer want hot water. If yer lose yer key, it's twenty poonds to replace it. Yer room is upstairs on the right. Sign here.'

'I thank you most kindly,' I said. Everything she had instructed was for my comfort and to my satisfaction. Rules and order were to be welcomed.

My room was accessed via stairs of a mountain incline and perhaps in need of supplementary lighting but, in fairness, I was glad to be out of the lights of the dazzling city and was ready to sleep after the exhilaration of my travel and my relentless anticipation.

I laid my compactful case on the end of the bed so that I did not have the minor inconvenience of climbing over it to reach the neat washbasin beyond the bed. I discovered two coat hangers in the cupboard behind the door which was exactly sufficient for my wardrobe, namely my matrimonial suit and one pair of dress-down trousers and a white shirt. The window above the basin grandstanded the Grand Circular Road and I saw that it opened by means of a pulley and a rope. A nostalgic feature perhaps. I could only note one omission. There was no iron.

I washed in the shower chamber off the landing but first thought the water burning hot before comprehending that the paining sensation was due to the opposite, namely freezing to the degree of a showering of ice. I had heard of this custom of cold dipping in northern countries and found the report was true: that you felt good and invigorated when you had towelled afterwards.

The hollow of my mattress made for a comfortable repose and I lay listening to the hurry of the cars that passed below the window, their drivers and passengers impatient, no doubt, to achieve important ends. I thought how none of those travellers in their cars were concerned about encountering a buffalo on the road on their way to and from work. None need be concerned at being chased at peril of their life and having their transport smashed by a beast. No, all were purposefully fulfilling their ambitions. Reduction in the difficulties of living and safety from predators were the undoubtful benefits of civilised society. I slept well, dreaming of cooking for discerning and deserving diners. My first night in a city in the progressive and comfortable West.

My Casio timepiece was in need of battery replacement, but I woke before dawn as was my custom. The thunder of the traffic was even greater than the previous evening. I let myself slumber somewhat, waiting for sunrise. Later, I noted a lighting of the curtain, indicating dawn approaching. I allowed myself a little more rest to prepare myself for the next phase of my journey. I guessed I would be on a flight to Boston that evening and wished to be well rested. When I noticed a prick of light on the wall, I left my bed and drew the curtain to see the sun just above the horizon.

I heard a knock on the door. 'Mr Tooshy? Your taxi's here. Close the door when you go out and don't forget yer key.'

I had not anticipated how low the sun would be in the north countries in March at nine fifty-five hours. My novelty mistake.

Chauffeur Jordon, still down-dressed to my disappointment, dropped me at a headquarters in the city. I passed through plate glass doors to a reception furnished in executive-black and polished timber. I had become like Monica at the bank in Romaji, I was on the inside of the glass of modernity —only better, as for me there was no anthill outside or boys selling recycled shoes.

A motherly lady with a cushion-soft face and figure welcomed me warmly.

'Mrs Camlyn, I'm enchanted to meet you.' I spoke with a certain over-eager. 'I've been fantasising this occasion.'

'Ooh, I'm not Mrs Camlyn. I wish! I'm Brenda. I'm only a colleague. That's what they call us. But I'm awed to meet *you*. A real safari chef!'

'A chef who apprenticed in a tourist establishment, true.' I could not deny my ignoble beginnings but did not wish to be characterised by such past, to be labelled as a camp cook from the bush who had never seen a double oven or a blast freezer.

'Let's hop along straight away. The photographer will be here any moment.'

'The photographer?'

'For the promotional. You're going to be recognised all over Britain. Quite a celebrity!'

I had read that many head chef's had celebrity status, their faces front-paging magazines or on Facebooks and Twitters, pursued by millions of adulating stalkers. I was not seeking such for myself. I did not approve of a look-at-me vocation, my face more famous than my dishes. But if this promotional was a necessity for a head chef position, I would accept with all humility.

Mrs Brenda took me through to a dazzle-white room statued with chrome technical equipment of the lighting variety. In that finely engineered bright space, I felt yet again the thrill of my posting. The environments were going to be conducive to excellence. There would be no ants, pets, peeling ceilings, cracked floors or bare-foot employer.

'There you are now, my darling, pop into the booth over there and change into your uniform. There are three sizes to try on.'

I was at last to take the vestments of my calling, to become an archbishop of the culinary catechism dressed in holy whites and a high toque. As such, I would cook for my diners the most sublime creations, the divine summit of my skills. I saw myself in the promotional in my finery, arms folded in confident and relaxed but quietly dynamic pose, professional and reliable hands on show, countenance set to convey that of a man knowing himself to be greatly respected, but knowing himself not to be haughty, indeed approachable and not affected with pride, however justified.

In the booth I found three pegs with clothing hanging from each, namely a green flop-brimmed hat, a Swahili-style collarless shirt patterned with leaves, red flower blooms and birds with banana beaks. I took note of the green shorts with matching long socks. I looked in vain for my chef's uniform.

I exited the booth and said to Mrs Brenda, 'My regrets ... I cannot find my uniform.'

'This is your uniform, my pet. Right here.' She indicated the jungle-themed attire. 'It's fun and sunny, don't you think? You can wear it with pride.'

'Do I not wear white? A head chef wears white, properly ironed.'

'I guess a head chef would. Hurry please my love, the photographer's arrived and he hasn't got a lot of time.'

Unless I was mistaken, something was mistaken, unless there was a trending fashion for top chefs, which I was unaware of, and certainly did not approve of.

I tried on said party clothing and came out with the one least tight and least loose. It was the first time I had worn shorts since I was a child. I had a disturbing presentiment that I was to be asked to dance for the photographer. To prance moves of primitive culture for party entertainment. Was I being pranked?

Mrs Brenda placed a yellow sash around my neck and shoulder, patting it flat with her mother hands, and stepped back.

'Perfect! So Safari Cubs!'

Said sash was designated 'On safari, grrrr!' All was highly irregular.

The photographer had black eyebrows but bleached hair or maybe painted eyebrows and blonde hair. He said, 'Sit on the stool. Turn slightly. Look towards me. Look into the lens. Make your eyes sparkle. Smile. Make your cheeks like a bunny.'

I complied to the most of my understanding, but I was bewildered and disturbed of mind. Events were not to my expectations. Had I been chauffeured to the wrong location? Was I mistaken for some other? When would I travel on to the USA?

'Good job. You're a natural.' The blanched photographer disconnected his camera from his tripod, concurred with Mrs Brenda and left.

'All finished now duck, change back again and leave your uniform there,' said Mrs Brenda.

'I don't take these clothings with me?' Perhaps this party dress was a one-off side matter, said my hoping heart.

'No, the photo's all we need.' She sighed and smiled at me. 'Fancy being in the promotional! I wish I was you. Now let's go through and I'll introduce you to Dave. He's the Marketing Director.' She wink-eyed me. 'Very important, he is. Be on your best behaviour.'

I was eager to meet Mr Dave, to understand the irregularities that I had experienced that morning, but I declare that I found Mr Dave to be a let-down. I cannot exactly say why. Perhaps because his eyes shifted slyly —like a liar's— in his doughy face when I polited, 'Most pleased to meet you.' I shook him, but found his hand curled disagreeably around mine, soft and damp like an ox's tongue. Neither he nor his clothing appeared straight and upstanding. As example, his thin red tie traversed at an angle over his gestationing white shirt to be tucked into the side of his trousers, but the end stuck back out like another tongue, dangling limp. His sleeves were untidily furled up his forearms. In all, it appeared that he did not appreciate that he was in the exalted position of Marketing Director to the great Mrs Camlyn, that he had a position of office to respect. Even Mr Bin had sometimes looked more presentable.

Reciprocal greetings were not his style, instead he scanned me lazily up and down. Was I a product for sale? Would he part my lips to check that my teeth were straight and white? My impression, I could not deny, was unfavourable. He did not inspire me. Where was the praiseworthy Mrs Camlyn?

'Mr Toothy,' Mr Dave said, speaking high through his nose, 'you're a damned lucky man, but I know you appreciate that so let's cut tedious niceties and go straight to the eatery. Mrs Camlyn thought you ought to see it. It's across the road.'

Said eatery was entered via an eye-sore frontage debauched in the style of the party clothing I had attired for the photographer. Across the door was a flashing sign, surrounded by grinning and mocking monkeys. *Party Places. On Safari, grrrr!* Mr Dave turned on lights and I found myself in a room teeming with plastic animals deformed into chairs. Zebras, warthogs, buffaloes and such around picnic tables in the same party-themed colours. Mr Dave operated switches. A curved wall of glass leading up to the ceiling at the end of the room glowed with a scene from a misleading tourist brochure. A big red sunset somehow cast a strong green light on a lushful savannah with giraffes and wildebeests fatly grazing. Off to the side, elephants squirted water at each other from a blue waterhole. Sounds of the bush came from all angles, no escape, causing me to startle and rubberneck from side to side.

'There we are!' Mr Dave beamed. 'I hope you're absolutely wowed.'

'This is for children?'

'We call them Safari Cubs.'

'May I ask my duties?'

He made a theatre of saluting me. 'You're our genuine safari-chef! Respect! Respect!'

'I'm cooking for the Cubs?'

'No, good god no! We've got our own chefs. You're our promotional. Thing is, Mr Toothy,' he pinched my neck and pinned me with his button eyes, 'you have twenty-four carat cultural identity. One hundred percent authenticity. You're from a genuine African safari location. Totally credible. We're not going to dress up some Brit chef from Hackney. There'll be no cultural appropriation from us. Mrs Camlyn insisted on you.' He waved his hand at the eatery. 'So, quick now, what do you think of our Safari Place?'

'In the safari locations, it's bushy, stony and dry. It's a hostile environment. The animals live in fear and often starve.'

'Which is why this is so much better than the real thing, don't you think?' He had a debating point, certainly. There was no dust, no flies and there was no danger from the plastic beasts. 'It's the make-believe the kids want and it's got the wow factor for parents who want to impress other parents with their choice of venue for their kid's birthday party. Luckily for us, the more it costs, the more they can impress.'

'This is … like a party place for kids.'

'You're damned quick on the uptake, Mr Toothy. Party Places are party places!' His grin was that of a patronising hippo. 'We also have Ocean Party Place, and Antarctic, and Mountain. Not to mention Mars, so I will!' He laughed at his wit. 'Every city's going to have them.'

Maybe my reaction was not as appreciative as he expected because he came close, personal-friendly, wrapping his soft hand around the back of my neck and delivering to me a sweat and fresh meat odour. 'Of course, we'd appreciate suggestions you have to make it even better. You've got first-hand knowledge of the environment we're virtualing. Are there any little authenticating details that will help? Have we got it right? What are we missing?'

I stepped back. 'But safari chefs, they wear white and wear a toque. I'm to wear party clothing?'

'We are what it says on the tin!' I had the impression that I was amusing him. 'Let me present to you the menu. We'd value your comments … although we'll not be allowing you into the kitchens. Health and safety and all that. Are there any tasty items you serve on safari that we could do a Party Places take on?'

Said menu read, *Giraffe Juice – The tallest drink on safari! Lion claw nibbles – Nuts, Party Places style! Buffalo Bangers – Big bangers for little cubs! Elephant Trunk – Chocolate roll! Tiger Tasties – Stripy cheese straws!* and such.

'We don't have tigers in Africa.'

'So wouldn't it better if you did? Proves my point. Party Places improves on the real thing.'

'When am I taking my appointment in Boston?'

'Boston?'

'Your high-end restaurant in Boston, USA.'

'Major confusion here, Mr Toothy. We don't launch in the States until next year. Mrs Camlyn recently opened an Ocean Place in Boston, Lincolnshire. Whatever you've heard, it's not a backwater surrounded by stagnant ditches. But it is a long way out of town. Our waiters wear wetsuits and the kids sit in submersibles.' He slapped his chest. 'My idea that.'

Why had I been assigned to the Dave Division of the company? Was this a test? A temporary holding?

He fake-consulted his watch as if he had become bored and wished some other amusement. 'I've got work to do. The taxiwaala will take you back to your lodgings. We'll be in contact before long. About three weeks, I'd say.'

He was exiting but I was not so perplexed and disturbed as to forget to say, 'I have a delicate matter to ask. Can I receive an advance on my remuneration?'

'Nice try Mr Toothy! I'm sure Mrs Camlyn would have explained it's illegal to put you on the payroll when you're on a visitor's visa. Don't want to break the law, do we?'

I stiff-faced to assimilate this information.

'Give us a break,' said Mr Dave. 'Your accommodation and return flight's on us. You've been given a rare privilege. Your name and picture on our promotional material will be reward enough for your co-operation. You can't even put a price on its value for your future career, wherever that is. Many of our local chefs would love to be on the poster but bringing you over is our —what did Mrs Camlyn say?— contribution to a fairer world. We like to be seen to be doing the right thing. We like to promote it.'

He scratched around in his back pocket and passed me a sat-on envelope. 'But lucky you reminded me. Here's cash for your bus and living expenses. Strictly a gift to compensate you for your informal voluntary role.'

'I'm grateful.' I had been well brought up.

'Good to hear it, at last.' He grin-faced. 'Enjoy London and don't disappear or apply for asylum.'

Chapter 13

After I had drunk from my basin tap to ease a thirst, I perched contemplative on the edge of the trench of my mattress in Lochview Guesthouse. My situation had admittedly upended. I enumerated what I had learnt that day. There was no white toque to wear, no fresh-pressed apron to attire, no stainless-steel kitchen to work in. There was no head chef position to fulfil, or even sous chef. There were no VIP guests to please with superlative creations. There was no USA posting. I was to be seen in fanciful dress on a promotion for Party Places. I came to the judgment that the promises I had been given had been withdrawn or, at the best, postponed. Furthermore, there would be no remuneration to send to Dorothea. The envelope moneys were only enough for minor transport needs and staple food sustenance. Dorothea would not be able to pay for the most expensive brick in history or to honour our overdraft. Yes, my journey to success had suffered a road-block. If I had been a man of superstitious belief, I would have concluded that Dorothea's holy brick had brought a curse.

Some people faced with a difficulty, with a setback, ask themselves, 'How do I feel?' Such a question is without rewarding purpose, of no profitable benefit, and liable to cause a fit of pessimism followed by melancholy. Far better to ask, 'What shall I do? How shall I proceed?'

I wished to cook. Even if only to comfort myself. But tartan-woolled lady had instructed 'no cooking'. The traffic on the Grand Circular Road was somewhat moaning and discordant and there was a cold draught through the nostalgic window making further sitting unappealing, so what I did was to go walking.

I footed all over London in those days and only returned to my room to sleep. I walked away from the Grand Circular Road whose rubber and diesel vapours caused a thickness in my nose and a scratchy cough. I walked for many hours but never came to the end of the city. I discovered the great river, named The Tems according to the native peoples. When no one could tell me the source of the river —it seemed that they had never even asked themselves the question— I followed it up upstream like a colonist explorer. But without porters and provisions, I became somewhat tired and lost motivation. In any case, I had no one at home who would be lionizing such a venture.

I encountered a high number of persons in my footings. Indeed, London teemed like an industrious ant nest, there being even a labyrinth of tunnels underground for transportation named —to make plain— The Underground. All the people in the city were fortunates living in that go-ahead place like myself and from every sociology and geographic as if the dream of living in a foremost city was common to all the world. They had achieved such, but I observed a certain anxiety, a fidget, even a certain dissatisfaction, as if their hopes had not been realised. It was a disappointment to see such discontent, indicating a lack of appreciation of their good fortune. I made a personal note not to fall into the same error.

I had only one difficulty on my footings. Without the duty of work to occupy me, I wished to greet and converse with persons, but their ears were spigoted with phone buds and their legs hurried them to private destinations. If they looked my way, they looked away again as if they had seen nothing there. As if

I was just another scurrying ant. But I was the only ant in the colony who wished to touch antenna with other ants. Once, I turned in gladness to the sound of a man happy-greeting me to find him speaking to his phone. All these livings, I was close to them, brushed them, but I was in solitude. London trumpeted and clacked, not to forget rumbled and squealed so that some days my tympanics hurt but, without conversation, it was also a great silence. I had previously thought that the only place to be alone was in the cursed wilderness, but no, the modern city could also deliver. Sure, I had short interplay with whomever I could. For instance, I greeted people bedding on the street, being not surprised to see the lengths some went to live in the city. Better to be sleeping in the city than sleeping in the bush. I have very little money, I told them, I'm sorry, I cannot spare you. They were pardoning, but not inclined to chit chat of my employment confusion or to enthuse on their own grand plans for their futures in the city. One gifted me a coat to go over my wedding suit jacket, which he saw was too lightweight for the cold winds afflicting London. This kindness stirred in me a soft yearning, a misty wanting. To what, I could not exactly say.

I received a text from Dorothea.

I imagine ur working hard. Any BLESSING to send yet? Your good wife, Dorothea.

I could not answer in the affirmative to her question because there was not yet any capital advancement to remit. I had not even met the praiseworthy Mrs Camlyn. I could only remain expectant that Mrs Camlyn would hear of Mr Dave's error and rescue me. I wrote, *Awaiting a start date. Your faithful husband.*

I continued street after street every day until evening, having to slurp water from drinking fountains and snack bread baps from stores named Convenience, whose owners watched me closely until I had paid. I missed Dorothea. I wished to be joyed by her. I wished her excitable company, her bright and dancing eyes. A week later I received another text of a brief and bare nature.

Please ask for an advance. Pastor Cain is pressing.

After much roving and ranging to discern the truthful way to reply, I wrote, *Keep faith.*

Immediately she wrote, *No need for you to instruct me on my faith. My faith is strong.*

Was this a reprimand or a reassurance? I replied, *Of course, dear wife.* Then I wrote, *I'm missing you.*

It was three days before she sent another text. *Anything yet?*

I could not find a satisfactory reply as it would be too costly in texts to explain in unbelievable missives about promotionals, kids' parties, fancy dress, plastic animals. I had to wait, expectant for my fortunes to turn. I could not 'dear wife' her again as yet. All pleasantries would not get past the elephant of her unanswered question, waving its urgent trunk at me.

Several days into my footings I saw a man in a thick black coat and black knit-hat sitting on a bench in a park named Kensington. I perched on the end of the same bench and after some moments to allow him to become comfortable with my proximity, this being the culture in the city, I said, 'Good day to you, I'm Savalamuratichimimozi Mlantushi.' I had to repeat.

'Yes?' he said, into his lap.

'Yes indeed, it's very sunny but strangely cold, is it not?'

'Yes?' He still did not look at me. He spoke as if I was disturbing him or wanting something from him such as money or that I wished to put him under obligation. The city created suspicions. From his accent on his singular word vocalisations, I identified him as an offspring of the southern part of the same continent as my own.

I waited for him to show friendly but when he did not, I tried again. 'May I ask your profession?'

He looked only at his hands and rubbed them together. 'Teacher.'

'A fine profession.' I waited again but he needed facilitation to talk. 'You have pursued an honourable ambition and achieved.'

'I thought,' he said.

When he said no more, I said, 'I'm a chef. I journeyed here to take employment in a high-end establishment, but I've been delayed in that regard.'

He remained lip-shut.

'Perhaps you have advice for me on how to proceed.'

'My break's up, I'm going.' He stood and moved to depart, but said without eyeing me, 'Very well brother, let me advise you. Take what you can. Any work. I empty bedpans. It pays.' He footed away.

I stayed fixed to the bench. We were alike, him and I, in nativity, in anthropology and in pursuit of a high profession, but that man —yes, a man not unlike me— had lost all expectation. He had abandoned his dream. He had taken a side path downhill. I was not like that man; I was always in sure hope that tomorrow would deliver. But I felt a little apprehension that I could become such a man. I had encountered a dark potential for myself and I determined not to allow it. Yes, I had suffered every setback in the book, but the most needless and ill-disciplined thing to do would be to lose my vision, to swerve from the path to my destination. Had I not lost my father to an instance of deviation? Not again. I would stay on the straight. I would not quit. I had been disconcerted beyond strict necessity.

I heard a bird somewhere near, the first bird that I had taken note of, maybe even heard, in London. A certain surprise came to me that I liked to hear it. I found it somewhat pleasing, this dainty, bright, chirrupy singing. Surely it signified that the promised spring would arrive soon and with it my destiny. The small bird dropped from a tree and hopped nearby. I held out my hand to it. Come here little scrap of all living things, be a companion to me, sing to me. My movement frightened it. It flew away.

Maybe my encounter with the bird explains what happened next. Close to Lochview Guesthouse I was in the custom of passing a shop named Pet Paradise. Small children pulled at their seniors to look in the window. I saw how eager they were to possess a pet. They wished a little friend, something dependent on themselves, something they could talk to as they pleased. I remembered Mr Bin and his pets. They were his friends to talk to. They were his companions in the solitude of that lonely house in that empty place.

A juvenile impulse came on me and I pushed open the door to encounter an odour suggestive of hay, sacks and dusty seeds. A hamster ran down its short life, spinning its wheel. A rabbit big-eyed me, but without malice.

The shopkeeper was a man of fisty features, namely a sharp nose, hard-bead eyes, oiled-back black hair, and a thin bar of a moustache. He wore a black-leather jacket with dull-metal buttons and a scorpion badge on his lapel. Would he not frighten little children coming to buy a hamster? I already regretted opening the door to his pet zoo.

'Can I help?' he said, eyeing me doubtfully, his up-lip presenting to me a chipped tooth.

'I'm looking for a pet,' I heard myself saying.

'How old is your child?'

What a fine-most question. I had no child except the one that I remembered from years ago. Namely myself. It seemed to me that this child was not older than the day of his father's brain stroke when he had to take leave of his friends to look after him.

'About maybe thirteen.'

'Too old for a hamster or a guinea pig. We're talking tropical fish.'

I thought that tartan-woolled lady at the guesthouse would not permit a fish tank although she had not specifically forbidden such to my remembrance. I heard the boy speaking. 'He wants a pet that can be a companion. Like a friend.'

'We're talking dogs. I don't do em.'

'I thank you kindly. Not to mind.' I had come to my sense.

He bead-eyed me hard across his dagger nose in the way of making an opinion on my good character. Reassured, of course, he locked the shop door and turned the sign to indicate that the establishment was closed.

'Are you a discrete man?'

'Discrete is a core principle of mine.'

'You'll be interested in exotics then. Thirteen-year olds love exotics.'

'Exotics?'

'Don't blow the gaff on what you see. Follow me.'

He signalled me to a door at the back of the shop and unlocked it with a large key. We passed into a confining and dim space smelling somehow of a public urinal. The walls and ceiling were tar-dark, but cages of wire and glass glowed under dim green and red lights.

'This is my jungle.' He beckoned me to a glass.

I held back to see such a creature in the green light with its crocodile tail and clawsome feet. As I approached with caution, its jungle-glowing eye watched me unblinking like an evil animal spirit —although I did not believe in such things. 'This is a lizard.

We're talking fat-tailed lizard here. Vicious, but absolutely safe as long he's kept in his cage. Your thirteen-year-old will love him.'

I wished to run. How could such a place exist in the modern city? He had brought danger to the city with the worst of the bush. He had brought Mr Bin's garden to the city.

'What about this beauty?' He signalled me to look behind the next glass. 'We're talking a blue-necked snake here.'

A serpent with a blunt jaw resided there in a red light like a glowing branch in a fire. A twitching tail stuck out of its mouth.

'Look, it's just eaten its mouse. Your kid will find that gross ... but irresistible.'

He moved to the next cage, but I backed away.

'We're talking a yellow-banded spider here. Huge all-seeing eyes. An incredible turn of speed! They've got great personality.'

It had been an error to enter his exotic room to be faced with such mutational and murderous creatures. That place was even worse than Mr Bin's garden.

'I thank you ... but on reflection I think that my boy should work and not play.'

I passed hastily back into the shop, but my eye was captured by a small bird in a small cage high on a shelf. It sat still and alone. It cocked its head down at me and we met for just one moment.

The shopkeeper said, 'You can have that for free, if you want. Shouldn't die on your kid. He could release it when he gets bored with it. We're talking garden sparrow. They're as common as cats here. I don't normally have sparrows ... but let's say someone brought it in injured. Was going to feed it to a snake but this morning it perked up. What a coincidence that a fellow with a kid like yours should step into the shop right now and want it. It's meant to be.'

Naturally, that did not persuade me. I declined. A bird is a fowl, a variant on a chicken, and this one was so small that it would not even make a snack for a small man. Not that I would have eaten it of course. I was civilised and humane towards all animals designated as pets by whatever the prevailing culture. I excused and exited the shop as fast as was polite.

On the edge of my bed again I listened to the traffic, a factory of droning pistons ceaselessly running. I lay down for a minute, but my limbs prodded me to move. I was not tired to sleep and the ceiling had no interest in it. I stood. It seemed, all sudden, that I desired the sound of a bird. The harmless and reassuring chirrup and tittle. The flutter of another heart in my room. I fell for a simple and natural temptation. Somewhat ashamed, I returned to Pet Paradise.

I turned my suitcase on its side end on the floor by the basin and placed the cage on top. The adjacent window would gift the sparrow a view of the sky, grey-nothing up there notwithstanding. I lifted off the covering cloth. The sparrow flapped about in surprise.

'Don't fret. I'm like a companion for you and you'll be a companion for me. We'll talk to each other.'

It sheltered tight on the floor of the cage as far from me as it could achieve and I could see its seed-sized heart trembling.

'You're safe here.' Still it trembled. 'I have no snakes. We both hate such things. In that respect, we're alike. We concur on this.'

I took my face away to give it space and it flapped to the end of its perch and stood on its pin legs, eye on me.

'That's better, little bird.' The power-most tranquiliser is the human voice. 'I'll feed you. You're lucky, I'm a chef. All I ask is that you sing for me.'

It was unblinking at me.

'I'll be your head chef. What dishes do you like? I can cook international, but now I'll extend myself to interspecies.'

It remained highly attentive.

'You said seeds? That's no problem.'

I opened the cage door with caution and took the food tray. I arranged the mixed seeds, which I had bought —at the expense of my lunch— from Mini Mart, in its tray. The dish resembled, with the eye of deep faith, a risotto of whole grain rice peppered and garnished with garlic, onion and parmesan cheese. It was not my finest creation, but was a respectable plate.

'Bird, you can now dine. This is my signature dish for sparrows.'

It stayed, watching me. It took no notice of my dish.

'It's always a big deal with sparrows.'

Perhaps it did not want to eat in front of me, so I excused myself whilst I used the comfort station on the landing. When I returned, the dish had not been touched.

I apologised that this was not up to scratch, footed to the Night Glow Food Locker and bought oats, raisins and ground nuts. I cleaned the food tray and arranged such. I saw a dead spider in the corner of the room. With aesthetic consideration I arranged this in the centre of the dish as if it was a sprig of rosemary.

I excused myself again. On return I saw that the spider alone was gone. The sparrow was back on its perch and did not flap at my presence. I felt satisfaction at my discovery. The sparrow craved insects.

I bought a small packet of Dried Bug Bird Feed and it ate hungrily. However many dried insects I offered it, it ate them. To leave me cash for feeding myself I invested in a butterfly net from a retail called Pound Shop with the intention of catching insects in the park. There were no 'No poaching' signs, no 'Keep out. National Park'. I found the reason: there were no insects in the park. The only sound was that of the big bug vehicles on the roads. There was no buzzing and whirring of little wings.

What to do? No matter, under the lights in the park at night I found the occasional moth. The beautiful tents of light were a fatal trap for the remaining insects of the night. At first I arranged said moths freshly slaughtered in my bird's food tray, but I discovered that it liked them most when still flapping. Of course, an insect could escape through the bars, but the bird was quick and hungry. Each night I supplemented Dried Bug with live moth. As the days counted the sparrow became familiar with me and listened ever more carefully and politely to my talk. It never argued against me. It took my point of view. I hoped that one day it would show its appreciation of my dishes by singing, even a simple chirrup would do.

I still walked the streets to move my limbs, but I was always eager to return to my room to talk to the bird, to tell it of the surety of my future destination and to promise that it could stay with me and even be upgraded when finances allowed to a high vaulted cage with space for a companion sparrow. I would purchase a fancy cosy for the cage for night-time to prevent the glare of the moonlight through the grand windows of my upcoming abode.

I smiled to think how Mr Bin would have been unbelieving to see me with a pet. I had indeed surprised myself. I needed to understand why I was appreciating the companionship of a little fowl. It had no conversation, no laughter, no sharing of its food, no hand shaking. I concluded this: the bird was a living. All livings crave interplay with another living. We were both livings, the sparrow and I, admittedly of differing sizes, shapes, body clothing and ancestral history, but as a consequence of being livings we needed each other for serenity of the heart, even to comply with the natural bias and needs of being a living. I only craved that it would sing.

CHAPTER 14

One auspicious evening, tartan-woolled landlady knocked on the door with a hard knuckle.

'Mr Tooshy?'

'Yes? I'm here.'

'I doon't like being yer receptionist, but I've had a call from a lassie. An Ella Camlyn. She'll visit tomorrow afternoon with her grandfather. I have her number if that's nae alright, but yer'll need to ring her yourself. I cannae be your telephone exchange.'

Of course, I did not call to decline the appointment. I would be present, for sure, waiting for my VIP guests. I told the sparrow and it saw me wipe a tear from my eye to think that I had visitors to my abode, my first, and they being special persons, taking the trouble to come and see me. It did not laugh at me or side-glance me.

And so it occurred that I found myself the very next day waiting outside the front door of the guesthouse in the flappy wind and spilling rain for the arrival of VIPs Miss Camlyn and Mr Summerberg. My heart beat with a longing note to meet guests from those previous days. How unexpected, I thought, to look back to the time when I was professionally unfulfilled and living in the barrens to now believe that those were tolerable days. How could that be? Those days with the disorderly Mr Bin, with the pestful little ape Freddy and the moulting feline. Where had this confusion come from?

My guests could not stop outside the guesthouse as no one is permitted to park on the Grand Circular Road. They appeared from a side road, Mr Summerberg with a wheeled frame pushing forward against the blowing and Miss Camlyn with one hand behind Mr Summerberg's back and the other tight on her rain hood. Myself I got wet under my plastic bag makeshift umbrella, but that was of no concern to me.

Miss Camlyn hugged me, so much so that I was tempted to weep, experiencing her warm personage again, touching antennas once more with a person. We could not hear what we said because of the barrage of the traffic, but it was certainly sincere felicitations.

It took patient efforts to assist Mr Summerberg up the steep stairs to my chamber. 'When will you make luncheon for me again, Mr Mlantushi?' he said as he attempted command of his wavering legs on the last step.

'I'd take immense pleasure in cooking for you again Mr Summerberg, but no cooking is permitted up here.'

We took off our plastics and coats and draped them on my wardrobe door and sat ourselves in a row on my bed as there was no chair. Miss Camlyn was smiling and scented, attentive to her grandfather, and bringing a full winter-statement black and white sleeve dress, warm gilet and pearl strap boots to my dull room. Mr Summerberg wore a dark navy suit, braces and white shirt with burgundy tie. Dignified, for sure.

'Mozzy, I can't believe this is where you're living, this poxy cupboard of a room,' Miss Camlyn said. 'I did warn you about my mother.'

I shrugged. 'My father used to say, *A small house will hold a hundred friends.*'

She sighed. 'Seeing you Mozzy, has reminded me of my little fantasy of escaping to a different life, far away. Saying goodbye to ball bearings.' Then she saw my sparrow. 'Aw, you've got a little bird. How sweet.'

'A sort of friend,' I joked, light of heart.

Mr Summerberg purged his throat. 'Let's not waste the sands of time like beach bums. Mr Mlantushi, we've come to ask formally for your help.'

'My one desire is always to help.'

'Ben has my recording equipment. I want to know if he's recorded the akalat. He won't reply to our emails. I'm minded to just fly out there. El's reluctant.'

'We don't know if Ben's still guiding and we shouldn't be flying so much. Only birds should be allowed to fly.'

'The brackish akalat has to be played at my funeral. We can't have my funeral until we've got it.'

'Grandad! Stop it! You do make me laugh.'

But I did not think that Mr Summerberg was jesting. It seemed to me that his desire for the bird to be played at his funeral was for some other reason than the trivial matter of having a musical decoration to the proceedings.

'We're requesting your help, Mr Mlantushi,' said Mr Summerberg. 'Will you contact Ben? We're sure he'd reply to you.'

I had not spoken to Mr Bin since I had left. I had said my final goodbye to him and left him for this other future of mine. This life here which too many times, I had to admit, meant staring at a wall in front of me —which I could touch from where I sat— and experiencing the unending drone of the road, twenty-four seven. As intolerable as a tinnitus of cicadas and flies.

'Is Ben alright, Mozzy?' said Miss Camlyn. 'I tried to help him when I got back by posting crazily good stuff about his safari walks. But nothing. It's like he's died.'

I pondered what feeling she had for him now, whether she still loved him with blind adoration despite his contracted matrimonial status or if she had finally understood his true character. I conjectured that she might not know yet what she felt about him. The fluctuating and inscrutable sentiments of ladies could swerve about, even wax and wane over many seasons, before they finally settled into a fixed and categorical position.

'He was alive the last time I saw him,' I said. 'Of course, I delivered your recording equipment. He said he'd been looking for your bird. That gives us certain hope he's recorded it by now.'

'I love you Mozzy! So, so, optimistic on everything.'

'Optimism is his opium,' said Mr Summerberg.

My guests' request reminded me how Mr Bin had asked me to find the bird with him and to record it. I felt a certain discomfort at the memory, not only that I should have assisted him in fulfilling the wish of Miss Camlyn and Mr Summerberg but also that, maybe, I had been cold to Mr Bin. Had I misunderstood him, even knowingly misunderstood him by telling myself that he wanted a porter to carry the recording machinery? More likely he wished a companion. Someone to ease his solitude. I wondered if I myself had been infected with colonial-era thinking —assuming a master-and-his-house-servant situational.

'Do you talk to your sparrow?' said Miss Camlyn.

She had to repeat as I was still distracted of mind. 'He just shares the room rent.' I ha-ha'd. 'But yes, I confess I talk to him. Of course, he doesn't answer. He's just a little fowl.'

'Oh Mozzy, how heart-breaking. Is he your only pal here?'

Mr Summerberg was causing the bed to complain with his efforts to stand up. 'Did you say a sparrow? Doesn't look like a sparrow to me. Let me take a closer look. El, where's Ben's walking stick?'

'You use a frame now, Grandad. Don't you remember? We left it downstairs. Here, hold my arm.'

Mr Summerberg shuffle-shifted along beside the bed towards the cage. He bent to look.

'This is not a sparrow.'

Miss Camlyn lent over. 'It's small like a sparrow. They're small, aren't they?'

'I assure you, sir, it's a sparrow,' I said. 'The seller of both exotic and mundane pets confirmed its provenance.'

'It's not a sparrow.'

'It's not an ostrich, Grandad. You're not going to fool me again.' She laughed loud, but Mr Summerberg was not laughing. 'What is it, Grandad?'

Mr Summerberg peered and peered. 'Where are my glasses, El?'

She reached in her bag and passed them. Mr Summerberg adjusted the round frames to be concurrent with his eyes. He had become a professor, white-hair-thinking.

'What is it, Grandad?'

'I'm not sure. It's not native. Maybe a migrant.'

'I was misled by the retailer?'

'You were. Only a foreigner would mistake this for a sparrow.'

'*Et moi*,' said Miss Camlyn.

'Is it a brackish akalat?' I said. I knew Pel's fishing owl and hornbill and it was too small for those. 'It's certainly a brackish akalat, if it's not a sparrow.'

'I would bet all my rare collectables that it's not,' said Mr Summerberg. 'It would be an impossible coincidence.'

'Like the flukes in my trashy book *Into the Red Sunset*,' said Miss Camlyn.

Mr Summerberg asked, 'Does it sing?'

'It refuses. I've had it for weeks. It's silent. Very silent.'

'Maybe cos it's upset,' said Miss Camlyn. 'I don't think it likes being in a cage.' She put her finger between the bars of the cage and wiggled it. The bird remained calm. 'Ooh, you are a cute little thing.'

Mr Bin had said that birds learn their songs from their fathers. Maybe it had been an orphan, so never had instruction.

'Could be a female,' said Mr Summerberg. 'Female birds don't always sing.'

'What's a bird's life without it singing?' said Miss Camlyn.

'Even if it was a brackish akalat, and it can't be, if it doesn't sing it's not much use to me.'

'Let's believe it's a bracky one!' said Miss Camlyn. 'It could almost be because it's also small.'

'Good thing it's not. My equipment's in Africa with The White Tribesman.'

We were quiet, I think waiting for the bird to change its mind and sing. The silence was not for long. 'What does a bracky one look like, Grandad?'

'I couldn't be sure. I've never seen one. I don't need to see it, just collect its song.'

If Mr Summerberg did not know what a brackish akalat looked like and so could not deny the opinion of Miss Camlyn and myself, the bird could certainly be bone fide. What a fortuity! A brackish akalat! What an excitement for my guests and a noteworthy surprise for myself.

We watched the bird doing nothing for a while and then Miss Camlyn said, 'Well we never! It's a bombshell a minute with Grandad.'

We helped Mr Summerberg's chicken weight back to the bed. Miss Camlyn turned to me and looked into my eyes. She placed a hand on my arm. 'Mozzy, I'd no idea things were so pants for you here. I want to help.'

'Please, I'd only like the opportunity to prove myself in a kitchen. I'm in joy when I'm cooking good food for guests.'

'What if it were a brackish akalat, here in London,' Mr Summerberg said to himself, 'but it won't sing. Haa, haa, haa.'

Miss Camlyn thought-faced and said, 'I have an idea, Mozzy. I don't know … maybe. I'll try. It's not much but …'

'An idea?'

'Let me follow it up.'

I assisted them to their car, the cold rain sponging my back, the sky a ragged grey fleece, the trucks making thunder on the road.

Mr Summerberg said, 'You must contact Ben, Mr Mlantushi. He must record the bird for me.'

Miss Camlyn took the driving seat and said to me. 'I'm worried about you. You're all alone … apart from that little bird.'

'He's all I need.' But in truth, I was so sad that Miss Camlyn and Mr Summerberg were leaving. They were almost like … what persons called friends.

'Things are not turning out, yeah? It's no shame to admit it.'

'A turnabout is sure to come.'

'I can put you in touch with my life coach if you want. Because you're a sort of migrant, she'll probably give you a free session.'

'Thank you kindly, but no need. Life's already coached me.'

'Hmm, maybe. Look … I'll do my best, but don't raise your hopes.'

'I assure you Miss Camlyn that my hopes are always high. It's the correct way to live.'

I footed to the library to email Mr Bin as per my pledge to Mr Summerberg. I wished also to check out the old man's postulation that my sparrow was not a sparrow. I reckoned his eyesight to be failing. On my way I passed the pet shop. I saw that it was closed and looked in the window. The pets were gone. A child with a father also stopped.

'I wanna hamster,' said the boy, licking the glass.

'You can't. It's closed down,' said the father.

'Why?'

'The shopkeeper was a naughty man.'

'Naughty man?'

'Very naughty. He was selling pets from the jungle without a licence.'

'I wanna hamster,' said the boy.

They walked off out of ear reach.

At the library internet I prioritised a short missive to Mr Bin although had doubts that Mr Bin would be booting his old computer to look for emails. He would have to fire the generator. He would not want its howling to smother the indigenous whisper of the bush.

Dear Mr Bin,

I hope life is treating you. I have entertained Mr Summerberg and Miss Camlyn here in London at my abode. They are enquiring after your progress in capturing the carol of the brackish akalat. Please let me know your advance in this matter as it will bring them great happiness. Mr Bin, I beg you, this should be considered urgently as Mr Summerberg is even older now. I ask this as your late chef employee for your favour.

Sincerely,

Savalamuratichimimozi Mlantushi

(also known as Mozzy)

I had fulfilled my promise. Responsibility now lay in the careless and unreliable hands of Mr Bin.

I remained questioning of Mr Summerberg. I needed to be sure my bird was not a sparrow in order to narrow down to brackish akalat. Like a private detective, I searched *sparrow* on the Google. Straight away, it informed of two sparrows. The house sparrow and the tree sparrow. The portraits of such were not the bird in my cage. They were less dull, less brackish, more reddish, more black and white, more streaked. True, these sparrows were small like my bird, as Miss Camlyn had correctly informed us, but they were not my bird. Their expression was also less interested, less attentive, more off-hand and distracted. Further research indicated that there were many other sparrows, for examples the rock sparrow, the Somali sparrow, the Dead Sea sparrow, the parrot-billed sparrow, indeed more than twenty. I studied each. My bird was none of those. I could not find the 'garden sparrow' that the seller had referred to, but the Google was sure that there was no such. The most compelling persuasion against sparrow was this: sparrows dine on seeds. My bird was against seeds. It dined on insects. My bird was not a sparrow, for sure.

I searched for 'brackish akalat'. Said bird was known to the Google as without hesitation it showed me a page. Said page presented only one photo, surely taken accidentally by an amateur pointing at something else as the focus was off, but I could see a small bird with round black eyes, a small beak, a brackish-brown back and greyish underparts. It had the same attentive expression as my bird and was just as non-judgmental, but I had to admit that it was not an exacting match. My bird was duller in colouration, legs not as orange, beak perhaps a little thinner. Despite such, there was certainly a strong resemblance and no doubt each akalat would have its own family features depending on its parents.

The brackish akalat (Sheppardia eximius) is a species of bird in the family *Muscicapidae. It is found in equatorial and southern*

Africa. Its natural habitat is dry forests and scrubland. It is threatened by habitat loss.

Et cetera.

I checked on the diet of the brackish akalat. Insects!

I was disappointed with the pet shop owner, that he had misinformed me, perhaps with deliberation. The police were no doubt already investigating his falsifications. I would try to find the court judgement. It would no doubt result in him being caged. Rightly.

I paged to find further on the brackish akalat. Some academic named Gershenwald et al had troubled to research it. I learnt that the song is described as melodious. I did not know how Gershenwald et al could know that. To my knowledge it had not yet been heard by any except possibly Mr Bin and —there being no recording— no one could confirm Gershenwald et al's claim. At the end of the page there was reporting of folklore from Carter[5] (1931). I did not trouble to read the superstitions of the past.

I returned to the guesthouse and my bird in contemplative mood. I sat and studied the bird in a scholarly mindset as if I was Gershenwald et al. No, it was not a sparrow. I compared the remembered photo of the akalat with my bird. Yes, no one could deny that there was a similarity, particularly the attentive, even expectant, expression. I could only conclude that it was the brackish akalat. The retailer had been selling exotics. What could be more exotic than a brackish akalat? I felt a certain excitement. A brackish akalat, here in London! Here in my possession! I had to resist baked-loaf-of-blessing thoughts and a flirting with belief in supernatural causalities.

'I'm sorry, I mistook you,' I said to my bird.

It said nothing in reply of course although I sincerely wished it to speak. In truth I felt it needed to explain itself as to how it had found me, a living from the same country, also far from home. It was a living that knew the same sunny skies and dry timbered land as myself. Of course, it could not speak, but why not sing? Yes, I wished it to sing.

'Where is your melodious voice?' I spoke politely but sternly. 'I've fed you well. I've tried every insect menu to encourage your happiness. It's been exacting labour searching for your favourite dish in the cold park by night. I've spent my food money on you. I'm asking a small thing of you. Just one song.'

It remained dumb. During this hurtful silence, I had a curious pop-up thought. I remembered how my father had been silent after his brain stroke. The doctor had diagnosed aphasic. I had in truth willed my father to speak again, feeding him well in the hope that this would somehow loosen his tongue. I had prepared the best dishes to please him, to coax his voice in appreciation of my efforts, but he had remained dumb until the soil of the grave filled his mouth and he could never speak again, excepting in my remembrance of course. No matter how well I cooked for him and cared for him he had said nothing. That bird somehow reminded me of my father. It was silent like him, despite my supreme efforts.

CHAPTER 15

At last I received a call on tartan-woolled landlady's phone (to her displeasure) to request my attendance at the Party Places headquarters again. 'We're all ready now, Chef Tushi,' said Mrs Brenda. 'It's going to be so exciting.'

They sent aforementioned Jordon, dressed-down driver, to pick me. Of course, I had grave reservations and apprehensions concerning what this 'so exciting' occasion might be, but I was inclined to believe that Mrs Camlyn, the famous restaurateur who had invited me and paid for me to travel to London, had a confidential agenda that would be revealed at just the correct time. Chief executives must stay one step ahead of their employees, surprising them with the grand and ingenious plan just when they think all is lost and that there is no way forward. In that way, they justify their superior remunerations and receive the awed adulation of their staff. I had full confidence in Mrs Camlyn.

Mrs Brenda welcomed me in a new hair of a soft blue variety and a Sunday-best pink jacket and skirt with parrot broach on her mother bosom.

'Mr Tushi, you look so cute and lovely in the poster. I've been longing to show you, but Dave said we should wait until today.'

'What is today?'

'The marketing launch with the press! They're all ready next door. But first, here it is.'

She took me to a table. There I was on a poster in the fanciful dress, my cheeks chubbed like a fat rabbit, my eyes sparkling and my lips smiling. Yes, I had to concur with the photographer, I was a natural.

The poster stated CELEBRITY SAFARI CHEF Can Tushi says, 'PARTY PLACES will make you roar. I would serve nothing less in AFRICA.'

Mr Dave joined us with much excited breathing and collar sweat.

'Just gorgeous!' said Mrs Brenda.

'Totally authentic,' said Mr Dave.

'My name's not correct.'

'We made a small adjustment,' said Mr Dave. 'Man Tushi is very gender specific and has colonial era connotations —Man Friday and such— so we've adjusted your first name a little. Only one letter change so I felt it hardly worth mentioning.'

He flatted a paper on the table and placed a pen.

'What's this?' I said.

'It's a release form for your picture in our promotional. Should have got you to sign when we took the photo, but it's just a formality.'

I observed again my portrait. It was a high temptation to forget my calling, to embrace celebrity status, be a trending personality. Such opportunity for personages of my heritage was rare. I would become the internationally known face of Party Places, Safari. The celebrated safari chef for kids. But I would be the chef who did not cook. The chef who just had to look cute and bunny-faced, through no merit apart from being spotlighted as from AFRICA. The chef who had given up on his ambition, like the teacher in the park.'

'With respect, I cannot sign.'

Mr Dave tapped the designated place on the page for my signature whilst nodding to a gentleman at the door, indicating that we would be ready shortly to go through and meet the press.

'I was mistaken,' I said. 'I'm looking for a chef position in a restaurant of good standing.'

Mr Dave laughed. 'Instead you're going to be a superstar! What could be better than that? By the way we've printed out an extra poster. A souvenir for you.'

'I'll go and get it for you right now,' said Brenda.

'No thank you. Party clowning's not my profession. I have a dream that's certain. I'm unable to ink your document.'

Mr Dave held the tongue of his tie that protruded from his belt and lost vocalisation.

'Ah, you're shy, aren't you darling,' said Brenda. She put a mother-hand on my arm and turned to Mr Dave. 'It's daunting, his face out in public, being recognised everywhere, meeting the press. It's just understandable nerves.'

Mr Dave nodded in all insincerity. 'Mr Toothy, I totally understand. It's actually no big deal. You'll be fronting our Facebook newsfeed for a day or two, the adverts will be up for a week, the mailshot a one off, then you'll be over and done. Totally forgotten. Does that reassure you?'

'I'm thanking you, but I'm saying that I'm needing to excuse myself.'

'Are you worried about meeting the press?' said Mr Dave. 'All you have to do is mention your safari chefing in Africa, the cooking you do out there surrounded by lions and tigers eager to snatch the steak.' He ha-ha'd in a nerveful manner. 'Perhaps you've a sweet story or two to tell them about the cuddly creatures you've met so the kids will want to meet you and hear more. Don't forget, you're our genuine article!'

'I thank you again.' I turned to go.

'Mr Toothy, don't let us down.' He bulge-eyed and pulled his tie out from his belt and waved it at me as if swatting me. 'You've cost us. We've flown you here. We've put you up in a guest house. You'll not find another chef who wouldn't have paid us for this sort of publicity.'

'In that case I'm pleased to hear, knowing you'll find it easy to find another. I don't wish to inconvenience you. There are indeed hundreds of chefs in my country bicycling around looking for any work, but for myself I'm seeking bright prospects and masterful achievement at the top end.'

'Get Mrs Camlyn,' said Mr Dave to Mrs Brenda.

That stopped me. I was at last to meet Mrs Camlyn. Her very self! The praiseworthy Mrs Camlyn, the talented and productive owner of international restaurants of world renown, the exacting employer who only accepted the highest culinary creations in her kitchens. Surely, she would reprimand Mr Dave for misunderstanding her intentions over my employment. I was going to be rescued from Party Places, to escape the Dave Division. I would surely be on a jet to Boston that very night.

The door swung open. Out came a purpose-thighed lady, crew haired, powerly suited in black and violet, shoes matching, a heavy silver horseshoe bracelet on her wrist and silver horseshoe pendant on her necklace.

Mrs Brenda followed with hasty little steps. She mouthed, 'Mrs Camlyn!'

Miss Camlyn's famous mother. Mrs Zeto Camlyn! Yes, her very self! To rescue me. My heart was prancing in my chest.

But for how long did I feel lucky? Not so long. She did not see me or greet me but nodded impatiently as Mr Dave explained my objection. She was like her daughter only in one respect: she had bluish eyes, but then I saw that they were flecked with sulphur and black granite.

She said, '— !' Then, 'Forget it! It was only because my silly daughter pressured me … her childish enthusiasms. Told her it wouldn't work. I'm right, as ever.' She spiralled her eyes. 'She never listens.'

'The press?' said Mr Dave, pulling so hard on his long red tie that I worried for suicidal strangulation.

'Pff, I can handle the press.' She touched her horseshoe pendant, swung around and made for the door.

'Mrs Camlyn!' I called out in desperado urgency.

She pivoted back, but she did not meet my eyes although they must have bugled imploring. 'David … sort your tie. It's becoming an embarrassment.'

She exited, the door banging closed like a gunshot —directed at myself.

'That's it then,' said Mr Dave, dropping his tie as if he had accidentally picked up a serpent. He stared at the door.

'Oh dear … mercy me,' said Mrs Brenda, and a sad hand went out to touch my chubbed cheek on the poster.

I too stood stupefied, acclimatising to the new situational and in mourning for the praiseworthy Mrs Camlyn of my expectations and dreams. She had changed. How could that be? What had happened to her? She was a backslider. She had about-faced. She had mutated.

Mr Dave moved all of a sudden, ushering me with inconsiderate curtness, not even permitting me to bid farewell and apologise to the disappointed maternal.

'You'll have to make your own way back. We can't waste any more money on you for obvious reasons.'

At the glass door to the street, I attempted to shake his ox-tongue hand again, but he turned and left me without a farewell.

Notwithstanding the aforementioned embarrassment and the unmasking of the duplicitous Mrs Camlyn, I spoke proudly to my akalat when I got home. 'I've kept faith. I've kept belief. One day I'll be a chef in a high end. No evidence will persuade me otherwise.'

It agreed.

'We must look out for the next available opportunity. It'll surely come. Tomorrow will always be better than today.'

It agreed.

'By the way, I'm sorry I've been calling you sparrow. It wasn't your name. I can appreciate how grieved you felt at this misnaming, believe me.'

It accepted my apologies.

That very evening, after I had fed my akalat, Miss Camlyn called me. 'This is the last time,' said tartan-woolled lady.

'Mozzy, my mother just rung me and told me what happened today. I'm so sorry.' She sniffed down the line. I surmised she was upset. 'Mummy blamed me.'

I reassured her that the Party Places posting was a misunderstanding, that I had retained my dignity, and she was not to give it another thought of any kind, especially the sad kind.

'You did the right thing,' she said, 'they would have dumped you as soon as they finished their marketing. I know about these things … I'm in marketing.'

'You know, for sure.'

'Look, I've spoken to a friend's father. He owns Plume de Paon —a poncey restaurant in Knightsbridge. He says that if you're free tomorrow evening you can observe in their kitchen. He says it'll be an experience for you.'

'It's a top kitchen?'

'It's one of the top ten restaurants in London according to Tom Barstow, the celebrity food critic.'

'He's well known.'

'Oh yeah, very. He's even been on *Strictly*. I'm just sorry they're not giving you a job. Perhaps if you offer to be helpful, something will come of it.'

My heart kicked. 'They're likely!'

I thumbed up to my bird. I had been vindicated in turning away from Party Places, in refusing to lower my standards and become a kids' party promotional. I would never accept rock-bottom. At the top restaurant in London I would certainly impress. The dawn would break.

I thanked Miss Camlyn for not forgetting me and went to enthuse with my akalat and, in truth, I could not sit for runaway excitement but walked back and forward in the narrow gap beside my bed.

'Now that I've been gifted opportunity, my destination's very close. This is it! Super! Sharp-sharp!' I allowed myself to jabber. I was experiencing the sensation of thrill.

I texted Dorothea, my hands almost uncontrollable with dignified euphoria. 'High end kitchen tomorrow! Your faith is rewarded!'

There was no reply. Perhaps she had run out of credit. Perhaps she was waiting for remuneration. This would surely be forthcoming.

CHAPTER 16

I paraded to the famous London Borough of Kensington and Chelsea attired in my matrimonial suit with a purpose-making bearing, my shoes reflecting the bright and prismatic lights of the beautiful city. I was about to take up that lifetime opportunity in the famous kitchen of my destiny. There are perhaps only three days in a life that are truly exceptional, pivotal and singularly memorable, standing alone above the mundane run of days, and this day would be the most notable of those three. That was for sure.

Plume de Paon was positioned on a gardened square of stone buildings with tall doors and imperious windows, which would surely stir the public's respect for a thousand years. A sober-grey dome announced the entrance to the restaurant and a pulpit displayed a glass-protected menu, written in an ancestral font, perhaps with a quilled pen plucked from the fancy fowl that was depicted on the menu, every letter trailing tendrils like a climbing plant.

Finest Traditional English Cuisine

The menu presented many delicacies. *Breast of Pigeon in Brandy; Great Yarmouth Grilled Bloaters; Cauliflower and Fennel Soup; Lamb Cutlets with Laverbread Cakes; Devonshire Junket; Baked Custard Tart* and more. All reassuringly expensive. Yes, they served the ultimate colonist cuisine. I would not find better. The quotes of newspaper pundits were framed on a side stand. *A rich and refined banquet; Dining at its most royal; Restores the English food tradition.*

The door was locked and so I pulled politely on the golden tassels of the bell call. In point of veracity, I pulled politely three times before I heard from a discrete speaker by the door, 'We're not open until seven, can I help?'

'My name is Chef Mlantushi. I've been assigned to your kitchen tonight.'

I heard him call out, 'A man at the door says he's expected this evening. Jeffman Tooshy, or something.'

Someone shouted back, 'Oh god, not tonight. Mr Fairbrother mentioned him. Better let him in.'

A Chef Arthur —a commis chef, he informed me— escorted me through the restaurant, and what a passaging it was. All was deep-buttoned cattle hide, knotted timber panels, gold picture frames as big as rafts displaying dark portraits of pheasant fowl, hunting dogs and horses with proud faces; also Queens with waists as thin as a wasp's and well-fed button-straining Kings. Velvet curtains waterfalled in royal blue and crown gold and chandeliers made starry constellations above. The tables were draped in white silk and sanctified like high alters by silver candle sticks. The crystal-bright cutlery was hallmarked for sure. Two giant lion heads in black stone guarded each side of the cave-like fireplace where logs glowed behind iron spikes. It was truly a dining environment for monarchs, presidents, heads of states, served by the best chefs in the world, indeed the archbishops of the culinary catechism.

To avoid any doubt or misunderstanding, I informed Chef Arthur of my top credentials and cited testimonials from my diners, explaining that I had chefed clients who paid five hundred dollars each to eat at my table, including a supplementary guided walk in a local park.

'Very impressive,' he said, and I agreed.

When I entered the kitchen, I was arrested in my step and was minded to ask how they had exact-copied my dreams. They had done so without my permission! (This is a jest, of course). All gleamed in stainless steel: the preparation surfaces, shelves, trays, hooks, air extraction, electric sockets, scales. Chefs laboured in whites and strenuously ironed aprons of blue and white stripes, tied with bows.

'This is Jeffman,' said Chef Arthur to the head chef.

The head chef pulled a tray of the puddings from Yorkshire from an oven. He hurried with the tray to a surface. 'If you stand over there you'll not be knocked over. We're two chefs down tonight. We've a full house. I can't give you any attention this evening. You'll just have to watch.' He shouted, 'Margery, pastry egged?'

'Yes, chef,' she shouted back without hesitation. She had watched *MasterChef.*

Chef Arthur found me a corner and said, 'Stand there. I've got to move.'

Another chef shouted, 'Chef, oven two's on the blink again.'

'— it! What else will go wrong this evening?' The head chef went to investigate. 'I'll give it a kicking, it worked last time.'

Standing in the corner, ignored, I was thinking that surely my best lifetime opportunity was at risk of becoming compromised. Would I be invited to cook? To what purpose was the singular day if I did not deliver my dishes? Notwithstanding this, I was like a river bird watching the water without blinking, without motion, imperceptible in breathing. Over the following twenty minutes I noted the locations of every ingredient, implement and plate, the controls for the ovens, grills, hot plates and blast freezer, where the orders would arrive, where the food was plated out. Nothing escaped my sharp and obstinate gaze.

'Chef, we've no chestnuts for the stuffing. They've not been restocked.'

'— it! I'll strangle young Harrison.'

They all sweated too much. They were all of a certain mature and complaining age and I surmised that they had not left that kitchen for decades. They needed me. I had to be bold. I left my corner and stepped up to the plate, so to speak. 'Head Chef, I can help. I'm also a head chef. I've cooked fine cuisine for VIPs. They were kind and honest enough to say—'

'Can't you see? I've no time to supervise you.' He groaned. 'Edward, I have a migraine … I'm losing my vision.'

He staggered and then tripped, dropping a roast loin of pork. It exploded hot fat across the floor.

The chefs ran to give assistance. 'You have to go home,' they said.

'— it. I can't! Not tonight. I'll be alright. I'll lie down for a moment.' They led him to a door at the back and I heard them resting him down and then they returned to rush, rush, rush, shout, shout, shout. There was much ill-disciplined and unnecessary language in that kitchen. Chopped onions and carrots danced under thrashing knives. Spittle and sweat flew.

I was rising and falling on my tiptoes to assist. A failed pan was emptied into a bin. The sprouts from Brussels had been left to steam too long. Panic was rising. Chef Arthur conferred urgently with Chef Margery and Chef Edward. Then he came to me.

'Alright, we're desperate. You've been watching. The menu's up on the wall there. You claim to be good … see what you can do. Get on with it, chef. Then show it me. It better be fantastic. It must capture our traditional and revered style. Don't deviate from what you've seen.'

At last! All my studies, my experience, my dedication, my

unbreakable belief in my destiny were to be tested in a master dish. This was the task of my life, the entrance gate to my final destination. It would indeed be the most memorable day of the three of a lifetime. I felt that I was even acting as the head chef due to the infirmity of the incumbent. I had experienced an exact parallel situation at the start of my career. Had not the chef at the Tom Mbolo Overnight Motel (Cash Only) had to lie down and let me take over when he was incapacitated? And had I not made superlative dishes in the bush in Mr Bin's kitchen that was only one up from a campfire, the power having to be sparked on, the ingredients hard to source, surrounded by crawling creatures and a bare-footed employer? So I set to with a calm and light heart. It would be a piece of cake in the kitchen of my dreams.

Whilst the quilled menu was fine in its own paradigm —the glass cabinet outside the front door— my observations of the dishes that the chefs prepared had not inspired me. I would cook instead as if for favourite diners such as Miss Camlyn and Mr Summerberg, for they had been a queen and a king. What was unsurpassed for my VIP guests would certainly be sufficient for the diners of Plume de Paon.

My main was premeditated to guide the taste buds through multitudinous simultaneous sweet memories, technical complexities and indescribable ecstasies. In a calmly enacted frenzy of motion, I created my dish. Mangetouts, roasted red groundnuts, star anise, caraway seeds, duck breasts, kumquats, red chillies and more, I hardly remember. Heating, cooling, seasoning, slicing … I was in a zone, a trance. The cursing and clatter of the kitchen fell away from me. I was touched by the hand of an Almighty. I was a channel for the pouring out of perfection and glory. I was Master Chef.

The chief maître, stiff-gaited and attired in black and white like the conceited fowls I had seen in Kensington park, came to the order window.

'Table four's arrived and Ted Barstow is with them,' he said fearfully and remorsefully as if breaking news of the loss of a loved one.

'Not tonight, surely,' said Chef Arthur. As he passed me, he said, 'He's the most influential food critic in London, but a right barstow.'

I was of course delighted. Every star was aligned for great success (although I did not nod to astrology). Mr Barstow was my dream diner. A famous pundit with a discerning palate. I would rehearse the superlatives he would write in the national presses when I got home in the early morning, but now I had work to do.

The orders came through. The chefs ran about but I completed in calm and without sweat. Still the orders went out from the menu, no one came for my dish. I was about to politely admonish Chef Arthur when the maître came again to the window. His face was as pale and drained of health as skimmed milk.

'Ted Barstow has sent back the main. He says it's burnt. *Incinerated* was his specific judgement.'

'Oh — ! It's that oven two,' said Chef Arthur. 'What else is ready? Haricot mutton ready, Margery?'

'Fifteen minutes, chef.'

I said to Chef Arthur, 'I'm geared to plate right now. Let's not delay.'

Chef Arthur was paralysed, staring at my pans.

'He's in no mood to wait. What shall I tell him?' said the maître.

'Kindly inform him that we have a special,' I said.

'But what is it?' said Chef Arthur. 'It's not on the menu.'

'It's Breast of Duck with Kumquat and Chilli Marmalade accompanied by Minted Pea and Roasted Red Groundnut Salad. But its presentation and taste will be worth a thousand words.'

'Not on our menu,' said the maître, eyes sunk in deep woe. 'I don't know how I'm going to explain it. His table's gone quiet. He's stabbing his fork into the tablecloth with impatience. Even his companions are terrified.'

'If he won't wait, we'll have to serve Chef Jeffman's,' said Chef Arthur. 'Tell him it's on the house. Tell him it was a favourite of Thomas Cromwell's grandmother.'

I plated out in one minute thirty and the maître took it, muttering, 'Oh no, oh god no.'

I hummed one of Dorothea's songs of blessing to myself.

For dessert I created orange pistachio pastries, soaking the oranges first in Amaretto before mixing pistachios, nutmeg, cinnamon, ginger and cardamom in a particular and necessary sequence with aerations and blanchings to cause the receiving tongue to linger in intoxications and ravishments, past lovers brought to mind. I baked the pastry squares in oven number one until a light golden in colouration, in layers as thin as gold leaf and dipped in maple syrup, orange albedo and nuts. I scattered the completed creation with fresh shredded mint leaves.

When the desert orders came through, I was ready and already plating. The head chef reappeared from his lie down, recovered somewhat. He came to my plates.

'What are you playing at?' he said.

'It tastes heavenly, sir chef. It's a big deal with VIP diners.'

He put his hand to his forehead as if I had recurred his migraine. 'That's not a Plume de Paon dish. Bin it!'

'But—' said Chef Arthur.

'Bin it! I'm not having our reputation trashed.' He regarded my dish as if I had plated a Safari Cub menu from Party Places. Lion Claw Nibbles or Tiger Tasties. 'It's horribly gaudy.'

'But Barstow—'

'It's voguish, it's fashion conscious, it's upstart. It's too … frivolous.'

'But Barstow—' pleaded Chef Arthur.

'Offer Barstow our traditional vanilla ice cream with grilled peach. On the house. Who let this amateur cook loose in the kitchen of the great Plume de Paon?'

He snatched up a spoon and scooped up a corner of my dish, his hand shaking. He tasted. Surely he would be blown away, he would be silenced, he would drop to his knees in apology. He would offer to employ me. I had poured my very soul into that desert.

No, he gagged. He lifted a tea towel and wiped his tasting into it. 'Vomitable!'

I remembered the sicking bird that had troubled Miss Camlyn. My dish tasted of gizzard food?

He scrubbed his lips clean and turned to me. 'You've got a — cheek, Jeffman, after I ordered you to stay out the way. There's no excuse. Four hundred years ago I'd have petitioned to send you to the tower.'

There was a hush in the kitchen at his words and clandestine glances over the beating of the creams and the stirring of the sauces. There also came a bottomless hole in my heart into which my only chance and my grand hopes slid. I excused myself in a somewhat high voice and departed, exiting the kitchen of my dreams, passing through the high-end-dining where those who noticed me gave me a hard stare as if I alone was responsible for their unfortunate dinner.

A thin rain smeared my shoes on the long walk back to my room through the abandoned, cold, slimy city suburbs; their closed curtains and doors as unseeing as shut eyelids. Crossing a road, I almost collided with a late-night bus that loomed as big as an elephant and splashed me as it passed. I tried not to dwell yet on what had transpired that evening. Nobody should howl out in a public location. No one should howl like a lost soul falling into a bottomless abyss. I would wait until I got to my room where I might utilise a smothering pillow if I lost control of my vocals. How had I come to this, that I planned how to release feeling without dignity? To lose decorum. It was surely because of this: I had been butchered in the beautiful kitchen. Was it my father who had said, *It's only a stupid goat that rejoices at going to a beautiful abattoir?*

CHAPTER 17

The dimly lit entrance hall to Lochview with its dark textured wallpaper was a grave with pitted and eroded walls from which I would never escape. But I was mistaken. Post awaited me on the desk. I took it with automatic hands and opened the envelope as I wearied up the stairs. It was a 'Dear Mr Tushi' letter from Party Places, Going Places. I was directed to check out of the guesthouse by said date, which I noted was that very next day. They had additionally reissued my return air ticket, giving me a replacement for two days' time, with no provision for the interim. It was signed by Company Accounts. There were no felicitations.

Despite the forthcoming accommodation difficulty, it was in no way centre-mind. I sat feeble-bodied on the end of the bed in the brown gloom of the room's economy light bulb, close to my bird, with my head near the cage bars so that we could converse in confidence, one to one. This was a private matter, but my bird had what I imagined was, by public convention, the qualities of a friend, namely discretion and a propensity to listen without prejudice. It would not blab to anyone; of that I was sure.

'I'm sorry to disturb your sleep,' I said, 'but I beg your ear. I must speak veracity to you … my akalat.'

I needed to logic and in small steps so as not to come to an irrational conclusion.

'These are the facts. Number one: I endeavoured to help.

Number two: I enacted my uttermost. Three: I thought my dishes superlative. Four: my creations were not appreciated.' The bird still listened. 'Why?' I could hardly verbalise the next logic. 'They were not good enough. I was not good enough. Yes, my dishes were only fit to be sicked-up for birds.'

The bird did not catastrophise or get excitable to hear the worst. It stayed calm. 'This then is the conclusion of my analytic. I'm not a high-end chef.'

I heard Mr Makata's nonchalant opinion. 'Potato scrubber. Sandwich cutter.'

The next logic was not easily discovered. It required the knight's move of a chess master and the intuition of a solver of a mathematical theorem.

'If I'm not a high-end chef … then I've been living an illusion. A fantasy. Yes, living a fantasy.'

The akalat cocked at my hand, the hand that fed it.

'I'm only good for feeding you, a bird. That's the topmost of my skills. I can arrange insects on a dish.' I stared at this truth in the feed tray of the bird. 'My achievement? A celebrated chef in a skyscraper city? No. My terminus had always been gizzard-food cooker and bird feeder.'

Now I understood. The consummation of a hope is only known on arrival, it cannot be foreseen. Yes, to walk is not necessarily to arrive at your assumed destination. There may be another terminus, far from glorious. I had known my road would be arduous and long, but I had believed that I would finally walk through a shining kitchen door. But the end of my hard path had led to this; this cupboard room, in solitary, serving a small bird its bug dinners.

I tried to think of one of my father's sayings, one that would impart me some alternative wisdom, but it seemed that such a catastrophic position had not been envisaged by the erudition of the elder. There was no knowledge for such a circumstance.

The bird flapped in a sudden flurry about its cage. It was trapped of course, and it exhausted itself. It believed that if it flapped hard enough it could one day free itself and reach a sky. It was trying always for this impossible utopian destination. There was some concordance between us in this respect.

'I'm going to release you,' I said.

I had surprised myself, by saying such. I said it again, louder, so that I could hear myself confirming. My own hopes were lost, but why deny it to another living? I felt a little soothing of my pain, a distraction perhaps.

The bird flurried again. I alone could give it its dream: open skies, the freedom of unbounded air under its wings, live dinners flapping past.

'You've shared my loneliness. I've fed you and you've been my companion, but that's not what you wish for.' I felt an ill-disciplined tearing of my eyes. 'I apologise for holding and confining you. I'm going to set you free.'

Of course, the bird did not understand. It did not know to joy at my words.

'Maybe you'll sing when you're free of your cage. Maybe Miss Camlyn was right. You're too sad to sing.'

It fluffed itself and I brought my other shirt from the wardrobe to shelter its cage from the cold-seeping period-piece window.

'Don't worry, I'll not release you here in this chilly climate where you'll die in the winter, where insects are few, where you'll not find a mate. I'll release you at the homeland you fly to in your dreams. Where your kind was made for. I'll free you in the bush, in the wild and insect-bounteous lands beyond Romaji.'

I remembered the bird in the Kensington park, flitting from

here to there, busy without ceasing, fulfilling its desires, pleasing its instincts, feeling its wings utilised. But my bird was restrained in its cage, unable to busy, unable to purpose. It could not achieve the functions to which it was born. Without purpose, there was no meaning to its short life. Surely a tragedy for any living thing. I laid my hand on the cage as if I wished to reach the bird and hold it in my hand. My cheeks tickled and I found that they were wet. Yes, I had lost my senses. I was indeed weeping, losing personal control. My tears poured. I did not know why I felt so deeply for the bird.

I laid myself on the bed without disrobing or taking off my shoes, not thoughtful to creasing my trousers. Despite such, flopped in the bed, I felt somehow relieved to submit myself to disorder, to be abandoned to silly crying and to a sentimental desire to free the bird. I had no dream to keep discipline for anymore. I closed my puff-eyes and slept the deep sleep of a soul resigning itself to freefall in the bottomless abyss without care.

Tartan-woolled lady told me to wait outside my room at the hour ten departure time with my case and my bird. She eyed the cupboard, wiped a scrutinous finger along the shelf, shook the pillow and inspected the sink. She ticked a paper on a clipboard.

'Two coat hangers, one pillow slip, one duvet cover, one sheet, one towel, one soap. Och, seems the entire inventory's present, clean and correct! Sign here Mr Tooshy.'

'With pleasure, of course.'

She followed me down the stairs in silence, but at the front door she said, 'I'll be sorry to see yer go, Mr Tooshy. I'm Morag, by the way.'

'Please call me Mozzy.'

'May I? Yer've been a satisfactory boarder, Mozzy. I hope yer've found yer stay here to yer liking.'

'Very excellent, Miss Morag.'

A somewhat cautious smile, which appeared offered to myself, crept about her lips and I surmised that if I had stayed longer, we might eventually —after such polite interactions over many months— have become friendly to each other. This was how it was for those aspiring to live in a big progressive city. Little by little to gain familiarity so that, in due time, they would feel free to introduce themselves to each other by name.

I footed to the park, carrying my net, my suitcase containing my matrimonial suit, and my bird. I had covered the cage with my spare shirt to protect the bird from fright and chill. We would find a sheltered place in the park for the night and then the next day I would walk to the airport, the cash in my pocket not being sufficient for the bus. It was not more than twenty kilometres or so and there would no doubt be food served on the jet, so I only needed patience. I had no concern —patience was one of my core attributes. In the meantime, the park had all necessary amenities: a drinking fountain, public ablutions open during the day and a bench fitting my compactful body. A blanket for the night would be desirable, it still be cold in May, but I had no wish to beg and, in any case, I had the warm coat kindly donated me by the street sleeper. Surely things were not so bad as I had been tempted to believe the previous night. There was no drizzle and no wind, and this was a new day; a new opportunity would surely arise. I had catastrophised too much. I must restart in faith, not dwell on the inconveniences of the past. I should let bygones be bygones. Yes, my habit of hope was hard to suppress. After all, it was my irrepressible hope that had got me all the way to London from the bush.

I had not long taken up residence on the bench, finding a patch to sit on which was dry and not too lichened and bird pooped, when the teacher who had accepted to empty bed pans, although his vocation was professor, came walking by in his black knit cap. He stopped and bent to look at the akalat.

'A bird?'

'He's my companion,' I said.

'Where are you taking it?'

'Back to my country. I'm releasing it home.'

'They won't let you take it on the plane. Can I have it?'

'No, I've promised it freedom.'

He knelt down beside the bird. 'Your companion you say? Maybe he's even your friend.'

'Teacher, I can understand friendly, but what is this friend thing? It makes me somehow troubled and perplexed. I don't trust it. I have reason not to. What is a friend? What's its meaning?'

'Are you asking me as a teacher?'

'That's your profession, no? Yes, I'm asking the teacher.'

He stood and footed back and forward in front of my bench, eyes to the ground, arms clasped behind his back, his brow in furrow. He imagined an eager class awaiting his instruction. He cleared his throat and spoke clear. 'A friend is someone who forgives your faults.'

'But teacher,' I said, 'I'm happy to enact such for my acquaintances. I don't need them to be friends to forgive their faults. In point of fact, this bird and I have forgiven each other's faults, but a bird cannot be an actual friend, of course. It's only a bird.'

He continued to pace. 'You could call your bird a friend and no one would contradict you.'

'It seems then that friend is a careless term.'

'Let me see. A philosopher said that a friend is a second self.'

'I wouldn't want such a friend. I wouldn't like to find and tolerate the same faults as mine in another, even if they are few. I'd find it difficult to be friendly with a second self. They would surely be a rival, applying for the same high-end postings in competition with me.'

'A thought-provoking answer. Okay, try this. A friend is trustworthy.'

'So is the bank.'

He paced more. 'A friend is someone you'd like to see often,' he tried. 'Someone whose absence makes you feel wistful.'

'If I lost this bird, even though it's just a bird, I'd feel the same.'

'A friend is loyal.'

'That's duty, not friendship. I've always endeavoured loyal. For instance, I was loyal to my previous employer, despite provocations.'

'You're a bright and challenging pupil. How about this? A writer said that friendship is sweet and steady and so enduring that it'll last a whole lifetime.' He paused. 'If not asked to lend money.' The teacher chuckled and I nodded. He had told a fine and clever joke.

'But my wife and I are sweet and steady, even life enduring,' I countered. 'It's what's expected according to the duty and necessities of our matrimonial bond. We are friendly, but are we friends?' After I said such, I recalled that money was indeed a disturbance in our relations. The joke the teacher had told me was not so funny.

The teacher walked again, but now he moved his hand in a circle to encourage his brain processes. Eventually he said, 'Maybe friendship is just a treasured notion held only in the heart. An admirable idea that no one can define … a laudable thing that we think we should believe in to show we're good human beings.'

'I've no need for that reassurance, thank you.'

He stopped and gave me an uneasy eye. I also was disquieted to hear myself say such. It somehow sounded self-satisfied and presumptuous to set myself up as the judge of myself.

'Maybe it's just true that *to be without a friend is to be poor indeed*,' he said.

I was losing his logic.

'My break's up. Thank you for the chance to practice my teaching. It's made me want to apply again.' He turned to go, but then stopped and said, 'Personally I find birds too aloof, too distracted and busy to be friends with, but I wish you good luck with it.'

I tended my akalat, feeding it bugs from a packet, keeping it warm, waking during the night to check it was safe. I arose early. I had arrangements to make.

CHAPTER 18

Truly, we eventually and always return to dust. The road to Romaji village had still not been tarred and so the bus still crunched and grinded over mile on mile of gravel, travelling ever towards that heat-ghost horizon. But perhaps the Anthropocene had its rapacious eye on the village as there were now pylons marching beside our way, strung with the wire-tentacles of electric power. The orange wash of fires and kerosene lamps would soon exist only in the memories of the old.

At our village terminus, I stepped out onto the dirty earth. My shirt was creased and sweated, my collar, ears and neck were powdered grey and rust and the rough jolting had caused my nerves to become as tight as piano strings, but without the pleasant notes. Worse had preceded. I had bedded overnight in the capital in the bus station, but as I slept my case had been stolen. I was empty-handed apart from my insect net. My matrimonial suit was no longer mine. I had regret. How could I ever interviewee again? But in truth, I was glad to be away from cities with their hard concretes and metals, perpetual noise, harsh lights, swerving people. I was at last returning to the soft and abiding arms of my good wife. How I longed to see her. To be joyed by her.

I walked through the village. A news board informed that elections had seen the President ousted. The incoming President was to divert resources to more needy regions. Romaji would no longer be favoured. Despite such, the place of the anthill had been erased, built on by *House of Concrete. Buildings Merchants.* I noted *No Pain no Gain Investments*, and *WhatsApp Saloon*. New churches and assemblies competed for custom. *Apostles of the True Testament (Signs, Wonders)* and *National Prophetic Assemblies (Name It then Claim It)*. I stopped by a billboard-sized new sign. *Pastor Cain Assemblies (formerly Divine Prosperity Assembly)*. There was a photograph of Pastor Cain's grand assembly hall and Pastor Cain himself, attired in a gloss purple suit. *Blessings! Healings! Resurrections!*

Behind the glass walls and chrome shine of the bank I caught a glimpse of Monica. She was still decorated with gold hoop earrings, but her hair was now in lustrous ponytail braids. A fashion of the city. She was transacting smoothly in mutual respect with clients. But such places were shut to me now. We would be pursued by the bank for the loan. They might take our house. That is what I heard myself saying to said self, and it made me stop. I had reverted to pessimism. To a melancholic persuasion. Had I not become like the teacher in the Kensington park? A man not unlike me who had lost all expectation, who had abandoned his dream. Had I lost again my sure hope that tomorrow would deliver? Why was I thinking in such a defeated manner? Surely, I was allowing what had happened in London to cage me. I had had an unfortunate evening in a kitchen, true, but what was one day in the many thousands of days of an ambitious man? The future did not have to arise from the past. Had I not seen a new tourist lodge signed off the road? What opportunities would therefore arise? Yes, Chef Mlantushi would chef again. The beautifully-braided Monica would respect, would not side-glance me again. I walked on, stamping firmly of foot, shoulders military. *Return to old watering holes for more than water; friends and dreams are there to meet you.*

But despite my lion-hearted effort, it was hard to maintain a renewed expectation that tomorrow would be better than yesterday. My life coach had been stern to me. But one prospect was not in doubt: I would soon see my good wife. She would be delighted to see her steadfast husband and I would be uplifted by her dancing eyes and joying disposition.

Our house was small in comparison with the grand quarters, which I had footed past in London. But no room of ours was as small as mine in Lochview Guesthouse. The brick on the table still lay there, still brick-like on its gloss wrapping and its Chinese ribbon. The sofa was even larger than I remembered and was just as pink and opulent. Only the trumpet-like vase of unbreakable glass was missing.

'My dear wife, I'm home,' I called. I craved her good humour to bring light to my heart, not to mention too forwardly and suggestively, her kissing.

Dorothea came without greeting from the kitchen and stood in the doorway. She was attired in the plain and spiritless vestments of the Divine Prosperity Assembly and her hands were clasped tensely together in front of her white pinafore. I open-armed her, ready for her to joy over to me. She stayed in the doorway looking at me, but without expression. My hands fell.

'My late husband,' she said, 'it would've been better for you not to return to me —far better not to have come home.'

'Late husband? What's this?'

'Prepare yourself.'

'Yes?' I had a bad feeling. Was this not an irregular homecoming?

'Sit yourself on the sofa. I'm going to tell you everything.' I had no wish to sit. 'Sit!' she commanded. I sat.

'Yes ... prepare yourself.' She looked away to the window. 'And don't interrupt me.' She took a long breath and then her words fell as hard and loose as stones dumped from a tipper truck. 'When I knew you weren't going to send money, I begged Pastor Cain. I begged him to postpone the love offerings. I begged, I begged.'

She teared and was unable to speak. I made to get up to comfort her, but she put out her hand to stay me put. She was surely injured in her heart, but was refusing me.

'He was angry.' She stopped again and sobbed. 'He said the love offerings must continue. Otherwise there'd be no blessings. No hope.'

'Where was his charity? Jezek … fourteen or thereabouts, no?'

'Let me finish! I told him I'd forget the blessings. I'd forget the marble house with plush furnishings … the fancy car … the high walls topped by protective glass. All that. The praise of the Assembly wouldn't be mine. I told him I'd return the holy brick for someone else to benefit.'

She gave another sob, but I knew better than to move again. I had never before seen Dorothea weep. It was much more shocking and heart-moving than seeing a melancholic weep. That would be expected, even dismissible.

'Pastor Cain said he wouldn't let me break my commitment. If I stopped the love offerings … I'd be cursed. He would excommunicate me in front of the Assembly. A warning to others. An important lesson to the congregation on the dangers of disobedience. Of lack of faith.'

'Where was his compassion?'

'Shut up, will you? I haven't finished. I cried. He said there was more than one type of love offering. He would generously consider accepting another means of love offering.'

I waited, but she did not continue. She looked through me.

'Another means?'

'Yes, another means.'

I puzzle-faced.

'Do I have to spell it out?'

I felt my heart prepare to fall. 'You … I think I see … you accepted?'

'The bank was chasing me hard. You didn't send money. What could I do? I'd already prostituted myself financially. I had no choice.' Now her tears came freely; they flowed hot and steady as lava. She sobbed out, 'But I was used.'

I lost grip on my insect net and it dropped to the floor. I could not look at Dorothea and my vocals were paralysed. I stood up and, lacking knowledge of what to do, lacking previous experience of such matters, I left the house. I turned this way and that way on the stones of the road, on the grit and dust outside. My imagination took me to evil places that no faithful husband should have to go. I had deep feelings that I could hardly understand. How could our wedded bliss come to such? It was as if I was falling into the bottomless abyss of previous mention, but not in a free fall. No, every tormenting thought was like bashing onto a ledge which I then tumbled off to fall again onto another, and so on, down and down. Each thought contradicted the previous. I stumble-footed beside the thick-limbed barrier of euphorbia fencing, back and forward to the standpipe at the corner of the track.

Did she truly detest Cain or did she so desire a three-metre wall and a limousine that all was permissible? What could I offer her? What had I brought back from the city? An insect net! Had Cain in actuality forced himself on her, or did she in truth wish a child with him? Had she decided not to wait any longer for a child due to my prolonged and perhaps exasperating consideration of the matter? Had she thought I had gone astray when I did not answer her texts? That I had taken another? Would I have to tolerate that Cain snake helping himself to my wife in order for us to survive?

One who plants grapes by the roadside, and one who marries a pretty woman, share the same problem.

Late husband? Did she wish a divorce? Would she become his fourth wife?

Truly, I had serious personal matters in my marriage. I had become like Mr Bin. I had striven against disorder since my father died, but now I had disorder in both my professionals and personals and the personals, to my surprise, were the more heart-twisting.

I returned to the house for want of knowing where to go next. Dorothea had remained in the kitchen doorway and was tissuing her nose. 'You'll no doubt want a divorce,' she said.

'Do you wish it? A divorce? Is it Cain for you?'

'What?' Dorothea wide-eyed me, threw her hands up and beat the door. 'No, no, no! I hate that man.' She was crying so loudly that the neighbours could surely hear. The monkeys in the park could surely hear and would be laughing at us.

She quieted. 'Sava, I wish to stay with you. You have big faults —there, I said it— but you've always been the man I respect. You're not like Pastor Cain.'

I wanted to somehow comfort her, but there was a painful strife in my heart that I could not resolve.

'But it's more than that,' she said, 'I missed you. I have true feelings for you at last. Yes, true feelings. Now it's too late.'

I went to the window and looked out at the yard. It needed sweeping of the leaves and seeds blown from the wild. The dying sun caused the breeze block wall to colour blood. A ragged winged bird flapped towards the coming night. All was cut up, dark and disorderly. She had professed true feelings —even such a thing as love? But she had accepted the arms of another man for money. She lacked personal discipline. Could I forgive such?

'Maybe this is the rock bottom that Pastor Cain talked about,' said Dorothea. 'The previous was a false bottom.'

I raised my voice, lost to a sudden berserk emotion. 'No! There's no rock bottom to hope for. Cain's a fraud. A swindler! A trickster! If you continue to fantasise, we'll never find rock bottom.'

I saw the brick, squatting silent but somehow mendacious on its star-silvered wrapping paper and purple high-gloss ribbon. A false and cunning gift, a fantasy wrapped in the phony produce of the city. I went to the brick and snatched it up.

'You must no longer live in illusion. Cain has shot-gunned your mind with his lies. This brick is just a brick.' I spat at it. 'A brick from the village kiln.'

I turned and threw the brick out of the open window with all the force of my rage and, it is true, with all my disappointments and fears. It hit the breeze block wall and broke in two. It was just a misfired brick.

Dorothea gasped. 'You've cursed us! You've smashed the last of my hopes and dreams.' She stepped towards the window, but then she turned around and slump-armed on the table, her wet face down ways.

Seeing Dorothea collapsed on the table sorely troubled my constitution. It finally sunk the boat of my recent dally with self-belief and the float of my positive thinking on my prospects. Instead, I remembered my reasoned words to my bird on the night that I had returned from Plume de Paon. I recalled my logic. I could not deny it. Tomorrow would not be better than today. I was a no-good cook and now I had a no-good marriage.

'Let me inform you, Dorothea. I'm also at fault, yes. I've also been living in illusion. My fantastical fantasy of being a head chef in the USA, serving top VIPs, was like your cloud-cuckoo brick. A misbelief. A phantasm.'

'You don't have a job?'

'I have no job. My pockets are empty. I'm an unemployed cook and a poor fool.'

For a long time she was still and silent, her face down and her arms out. I stood nearby but was unable to move to her. Then I saw her shake her head. I did not know what she meant by that. We had both emptied of words. We were lost, conundrumed, knowing not what to say.

What to do? I needed perhaps to talk with an advisor, with such a thing as a friend. A person friend. There was no one. What to do?

'I'm going to cook for supper,' I said. But what of after? Mr Bin was not, surely, a friend, but we were well acquainted. 'Tomorrow, I may pay Mr Bin a visit.' He had once sought my opinion; he would not mind my asking his.

Dorothea lifted herself and wiped her eyes with the back of a hand. 'Don't you know? He's in the jail. He's awaiting trial.'

'Mr Bin? Jail? What's befallen him?'

'He's charged with attempted murder. He'll be locked up for life.'

'Impossible! Tell me, how and who and when and where?'

But Dorothea was not inclined to converse further. She snatched a tissue from the kitchen and entered the bedroom, slammed the door and locked it, leaving me in many uneasy and disturbed speculations. Attempted murder! Surely Mr Bin had not tried to dispatch a new cook? Perhaps the new cook had also refused to wake him. Then I paralysed. His wife? The well-dressed lady? Had she driven to his house with her fiancé and her papers. Shouted yellow jelly at him? Did he pick up his rifle? Had Mr Bin lost his mind and committed a crime of passion? I did not think the spineless, indecisive, useless Mr Bin capable of such spirit.

Chapter 19

I found that whilst in custody, Mr Bin resided in a shipping container. The village had no purpose-built correctional institution but, no problem, the said battered container had been requisitioned from a railway siding far away, transported, I guessed, by flatbed sixteen-wheeler truck in a storm of dust and then tipped with the sound of thunder next to the police station. A small window had been angle-grinded with accompanying flashes of light high in the side to prevent suffocation of the prisoner and thick bars welded in place to frustrate thin escapees. The visiting hours were written freehand by an apprentice writer in dripping green paint on the side of the container. *3.30 p.m. to 4.30 p.m. Mondays. Apply at Police.* I had arrived on a Tuesday.

I entered the next-door police station and found Mr Bambatiwe, the full-of-pastries chief of the two police in the village, sitting on two chairs in paperwork with his officer. He raised his samosa-eyelids to see me.

'Ah, Mr Mlantushi, you're back. Greetings, greetings. No doubt you're on leave from your chefing work in the US of A. Perhaps I can drop by your house so you can give me a statement about it whilst I'm enjoying one of your excellent cakes on your fine sofa.'

'Of course sir, you're always welcome, but today I've come to see Mr Bin.'

'Our prisoner, the offender Du Plessis?'

'I've brought him a meal.'

'Visiting is on Mondays but my officer will pass him the food. He must be tired of ground maize and water, although he needs to get used to it.'

'I'd like to give him the dish myself. I've taken some trouble to cook it.'

I showed him the pot, wrapped in a towel to keep warmth, and took off the lid.

Mr Bambatiwe waved the steam of my stew to his horse-sized nostrils. 'Ah! Leave the food with us. This stew's too good for a prisoner.'

'Sir, I beg you.'

'Mr Mlantushi, why associate with a criminal? You don't want to appear as an accomplice, notwithstanding your clever alibi of being overseas during the crime.'

'Mr Bin's a criminal? Has he confessed?'

'So far he's been exercising his legal right to remain silent. That's how guilty he is. Does not an innocent man protest his innocence?'

'I look forward to baking a large, showstopping cake for you, sir. But how will I achieve such if I'm fretting about not delivering to Mr Bin. The stew's getting cold.'

Mr Bambatiwe tapped his pencil up and down on his desk. 'Let me check for concealed weapons … files … drugs. Show me the stew again.'

He lifted his pencil and poked it about in the stew. Then he licked the pencil clean and poked in the stew again and licked again. 'Yes, too good for a prisoner.' He frown-browed. 'Cake is necessary.' He turned to his officer. 'Officer Geoffroy, let Mr Mlantushi deliver and say a few words of farewell to the criminal before his trial, and then he must leave.'

Mr Bin sat on a metal shelf at the far end of the container in a thin spear of sunlight from the high window. He appeared somewhat forlorn and pale skinned above an unkempt beard. He wore prison-regulation khaki shirt and shorts and a pair of well-used prison flip-flops. A chain ran from his ankle to a ring in the centre of the floor. This was truly a maximum-security establishment for prisoners with murderous inclinations. A lumpen mattress and a small brown blanket had been provided in a corner for his night-time comfort and there was a bucket in the other corner for his ablutions. In truth, I was most perturbed to see Mr Bin incarcerated so, and although I knew that Mr Bin cared nothing for material comforts, for Egyptian cotton sheets and ceiling fans, I considered his current residence to be somewhat unsatisfactory, even for him. Despite the crime that he had committed. Indeed, I forgot my personal affairs, seeing Mr Bin caged in such a way. He was like a trapped bird. He would never again have need of his long legs for walking just as the caged bird has no need of its wings.

He fixed on me, wide eyed, as if I was a ghost. An unexpected ghost at that. Officer Geoffroy closed the door with unnecessary banging and bolting and left me alone with Mr Bin.

'Mr Bin, I'm so sorry to find you in this place.'

'Mozzy, is this really you?'

'I've brought you a meal.'

'You've come back from Boston to bring me a meal?'

'Not exactly … but I wished to see my ex-employer again. Here, look, it's a simple stew with beef, carrots and potatoes. You can eat the meat … I've added no curries.'

'Do you mind if I start?' said Mr Bin. 'I'm ravenous. State food's horribly monotonous and gritty.'

I gave him a plate, ironed napkin and a spoon. 'Please, eat.'

It was a pleasure to see him appreciate my food. He had never before. I did not disturb him although my time with him would be short. I remembered Father saying, *Words are sweet, but they cannot take the place of food.*

Mr Bin paused to dab his mouth with the napkin. 'I'm going to be put away for a long time, Mozzy. It's ironic, as lately I've become less keen on solitude.'

'My father used to say, *Solitude is an enchanting mistress, but an unendurable wife.*'

'For once, your father was right.'

'I'm sure the Justice will release you.'

'No chance. It'll be my word against my accuser.'

Officer Geoffroy cranked the door open again. 'Time's up. You must leave the prisoner now, Mr Mlantushi.'

'So short?' I stood. 'Mr Bin, I forgot to ask. Did you record the akalat bird?'

'That's why I'm here in jail. My attempts to record the akalat.'

'Come now, Mr Mlantushi, no more stalling tactics. Let him finish his meal.' Officer Geoffroy swung his arms about, shooing me out as if I were a disobedient goat.

I heard Mr Bin say after me, 'You're my first and only visitor. I appreciate it.'

On my way home I experienced being alone again, as in London. I had no Dorothea; soon I would not even have Mr Bin; I had no bird companion, not as yet. Prospects remained compromised in every respect. In daze-thought I almost walked into Mr Makata at the door of our house. Dorothea was remonstrating with him. When she saw me, she said, 'Mr Makata says you've agreed to sell our pink sofa in exchange for this extremely sick little bird in the cage. I've told him not to lie! I told him that I know my husband. You've no time for sentimentality. You'd never agree to such a thing.'

I knelt to the cage that Mr Makata had delivered. Yes, I still had my bird companion! My little London friend had arrived safely. It had a bright eye. I thought it not sick as Dorothea had suggested, only ruffled from its long journey. It was flapping this way and that, excited no doubt, smelling the home air, testing its wings. It had eaten all its picnics, leaving only a few scattered wings and dry limbs in the bottom of its cage. Did it recognise me, its friend? If so, it made no indication. It behaved as a bird. I was pleased that it was so. Soon it would fly and become busy, it would fulfil its purposes. Its life would have a meaning. I experienced a happy moment.

I stood up and shook hands with Mr Makata. He had delivered as promised. I had figured this: if Mr Makata could export organic produce from Romaji, he could surely import organic produce to Romaji. What goes out can also come in. That is the logic in logistics. At first, he said it was impossible, but when I offered the pink sofa, he had said, 'No problem. Import-export, export-import, it makes no difference,' and had arranged a pick-up of the bird from the Kensington park. He had even sent a taxi to lift me to Heathrow, departures.

Dorothea said, 'Is this true?'

'It's true.'

She open-mouthed and then said with a bitter tongue, 'I didn't sell the sofa even when I was living off the charity of my friends and having to … give Pastor Cain love offerings. All I sold was that hideous, hideous, vase … but you've swapped our most valuable possessions, and symbols of blessing I might add, for a half-dead bird?'

'Yes.'

'All will know we're in poverty.'

'Yes.'

I took the cage and placed it on top of the gloss paper, which the brick had been wrapped in. The bird alone had been the blessing to me. A living that had been a companion to me.

Mr Makata sat himself on the pink sofa and stroked its ample thigh-like arm. He rested his head on the back of the sofa and closed his eyes. 'Very perfect,' he said. 'I'll watch Powers in the final in comfort. I'll send a team of strong men to collect it.'

He exited with a haughty head and a jaunty step. Dorothea stared at me for explanations.

'I'm going to release the bird,' I said.

'So … you'll not even keep this bird that you exchanged for our sofa.'

'No.'

She put her hands to cover her head. 'What's happened to you?' Then she picked up a More Blessings Campaign leaflet, but then set it down. She did not know how to conduct herself. 'Sava, you've changed.' She twisted her fingers back and forth.

'We've both changed. We're transitioning to something.'

'I'm fearful, Sava. Where are we going? What will we be?'

How was I to know? I wished I knew. I thought instead of my bird. I was mindful to release it straight away but peaceably looking at the living that had saved me from loneliness in London, I became reluctant. I would enjoy its company for just a short time longer before I bid it farewell. Maybe it would sing, now that it was nearly free.

I picked up my insect net and left the house to shop for the bird's dinner. Around Romaji there were millions of fat tasty insects to catch. It would be locally-sourced organic food for the bird. A harvest from the park. I would make a beautifully presented feast. I would be the best bird feeder in Romaji.

Chapter 20

The trial of Mr Bin for attempting foul murder was held in the court at the district headquarters two hours away by bus from Romaji. Although we were in no way in happy conversation and of convivial spirit, Dorothea wished to accompany me, and I was glad. I longed for the joyed matrimonial days of the past, but we were both in paralysed confusion, both in a fog of the mind that prevented vision. We had passed each other in the house like ill-acquainted persons, taken different bedtimes and eaten in eye-swerving silence. I had taken no pleasure in cooking. Somehow, I had lost my ardour and mastery. Neither of us finished my food.

We arrived early at the place of judgment and took a seat together behind Mr Bin who was chained to Mr Bambatiwe to guard against his abscondment. Mr Bin was not looking around, a solitary figure as ever. Mr Bambatiwe was fortified against a long trial with sodas and chapatis in fat-stained brown paper parcels, stocked under his chair. The prosecutor was a young man, no doubt hoping to send a murderer down and so to make his reputation, so leading to a profitable career in his exalted profession. He occupied a table to the side, his soap-scrubbed hands resting on neatly stacked pages of notes, his beautiful fingernails on show. I could picture him preparing his appearance before the trial, standing before a mirror trying an open neck and then a tie and then a bow tie. What would be the exact balance of showmanship and dignity for the district trial of the year? He had decided on a maroon bow tie.

The chair for the defence was empty. I was concerned that Mr Bin's defence team was going to be late. Surely he had hired the best? Perhaps they were coming from the capital. The public benches were busy with a high number of excitedly murmuring public members, no doubt without jobs, this being a weekday. It was not every day that an attempted murder trial happenstanced. It could not be missed. Above us, a fan turned too lazily to cool the room. Behind the public, a large black clock dealt the judgement of time on the court room and its proceedings.

After a suitably long wait to demonstrate the wide pecking order of the court personnel, the Justice entered in the green and black robes and the white fur ruffs of her high office accompanied by two lesser officials carrying reference documents of precedent. The court quieted and stood for the Justice until she sat and then we all sat. After necessary and procedural preliminaries, the judge asked the prosecution to present their case.

The prosecutor stood, and with a lingering and courtly bow of his head said, 'Your honour, the prosecution's case is that Mr Du Plessis, the defendant, attempted to murder my client, Mr Vupuma.' He showed a hand to his client sitting behind him. Mr Vupuma was holding crutches and his face was contorted with the most severe pain.

'My client Mr Vupuma is a man of no means … a humble peasant even … having to collect firewood in the bush to put food on the table for his family.'

The public nodded and muttered in consideration for the man of little means.

The prosecutor half turned away from the Justice towards the public. 'Whilst harmlessly collecting firewood, he saw a discarded net in the shrubs and thought it could be utilised for fishing in the river. A truly providential find. Now he could catch the food to cook on the firewood for his only wife and five children.'

The public nodded again in sympathy for the harmless man and his toilsome efforts to feed his family but Dorothea leant to me and whispered, 'Now he just needed to find a filleting knife, a grill and matches lying about in the National Park.' It was unfortunate that this attempt at cahooting by my wife was so hung over by recent dysfunctions and was at the occasion of the trial of Mr Bin. Otherwise, I would have nodded my agreement.

'And what river?' added Dorothea. Too true, our flash floods lasted only a day. The waterholes in the park were frequented by elephants and occupied by crocodiles and so not conducive to peaceable Sunday fishing.

'Now imagine this,' said the prosecution. He turned further to the public.

The Justice said, 'Address the bench Mr Karamagonga.' She loosened the fur over her shoulder and took a sip of water.

'Immediately, your honour.' He turned to face her and showed her the freshly washed and crisp hair of his apologetic head. 'As my client, Mr Vupuma, innocently collected the net, the accused approached him on foot with his gun. Your honour, a man approaching another with a gun can have only one intention. To fire it.' He gestured the firing of a lethal bullet, his beautiful hands enwrapping an imagined stock of polished wood. 'The defendant did not wish to leave a widow and seven orphans. He ran, terrified of course.'

The public nodded.

'By good fortune, my client reached his bicycle alive and fled towards the village.'

The public leant forward.

'About halfway to the safety of the village the defendant caught up with him in his four by four.' He half turned again to the public. 'Imagine the destitute family man's dismay as the accused bore down on him … holding the two weapons of murder. In one hand —the steering wheel of his gigantic and expensive four by four. In the other hand —he brandished his powerful rifle. Either weapon could send a man to his premature grave leaving eight orphans.' He glanced at his notes. 'Correction, six. Still too many.'

The public clasped their hands to their lips.

'He rammed my client at high speed with the rigid steel of the fender of his luxury vehicle.'

'Ohhh!' the public gasped.

'My client was sent flying.'

'Sheee!'

'Silence in court!' The Justice wiped her perspiring brow and took more water. Her robes had perhaps been designed for a cooler climate.

'I'd like to present the exhibit, your honour.'

'Very well,' said the Justice, signalling him to get on with it. Her fingers were fat with learning but impatient towards sycophancy.

The prosecutor lifted half of a bicycle with a cockeyed wheel from behind his desk.

'See, it snapped in half from the speed of the impact.' He lifted the sad half-bicycle above his head and turned a full three-sixty.

'That's ridiculous,' whispered Dorothea.

'It proves beyond doubt that the defendant's four by four was travelling at a high velocity at the moment of impact. It's clear that the accused intended to kill my client.'

'Yees!' whispered the public, not wishing to wrath the Justice.

'Fortunately … my client suffered only life-changing injuries.'

He pointed to his client who dropped his head in a side manner as if he was suffering a snapped neck.

'In summary, your honour, I'm looking to the law to protect the poor man against the rich man. The defendant lives in luxury in his country villa. He considers the National Park his own estate, which he prowls with his gun, looking for trouble. The accused is a recluse without friends. He thinks he can act with impunity because he only subscribes to the law of the jungle.' He clenched a polished fist and brought it down repeatedly as he made his final points. 'He ignores the law. The laws of this independent country. He did not think twice about running down my client. He valued my client's life as less than an old net in a shrub.' He opened his hands to the justice and presented a triumphant and self-congratulating face. 'I rest my case.'

He sat. The villagers started to clap. A clerk stared them to stop. The Justice ordered the defence to step forward, but a clerk stated to her that Mr Bin was defending himself.

'Are you sure?' the Justice asked Mr Bin. 'You're on trial for attempted murder. You should have had professional help.' I believed she thought herself to be in the midst of fools.

Mr Bin said nothing until Mr Bambatiwe prodded him with an oily finger. 'I should've been more organised, I guess, your honour, but I've been stuck in jail. I'm defending myself.'

I was aghast-hearted. Surely Mr Bin could not be acquitted. It was his useless-self against the eager and professional prosecutor and indeed against the court of public opinion —which the Justice would no doubt have to take into account.

'Stand then and present your defence,' said the Justice. She pulled the edge of her robes from the collar of her neck. Sweat oozed from her brow.

Mr Bin complied and spoke in a quiet voice without theatrics.

'I was on my way to the village in my *bakkie* —my vehicle— to buy food.'

A public member shouted, 'Lie!' Mr Bin did not counter. A clerk with a strong arm escorted the public out of the court. The other public members sunk their heads down into their necks. No one wished to miss out on the guilty verdict.

'I saw bicycle tracks leading off the road into the bush. There's been poaching in the National Park, your honour, so I left my *bakkie* and followed the tracks on foot. I found the bicycle leaning on a tree. Then shoe prints leading further. I saw my accuser pulling at a thin net strung up near a nesting site of the brackish akalat.'

The Justice interrupted. 'Explain this brackish akalat to the court.'

'It's a bird. An endangered small bird.'

'Dangerous? Speak up,' said the Justice.

'Endangered.'

'But only small. Continue.'

'If only it had been a rhino or an elephant,' whispered Dorothea. Her soft breath on my ear made me wish for past times.

'I challenged the man,' said Mr Bin. 'He ran to his bicycle, leaving the net. I found a brackish akalat in the net. It was exhausted … trying to set itself free. It was nearly dead. I was upset.'

Mr Bin stopped talking and I believed he was about to tear.

'You're telling us that the small bird was tired. Continue,' said the Justice.

She fanned her face with a paper. I feared she was becoming impatient. Mr Bin was weeping over a weary bird whilst the prosecutor's client was severely injured.

'I believed my accuser was a poacher … I ran after him. But he'd already reached the road. He was cycling away. I followed him in my *bakkie*. I wanted to overtake him and stop him … find out whether he was acting on his own or if he was part of a gang. I was close behind him when we reached a gully. The road was rough. He lost his balance and fell. I swerved and only just missed him.' Mr Bin trembled as if gripped in the memory of the near miss.

The public shook their heads.

'That concludes my defence.'

'You have nothing more to say?'

'No, your honour.'

She raised her eyebrows. She said to the prosecuting lawyer, 'You may now cross-examine the accused.'

'With pleasure, your honour.' He jumped up, eager. 'I'll not take the court's precious time or insult your honour's patience. It's a hot day. I have just one question for the accused. That's all that's needed to prove his guilt. The accused says he did not impact my client.'

The prosecutor signalled with his arms his almost fatally injured client and the broken bicycle. 'Mr Du Plessis, does my client and his transport look like they were *just missed*?'

He picked up the other half of the bicycle and raised it over his head, turning it about with its cockeyed wheel so that the whole court could examine it from every angle. He looked disrespectfully at Mr Bin. '*Just missed?*'

The prosecutor could not prevent himself joining the laughter. Even the justice permitted a little respite of amusement to escape her judicial face.

'Is that the only argument he has?' said Dorothea in my ear. 'Why doesn't he give us a medical report to back up the man's injuries? Pitiful.'

'Stand and answer,' said the Justice to Mr Bin.

'I deny I made contact with him.'

The public groaned and threw their hands towards the injured man.

'I stopped to check he was alright after his fall. He had a graze but he scrambled up and rode off again. I didn't follow him … I was shaken by having to swerve so suddenly.'

The prosecutor shook his head wearily. 'On which half of his bicycle did my client ride away on?' The public laughed without restraint, slapping their hands on their thighs. 'That's all I need to ask the defendant. He's condemned himself … but I'd like to call a witness.'

A man, grinning whitely and with a low-placed black brim hat, a sharp-cut dark jacket and a crimson shirt for the occasion, stood up behind the prosecutor. He said that he was a cousin of the client and that he could vouch for the client's impeccable character, sad poverty, devoted fathership of nine children and that the client went to church on Sundays —always twice. He also stated that the client should receive high compensation, certainly in six figures.

The Justice told him not to instruct the court. The Justice called on the defendant to present witnesses.

'I have no one,' Mr Bin said.

The Justice frowned. 'So that concludes your defence?'

'I guess, your honour.'

'Are you sure?' She wiped her brow with a silky handkerchief. I detected both exasperation and relief behind her words. 'Very well, the court is adjourned whilst I consider my verdict.'

I stood. 'Your most honourable, venerated and exalted honour. I'm a witness for the defence.'

Mr Bin turned surprise-faced to see me there behind him. Dorothea tugged at my shirt to sit me down, but I stayed. I was in nerves to stand in front of the Justice and the court of the law, but

I could do no other. There I stood. I had been following the case in every respect and there was fishy business.

The Justice looked askance at me, but said, 'Proceed.'

'I am Mr Savalamuratichimimozi Mlantushi … formerly the defendant's chef for his safari business. I was able to observe my employer's character at close hand. I can tell you that my employer was most desultory in his habits. He does not care to order his possessions or his time and his business skills are rock bottom.'

The public amused.

'I can confirm to you that he has no friends. I can tell you that he's running from his wife —a woman of impeccable modernity, wealth and good dress sense.'

Mr Bin hung his head, but the public chuckled again. This was surely a very fine day in court.

The Justice said, 'Are you speaking for the prosecution or for the defence?'

'The defence, honourable Justice.'

The public he-hawed again. The justice did not admonish them this time. Had she given up?

'I confess to the court the defendant's human failings only to demonstrate that I'm a fully honest and reliable witness. You can trust my word. I have principles. You should believe me therefore when I state that the defendant is not a violent man. In contrast, he's placid to the extent of gently treating the smallest of the animal kingdom … even tired birds. As to his weapon? It's regulation to carry a gun in the National Park when running a safari business. He's therefore merely abiding by the law of the land. As to his purported riches? His business was failing. Many times, I had to push-start his broken-down vehicle. I believe my own bicycle was worth more.'

The public were silent.

'He's so poor that he couldn't even afford to have his garden cleared and swept.'

The public exchanged shocked glances with each other.

'Despite such he gave me, a man of insubstantial means myself, a good living, sacrificing his own comforts for my sake. I was even able to purchase a magnificent pink sofa. As to his so-called country mansion? It's a shack that's falling down. There are cracks all over in which all manner of pests live, the roof is made of grass, the posts are rotting.'

I had the public's quiet attention, but the Justice was looking at her papers as if they held more interest than my statement, truly as if waiting for the idiot defence witness to stop droning and to shut-mouth. She sipped at her water and dabbed her brow again with her silky handkerchief.

'True he has had difficulty in relationship with his wife. Let's not judge him on that basis. Who's going to cast the first stone? Not me. Especially not me.'

Behind me, I felt Dorothea's eyes on me and the silence of the crowd. Only the tock of the clock sounded.

'He should be considered like us all, in that regard.'

The Justice said, 'Address the bench, Mr Mlantushi, and make your point or I'll instruct you to sit down.'

'Forgive me, your honour. My exact point is this. It's only because the accused was hiding from his wife that he had no friends. I declare that Mr Bin ... Mr Du Plessis ... made effort to be friendly to me, notwithstanding that I did not encourage that myself ... being his employee. I have regret ... in that respect.'

Mr Bin turned his head a little to me.

'You're still straying.' said the Justice. 'The court is not convened to judge on a marriage dispute or to listen to your personal regrets.

Have you finished?' She blew out her cheeks, not caring any longer for judicial decorum.

'One last argument for the defence, if I may, your honour. With dutiful respect to the prosecutor, I wish to politely disagree. That broken bicycle does not belong to the injured party and has never been ridden by the injured party.'

The court's eyes were fixated on me. The tock of the clock sounded louder and louder, like a drumstick beating out the lead-in to a grand finale.

'It's mine.'

The public made a great commotion in their surprise.

The Justice said, 'Order, order in court.' A clerk stared the public hard again.

'Yes, it's mine. I myself saw it destroyed by a buffalo in the National Park. I narrowly escaped with my life. You can see the bell's torn off. It's the buffalo that should be prosecuted for wrecking my bicycle. He'll be easily identified. The bell is on his horn.'

A public member laughed loud, but short.

'I've delivered my witness statement your honour.'

'Is the ... so-called ... defence all concluded?' the Justice asked Mr Bin. She showed no indication in her law-upholding face that she had recognised the decisive status of the information that I had given the court. The evidence of Mr Bin's humanity.

'I guess, your honour.'

I sat.

'The court is adjourned.'

Dorothea stood up. 'Your honour. I'm the other witness for the defence.'

Mr Bin turned, wide-eyed like me. The Justice put her hands down hard, annoyed-faced. 'Very well then, since this is a trial for attempted murder, proceed. And make your point.'

'I'm Dorothea Mlantushi, well known in my village for my piety and charity work. I recognise the prosecution's client. I saw him two days after the date of the reported collision. He was at a Pastor Cain's house in Romaji and looked in good health, skipping from the property after receiving an envelope, which I have reason to believe to be a regular payment from Pastor Cain. He showed no signs of injury.'

'Ohhh!' said the public.

Dorothea sat down.

'You've finished?'

Dorothea nodded.

'The court is adjourned,' said the Justice. I saw her trying to suppress a sigh.

The prosecutor stood. 'Point of order. Mistaken identity. Look at my client!'

Mr Vupuma lolled his tongue as if stupefied by a brain bruise.

But the justice was already moving. She departed in a procession of herself and her two law officers and we all stood in reverence for the robes of her office.

The public argued amongst themselves. Their noise became louder and louder, men stood and faced off each other, chests were pushed forward. Two policemen removed a fisty man and shouted to all to sit down.

I tried to reach Mr Bin, but Mr Bambatiwe told me not to speak to the 'guilty party'. Mr Bin turned and leant towards myself and Dorothea. 'I have your help, thank you.'

Mr Bambatiwe popped a can and said, 'It'll not be enough, the court will wish to defend the poor man, the father with dependent kids, however many. Perhaps you can appeal before sentence is enacted in full.' He made a pulling motion on an imagined rope about his neck.

A clerk filled the glass of water on the Justice's table and then the Justice came in again with her officers. We stood and then sat, Mr Bin with a certain stiffness which made him seem aged although his lack of agility related, I suspected, to his shackles and cramped quarters in jail. I found myself respecting his fortitude, his refusal to panic and rage. I was in pain to think of his likely fate. Was this an ordinary human concern for the fate of another, or was it the sorrow of seeing a friend wronged?

The Justice took a sip of water. The public were still, but Mr Bambatiwe tore off a piece of chapati from inside one of his greasy paper bags and chewed it unhurriedly. He had surely seen before the inevitable course of such cases in court. I found Dorothea's hand in mine.

'I've listened to the evidence set out before me by both the prosecution and the defence. I've come to my judgement.'

The public held their breath as she paused to take a sip of water.

'It's not disputed that Mr Du Plessis pursued the defendant in his vehicle. Both the defence and the prosecution agree on this. The court has been asked to make a judgement as to whether the accused deliberately ran down the defendant, intent on murder.'

A public member hit his palm against the metal rail in front of his bench as if enacting the terrible impact of metal on a soft body. The justice looked up and scowled, a snail trail of perspiration down her cheek. A clerk stared down the public member.

'Here's my verdict.'

She looked down at her papers whilst reaching again for her glass of water. 'Robert Benjamin Du Plessis, I find you guilty.'

The Justice calmly lifted her glass and drank thirstily. She showed, of course, no emotion, no sympathy. The law must only be the law; it cannot be a hanky. I gasped. Dorothea's grip tightened on my hand. Mr Bin bowed his head. Mr Vupuma clapped and skipped with ease from his chair to shake hands with the prosecutor and his witness. His crutches clattered to the floor. Mr Bambatiwe continued to chew his chapati, his head resting nonchalant on the doughnut of his neck.

The Justice slammed down her glass. 'Sit!' she ordered. She wiped her whole face with her silky handkerchief. 'I have a flu. I should be in bed. I've not finished. Guilty of careless driving.'

The public and injured party hushed in an instant. The tock of the clock failed to sound.

'I find Mr Du Plessis guilty of careless driving. I find Mr Du Plessis not guilty of attempted murder.'

She took another justified gulp of her water.

'I therefore fine the defendant one hundred. The court is concluded.' She collected her papers and stood quickly, blowing out her lips. We all stood and inclined our respectful and dumbfounded heads. She departed with her robes of justice and mercy flowing around her; a majestic, beautiful, solemn, gracious and lofty sight.

I went to Mr Bin. He turned to Mr Bambatiwe and asked, 'I'm free?'

'Unbelievable! Astonishing!' he said with his mouth full again. 'You're a lucky man to have such a persuasive defence team.'

Still Mr Bin looked about with a waiting-face.

'Mr Bin,' I said. 'You're free!'

'I'm free … yes … I'm free,' he said to himself and then smiled. He stood and shook my hand and went to shake with Dorothea, his chain complaining on the floor.

On the bus back to the village we sat together, Mr Bin, Dorothea and me. We said little, our thoughts balancing on many contemplations, celebrations, hopes and apprehensions. Mr Bin requested to sit by the window and could not drink enough of the dull scenery of endless scrub and vacant sky, although way ahead, far away, a rain cloud was pushing up like a small grey mushroom. Was the thirst of the land soon to be quenched?

Near to Romaji, I said to Mr Bin, 'I've even better news than your freedom. I've brought from London a brackish akalat. From a pet retail selling exotics. I'd like to release it into the National Park.'

'You're kidding, Mozzy! Are you sure? Are you absolutely sure it's a brackish akalat?'

'I'm so sure. It was confirmed by the Google. It's not a sparrow.'

He looked at me, hope and disbelief crossing his face like light and shadow on a breezy day.

'I'd like to enact said release with you.'

'You bet, Mozzy.' He was quiet again. 'A brackish akalat! Seems impossible. Two miraculous happenings on one day? Let's do it. I'll drop by.'

Back at our breeze block abode, I thanked Dorothea for standing up in court, for helping me to defend Mr Bin against such mendacious accusations. It seemed that even a discordant couple like ourselves could adjourn their quarrel for a necessary co-operation. Dorothea acknowledged and then was quiet. There were no dancing eyes, ululating, joying, singing. She was hurting, yes, but maybe she was also waiting. Waiting for something, perhaps even something from me, some words from me that I thought might be available somewhere, but I did not know what those words were or how to find them. I believed that she did not want to hear any more 'beloved wife', 'dear wife' and such. True, we had achieved together to free Mr Bin, but that was a side show between us. I had big faults; she had said. Maybe I needed to find those faults and fix them, but what if they were my dutiful nature or my need to cook? Maybe I was too short. What if they were something I could not alter?

CHAPTER 21

I fell asleep to the sound of faint thunder and woke briefly to the sporadic rap of rain on the roof. As was my recent custom, I was bedded on the floor where the sofa used to sit. The room had taken an eager breath of cool air so that I had to draw a blanket over me.

The next morning, up early, I footed out insect-hunting with my net, happy to sniff the rising scent of damp grasses and to see spider webs silvery with rain drops. Just beyond the village, where the land still reminisced of the wild, there was a plentiful harvest of organic produce. The insects were dizzy with excitement that it had rained. Indeed, a blind swing of the net could score. I let free the beetles —too hard and indigestible; the grasshoppers —too strong and sudden; the bees —too risky to hold by their wings; the stink bugs —of course. Flimsy-winged bugs with fat abdomens were the delicacy, sweet to the tongue of my bird no doubt, although it preferred to gobble quick. The best were the ants that fly. I also fried those for Dorothea and myself. A traditional snack. And we had no cash.

Out there in the scrub, I did not risk uncomfortable encounters with employed or nosey people. 'There's a rumour that you've had to sell your pink sofa.' 'I heard a gossip. Whilst you were overseas your wife attended long *private* prayer vigils with Pastor Cain!'

After all, I was now self-employed and it required my full attention. Although it was not strictly chefing, it was not dancing for tourists. I also hoped my solitude would gift a special discernment, which would lead me to pleasing Dorothea. I hoped in vain.

I returned home with a pot full of juicy bugs. No more dry bugs for my bird. Dorothea was watching a soap on TV, sitting lifeless with her chin on her hands, uncomfortable on one of our two wooden chairs. She did not acknowledge me, did not 'dear husband' me. Only the bird followed my every move. Only the bird trusted me now.

My phone rang.

A wrong number, surely. I was inclined not to answer, but that would have been discourteous to the caller. Dorothea muted the soap with a reluctant finger.

'Mr Mlantushi?'

'That's me.'

'This is James Fairbrother, owner of Plume de Paon. I hope you enjoyed your evening in my kitchen.'

What was this? Surely a prankster in bad taste? Ripping the scab off my wound. The last time I had answered the phone, it was that hoaxer Mrs Zeto Camlyn. I terminated him and I went to my bird. Dorothea unmuted her soap.

'Here's your dinner, little bird. Tweet, tweet, please. Won't you sing for me?' It was happy to snatch a green-winged insect from my fingers between the bars. Watching and waiting on it, I became uncertain on my conjecture on its provenance. I had enthused that it was the brackish bird, but every ardour of mine had proved false, had it not? Its provenance hung by the frayed thread of my belief. Mr Bin would know. I hoped I was not to let him down.

The phone rang again. Such a cruel caller.

'Hello.'

'We got cut off. This is James Fairbrother, owner of Plume de Paon. You helped in my kitchen.'

Something made me doubt my previous conjecture. He sounded like a mature caller, no giggling in the background from fellow conspirators.

I spoke polite, but guarded. 'An honour, of course.'

Dorothea blew displeasure and muted the TV again.

'I understand you helped us out when our head chef became incapacitated.'

'I apologise. Too forward of me.'

'Far from it. Let me explain. One of our customers that evening was a well-known food and restaurant critic. His review has recently been published in *The Times*. Bear with me as I read it to you.

'*One really has to arrive for an evening at Plume de Peon on an Anglo-Norman trotter dressed as a Tudor Lord or Lady in doublet and hose, kirtle and gown, such is its nostalgia for the long gone past and its uncompromisingly meaty tastes, rough-stone floors, log fires and pre-renaissance art on oak-clad walls. There was a time when I ranked it as one of the top ten restaurants in the capital, elevating unfashionable dishes of venison, mutton and pork to royal status, serving rich and succulent English banquets, which gloriously bucked every contemporary trend. It was the place to impress ambassadors and oligarchs, to fatten up investors when sealing a multimillion-pound deal in wharf-side property.*

There was a time but, like the Tudors, that time is long gone. Plume de Paon is now sliding down my rankings on its own goose fat. I believe the hake and haddock soup had been ladled from the bilges of a rotting medieval galleon. I found in its thick murky depths a sediment of rubbery fish parts. Was my fork grabbed by a crab? I sent it back to be slopped out into a gutter. What of the main? I ordered rack of lamb but was served thickly larded burnt timber from a mast of the same galleon. I returned it to be exhibited in an archaeological museum. I feared for what they would offer in its place. A glutinous pastry pie stuffed with partially plucked blackbirds perhaps.

But no! Holy Katherine of Aragon! No! I was served a dish so sublime they dared not list it on the menu because no words could do it justice, not even as penned by your eminent restaurant critic.'

'Are you still with me?'

'I'm here.'

'Mr Mlantushi, he's referring to the dish you made. Let me read more. *I'm sure that Henry VIII never tasted such a dish. His cooks would not have had the swagger, the science, the artistry. If they had, he would have been in better moods. It might have changed the course of history. Somewhere deep in the doughy bowels of Plume de Peon's kitchen, a chef has poured away the muddy gravy, buried the pig trotters and re-imagined English food.'*

'Are you still with me?'

'I'm here.'

'I'll skip forward. *Then there was the desert. By the same chef, I was told with an incomprehensible apology by the maître. Heavenly choirs! Hallelujah chorus! A sensory adventure, bordering on the erotic.'*

'My desert? I thought it was binned.'

'It went out in the end after the head chef was overwhelmed again by his migraine.'

'I'm so pleased to hear all this. Thank you for informing me.'

'He wasn't the only one. Other diners commented as well.'

'So pleased.' I experienced a warm professional pride that had been hard to find of late although it was rightly tempered by the thought that I was somehow confabulating the call.

'You could help turn us around, Mr Mlantushi. You could give us the missing ingredient, so to speak. We've been far too conservative. Too reliant on nostalgia for something, which only ghosts are nostalgic for. We have to change.'

'Thank you for letting me know. I'm delighted I was able to help.'

'Come and work in my kitchen, Mr Mlantushi. If you make the grade, you could go far.'

Of course, I was startled to hear this but at the same time I was cognisant of the false hopes and fantasies of my inclinations. I feared the same, that I was in illusion again.

'Is that of interest, Mr Mlantushi?'

'Forgive me … it's of top interest to me. I thank you. Is this for real?' I was still fearful that the caller would laugh, all hysterical, and cut me off. 'I'll be a paid chef in your kitchen?'

'You'll be a probationary chef on a probationary wage to start with, but if you can prove yourself then you'll be given a secure and attractive contract.'

Still, I had mistrust and doubts. Had I not misheard on a previous occasion? Had I not concocted? But I had to concede that there was something altered here. Mr Fairbrother's words were exact. They were his own words, not my fancy. Probationary but waged chef. I was not fooling myself.

'Unfortunately, I'm currently back at home.'

'We'll get you over here with a travel grant and work permit and so on.'

I was a man of little faith and was hesitant to speak.

'Let me know what you decide, Mr Mlantushi. I know it's a big decision. Ring me as soon as you can.'

'Yes, I will,' I said, hardly moving in case it somehow broke the moment and I found myself waking from an absurd dream.

Dorothea had stood up. She was looking steady at me, perhaps even pensive.

Then it arrived on me: my lifelong ambition was to be realised. The time of success had come after I had reached rock bottom. I had discovered that there was a floor to the abyss in which lost souls fell. Now I would climb out.

'Mr Fairbrother, I've decided. I'd like to accept your kind job offer. I'll not let you down.'

There was no reply.

'Hello?'

I had let him ring off, but no matter, I would borrow credit from Trust Me Loan Holdings, No Loan Too Small, and call back.

In truth, my doubts flew out the window like a thrown brick. I experienced an unruly desire to jump, to hallelujah, to run in the road, to beat drums, to roast a celebratory hog ... but of course I retained dignity. I told my dear wife, Dorothea, although I believe she had heard most and had waited, still and quiet.

She came to me and placed a congratulatory hand against my arm. 'You've proven yourself, Sava. It's something you can always be proud of.'

My superlative triumph would surely bring us harmony again. If my big fault was not achieving, then all would be well again. Had she not just said that she was proud of me? She would soon hosannah, even ululate. I moved to kiss her, such was my joy, but she stepped back. 'Are you going to take it?'

'To take it?' What was she asking? How could I not accept? The vapour of hope had become a waterfall of blessing. Not blessing: BLESSING! The perpetual promise of tomorrow had become a fulfilment today. She could plan again for marble and Mercedes. Why did she question? I looked at her for an answer, but her eyes did not meet mine and held unknown things to me.

She said, 'We're changed, no?'

We were not as cocky, for sure. We had knowledge that failure was possible, or at least that success could be long postponed. My head was no longer a beehive of fanciful inventions. But by a chance, no, by work and striving, I had regained my proper destiny. I had made my own lucky. A better tomorrow had arrived just as I had always believed. That saying was true: *No matter how long the night, the dawn will break.* Yes, the destination had been there all along. I needed to verbalise such to Dorothea, to remind her that I was Chef Mlantushi, what I had always been. A name that would soon be reverenced by Barstows everywhere, but as I formulated to speak there was a knock on the door. I opened and found Mr Bin standing there.

Chapter 22

'It's time to release your bird … um … akalat, Mozzy.'

'Now? I have some important business to finish.'

'Right now. What could be more important than giving a bird its freedom? I'm passing by. You said let's do it.'

He greeted Dorothea and she polited but did not give him one of her More Blessings Campaign leaflets, which she had previously pressed on guests.

He said to her, 'Before I forget … Officer Bambatiwe wants you to attend the police station. To give a statement on what you said at my trial. About Vupuma and the preacher. Pastor Cain?'

Dorothea nodded and her cheeks tightened. *A thief who injures a bee whilst stealing honey, incites the whole hive to sting him.*

'Bambatiwe says he wants to make his name with the apprehension of a criminal who ends up being successfully prosecuted, so that he can get a promotion to the capital. He says I was a disappointment. And when you go to give your statement … he wants you to bring him one of Mozzy's cakes.'

She flicked a little smile.

I thought also of Cain's accomplice, Mr Makata, of his bicycle logistics —but this was my bird's moment and I was impatient. I moved the cage to the edge of the table and stepped back. I held myself still. Mr Bin knelt and looked hard, he looked long. He said nothing. His face did not joy. All sudden, I lost all confidence on the bird's designation. He turned the cage. He looked from high, he looked from low. I had confabulated again. Mr Bin had an encyclopaedia of birds in his head. Of the thousands in his encyclopaedia, why would this be the brackish item? The rare one. I was no bird spotter. I only had the poor focus picture on the Google to rely on. Mr Bin was surely the foremost expert —the only one in the world apart from Gershenwald et al who could identify such a bird. I awaited his judgement with a stopped heart.

He stood up. He said nothing. My heart prepared to fall. Another fiction.

Then he activated and shook jubilant fists. '*Jislaaik*, Mozzy! It's a male brackish akalat!'

And so that is how I found myself temporarily diverted, walking with Mr Bin in the bush once again, far from the village. I was surprised to find that I did not, on that occasion, fear or curse the wilderness, perhaps because I had a sure escape. I even enjoyed. I did not agitate. The rain in the night had purged the air of dust and haze so that all was pin-clear and evidential. Little meringue clouds floated in the petal-blue sky. The primal earth on which I trod was damp and soft, scented of loam and marrow. The lichens were like molten bronze splashed over the rocks and pooled in the hollows. Leaves were drying out as crisp and golden as my pistachio pastries. Our path ahead was a mosaic in the chromates of plum, lime and pumpkin, and the white and grey trunks and branches of the forest surrounds were sculptures of nature that it would almost be shameful to cut for firewood. Nature had created beautiful order, tasteful decorations, and even sweet familiar aromas from the tangle of the bush —from the mess of the soil and its disordered ingredients. As a chef, I respected that.

Indeed, I had a certain relaxation, a certain contentment and ease in my heart, not only because of my upcoming posting in London, but for the bird. I was to release it to its rightful place, and I was soon to leave for my rightful place in the big city. I noted that I was thinking in balanced thought and having realistic musings on my future. I knew now what to expect living in the city: the people swerving away, the tight rooms with no companion, the transportations on black canals of tar, but at work I would be in the stainless-steel kitchen of my dreams, creating for appreciative diners, wowing Mr Barstow, no doubt. One day I could be a respectable and respected head chef, maybe with my own restaurant amongst the skyscrapers, or on a Kensington square. Maybe. One step at a time. Yes, I had self-reflected.

Mr Bin carried the bird in its cage and I saw it turn its head to hear the excited chatter of another bird and then lift its head when it heard a cicada start up its buzzing motor, and then turn its head again to follow a transparent green insect whirring past. It hopped along its perch. Its tail flicked up and down. The living little bird wanted to be busy.

We heard a bicycle bell some distance away.

I stopped. 'A poacher falling off his bicycle?' I asked.

'A buffalo with a bicycle bell stuck on its horn. A useful warning if it comes near.'

I was emboldened to speak of the private sphere with a man who had not been reluctant or too proud of his position as my employer to show friendly to me. 'What of your wife? Did she find you again?'

We walked further before he said, 'Something's happened to me.'

'Yes?'

'How can I explain?'

'I can listen.'

'I thought I was free. On my ownsome in the bush. My place of sanctuary. The wilderness didn't judge me. Pointed no finger.

It had no voices to accuse me. I thought Robert Benjamin Du Plessis could vanish … blown away like these dry grass seeds.' He indicated the sweep of lazy, luminous and misty grasses, eulogised as such by Miss Camlyn.

I was glad that he trusted me to hear his personal thoughts, whatever their soul-deep nature. This was surely the privilege of friendly relations.

'But no, I couldn't lose myself. There was that … voice in my head. All that spineless yellow-jelly stuff. It wouldn't go away. I was like this akalat.' He lifted the cage to see the bird. 'Trapped. The bars were the voices, my own and Jemima's.' His eyes darkened. 'Intrusive … relentless … ever-present thoughts. I had to free myself, bust out.' He laughed short. 'I had a lot of time to chew that over in that other cage, Romaji jail.'

'And your wife?' I said, to remind him of my question.

'I've settled with her. She's got her divorce and kept her money. I didn't contest it — spineless you might say. But … liberation! It opened the cage door. I'm free.'

'You're a happy man,' I said without necessity. I was not inclined anymore to criticise his marital failure. Was it not the case that Dorothea and I had been dancing on a smouldering fire of disharmony? Had we not rubbed flint against stone? Was it not true that Dorothea had not joyed at my ultimate posting?

'What about you? Are you going back to Boston?'

'In actuality, it's London for me as a probationary chef.'

'I was hoping you'd stay. I'd like to take guests again,' said Mr Bin.

'You're offering?' I laughed lightly, to thank his kindness, yes, but also to politely indicate that I had a better tomorrow.

'Just suggesting.'

'When do we release the bird?'

'This is a *lekker* place.'

He positioned the cage on a fallen trunk of timber, and I took one last look at my little bird. What was this strange experience that I had encountered? It had been loyalty through trouble, yes. I had not abandoned it for refusing to sing. I had done something to help it achieve its purpose. True, the bird had let me down, it had not sung, but I had not condemned it. I had not condemned it for behaving like a bird. I had not condemned it for behaving as its true self. Of course, this so-called friendship with the bird was one way. I did not know what it thought of me, if it thought at all, but nevertheless it had been a teacher to me.

'You release it,' said Mr Bin. 'You're the one that rescued it.'

I opened the cage door. The bird stayed unbelieving although the sky was no longer barred. For a while it seemed trapped in thinking its way was still closed, that it could not be free. It turned its head, this way, that way. Still the sky remained open to it. Then it was out, out into the wide as if blown by an eager gust of wind. We saw it vanish into the weave of the trees. Gone from sight. It had become a living out there with its own kind. It could now feel air beneath its wings. It could go on to live before it died. It had purpose. I had released it to the homeland it had flown to in its dreams in my cramped room in Lockview.

We rested quiet on the fallen timber.

Then I heard it sing; even though I could not strictly hear it. It was more a speaking to my heart. I could not say what it said, but it opened a memory, previously caged.

I recalled that night when my father died. I had allowed myself to be distracted from my duty to him. That evening I became like my mother had always been, in chaos and disorder. A friend had invited me out. I thought my friends had forgotten me, so I was flattered. I lost personal discipline and went out without a word to my father and without checking his needs were met for the evening. My friend and I visited bars, enjoyed music, enjoyed company, my old friends, flirted the girls. I had a drink and many more.

'This is like the old days, Sava. Glad you're back!' said my friend. The bar music knocked away my cares. In truth, I had a good time.

I returned home in no fit state in the pre-dawn hours. There I found my father on the floor. He had tried to move himself, perhaps to bed, but had fallen. Blood soaked the concrete from a broken head. He was soiled. He had died there. He had died without me. He had died because of me. I had been distracted from my duty by being friendly, by losing personal discipline. In truth, I had been unsuccessful in looking after my father.

That was the time, surely, that I decided never to risk too friendly, to maintain only professional relations for fear of catastrophe and failure. And from that time, I had also dedicated myself to the code of self-restraint, to personal discipline, so that I would never fall again. But now I speculated this: was this heavy thinking my own cage? Had I come to wrong deductions? Had I devoted myself to flagellation for a goal whose fist-tight purpose was to keep me away from risk? Was I fearful of the consequences of such? That it would lead to disaster, to failure? But was not Mr Bin free from jail because I had, in truth, been a friendly help to him —just in time? Was not the bird free because I had followed a mutinous emotion that had escaped from the locked door of my heart?

'It's getting dark,' said Mr Bin.

'Let's go. I don't wish to hear any soul falling into a bottomless abyss.'

Back at Mr Bin's house, I push-started his vehicle and he drove me back home. As the road declared itself ahead in the dim light of the headlights I was set upon by a surprising confusion, struggling to know my own road.

My father used to say, *Keep walking, the destination is ahead.* But what if I had been dreaming of the wrong destination. Why that far away, gloss-ribboned destination? I had never asked myself, although Dorothea had suggested that I do. Maybe another glorious journey's end awaited me, but it was not the destination that I had been offered. In London, had I not looked back at my time with Mr Bin with some reluctant affection, even when I thought of the little ape Freddy, even though I hated the flies and ants? Had I not missed the VIP guests to make their safaris worthwhile for them, conversing with them delightedly on their picnics? Were not my bush picnics as fine as any high-end dinings?

But surely not one in a million cooks looking for work would turn down the guaranteed place in a well-known restaurant in London. I thought again of wearing the finest, whitest, chef's toque and apron and arranging walnuts and dried cherries on a frisée and apple salad in that stainless-steel kitchen in that progressive city. I thought of Mr Barstow, struggling to pen adequate eulogies. Yes, I truly had the oven-ready posting of that dream to salivate over at last.

We pulled outside my abode. I could not avoid a thought, heavy enough to be considered a holy discernment. Since my father's death, I had believed my life to have been driven by the dream of advancement, but now I thought that this was not true. No, in actuality my life had been driven by the motor of a memory. The to-be-avoided memory of the circumstance of my father's death, my agency of it. But no, it was not a motor, it was a cage. Did I need to break the bars that that memory had donated me? How would I do that? I had no idea. What would the key on the inside of the cage door look like?

Mr Bin bade me goodnight and *totsiens*.

I said, 'If, if, if …' I stopped to vision the if.

'Go on,' said Mr Bin.

'If I was to work with you again … in concordance and mutual advancement for the business and in order to high-purpose our lives here, there would be a request, if I might.'

'It'll be pauper's wages for both of us Mozzy until we make some money.'

'No, not that.'

'I won't bring animals into the kitchen.'

'No, not that.'

'I'm not giving away Caterpillar or Freddy.'

'Not that.'

'I'm not going to become organised and tidy.'

'Not even that. This would be my request. You offer Miss Camlyn the position of Marketing Director.'

Mr Bin shock-faced and then laughed. 'I seriously need marketing, yes, but Miss Camlyn? I can't imagine her wanting to have anything to do with me. She saw my true character —as you so rudely but rightly pointed out.'

'Maybe you should try her and see.'

He slow-played his fingers on the steering wheel and said, 'Perhaps I should. Maybe she'll find I'm not the character I was.'

'That might put her off. She liked you as you were. She believed you had righteous convictions and concealed fortes.'

He smiled. 'I'll invite her and her grandfather out to have another shot at recording the akalat. I found your email when I was released from jail.'

'That would be a good start,' I said.

It was time to choose my destination. I had all opportunity, two noble destinations. I thought of Dorothea. She was waiting for something that I had not so far discovered. It seemed close, that if I thought freely, uncaged by painful memory, I might find it.

Mr Bin waited.

'I'd therefore like to apologise for my previous dismissal of your kind suggestion. I'll join you again.'

Mr Bin punched my shoulder and then moved to shake my hand. He beam-faced and almost teared. For myself, it felt like I had indeed unlocked the cage door. I had air under my wings. I was as free as my akalat, and just as purposed. I experienced a sensation of relief. I felt it deeply.

'But only if I'm appointed as head chef.' I gave Mr Bin a raised eyebrow to signal an indication of attempting funny.

'You shall be,' said Mr Bin. 'Top, top chef and chief host for the guests. You were always the better half of Bird Observation Day-Walk Safaris.'

Return to old watering holes for more than water; friends and dreams are there to meet you. Was it true?

When he departed, I stood there seeing the red light from the single working bulb at the back of his vehicle glowing like a warm ember in the night, like a welcoming campfire in the dark where persons could be convivial to each other as they partook of dishes so sublime that words could not do them justice, not even as penned by the most eminent food critic.

At home, Dorothea was sitting on the chair at the table, her head scarf off but still in her shapeless purple dress, tearing up the prosperity leaflets. 'I'm making firelighters,' she said. 'It's to start the fire for an oven that I'll make from bricks. Bricks! That's full circle, is it not? I'm going to bake bread for the safari businesses.' She tore them with force.

'Dorothea.'

'The hotels are always complaining they can't get good bread.'

'Dorothea.'

'I'll make wholemeal. They say the tourists don't like sliced white. I thought it was a luxury.'

'Dorothea.'

'Yes?' She stopped tearing papers.

'I have my dream posting.'

'Yes, you told me.' She carried on tearing.

'No, it's not in London. It's not in a city. I'm staying here. My dream posting is here with Mr Bin.'

She put down the leaflets.

'And my dream place is here with you, my sweetest Dorothea.'

She lifted from her chair. 'Sava, is this true?'

'I no doubt still have big faults, but I'm changed.'

She clasped her heart to hold herself in check. 'Why?'

It was too long a story to recite by voice from start to finish, from my happy childhood kicking footballs in the dusty roads, to my father's brain stroke, to the years learning my craft at Tom Mbolo's, to my father's death, to my mother's abscondment, to Mr Bin's employ, to the lonely days in London, to my recent illustrious appointment as chef to VIPs in a top kitchen; to recite about my little teacher the akalat, which had released me from my cage; to tell about my long road to success, notwithstanding every setback in the book.

'I thought that if I leave you again then we cannot try for a child.'

She came to me. 'You wish?' she said.

'Yes, I wish as much as you ... I should be here for the attempt, no?'

She was smiling, had joying eyes again. 'Wait there.' She exited.

I sat on the chair and completed the shredding of the fantasy and false belief. It made a tatty heap. Then my hands paralysed. A shock speculation came to me. We had at last received a Blessing. Major league. Was this *the* Blessing? Dorothea and I were now both in a prosperity of an unexpected kind. Maybe the brick had indeed acted. Perhaps that brick needed to be thrown away, had to be smashed, before it could let out its blessing. It needed release. I looked at the prophet's leaflets, torn by our hands. A panicked confusion came on me and my hands fumbled to fit the pieces of the leaflets back together again. Did we have any tape to stick them? What about a stapler?

I came to my senses, laughed at myself for flirting with superstitious thoughts of trickery. I continued tearing the paper.

I heard Dorothea say, 'Sava?'

I turned to her. She was standing near. She could have been the young lady on the lime-green Zapp Phones billboard: her face lively, romantic and smiling. Her eyes dancing again. She was gold bloused, pepper-red-skirted and sheer-tighted, just as she was when I first met her at Tom Mbolo's. She had cast off the regimentals and bindings of the false prophet.

I went to her and we tender kissed in each other's hold. We retired to our bed because we had no pink sofa. But was not that pink sofa hideous?

CHAPTER 23

I cycled out to Mr Bin's abode at four thirty hours on a bicycle bought for me by Mr Bin from Bicycle Repairs – Any Damage. Today, elephant delays permitting, I had chefing to do and we had VIP guests.

No creature barred my way, but I was surprised by a bicycle that darted silent as a bat across my path at a junction. It had no light. Above the flurry of the pedals and twirling wheels was the black shape of a rider, a shape not unlike that of Mr Vupuma, and behind him the square of a box on the carrier. He did not stop, did not greet. Maybe he had not seen me. He vanished as quickly as he had appeared, but I had no doubt that I had witnessed bicycle logistics. What organic produce was in the box? A bird?

I paralysed. The bird we had released was a brackish akalat, Mr Bin had confirmed it. But had the bird come by bicycle logistics, not via jet travel? Had Mr Makata cunningly delivered me an akalat from the National Park? Had my bird in London been sold on to some other lonely in London? The bird that Mr Makata had delivered had resemblance in configuration, true, to my London bird. But it was somehow more lively, wilder, stronger, less calm than my bird in London. I had put that down to it being excited, maybe also agitated to be jet-lagged. But was it truly my bird? Was it a lighter colour perhaps? Had my Lockview bird been some other type of insect scoffer that was still in London? The more I stared down the road at the disappeared logistics, the more I doubted that Mr Makata had delivered me my own bird, the more I thought that Mr Summerberg had been correct in doubting that I had an akalat in London.

And if the akalat Mr Makata had delivered was not my London bird, would it matter? Sure, I would grieve for my bird friend, but did my altered frame of mind depend on which bird I released or on a complicated and weighty psychology? I put my feet to the peddles again but hardly noticed the rest of my journey, despite passing an elephant, and came to the conclusion as I approached Mr Bin's property that these were questions to which there was no right or wrong answer; even that no wise saying could illuminate. Such would be the theme of the day.

I sparked the generator awake and then woke Mr Bin — disdaining but forgiving of the shanty in his room. I polished, ironed, cooked, plated. I had air beneath my wings. Mr Bin left for the hotel and arrived back with our VIP guests in his beaten *bakkie* just prior to sunup. The birds had started up in an unusually excitable fashion that morning as if they had a premonition of the felicitous occasion —although I did not believe in divination.

I stood behind the beverages on the veranda with repressed but undeniable excitement, attired in my double-breasted white jacket and my high head-chef's toque; chin up and chest puffed out. A fine sight, no doubt. A luxurious display of scarlet and white flowers from Mr Bin's unruly but convenient garden were hard to experience in the low light but they pleasured the still air with their scent of African wild honey and Seville marmalade. My perfectly-crumbling golden pinwheel shortbread creations awaited Mr Summerberg's discerning palate.

The doors of the vehicle opened and Mr Bin and Miss Camlyn stepped out but she did not 'wow' as previous. There was no blabbering or laughing. She only lifted a small polite hand to greet me. Where were her bird-of-paradise colours? She was in nettle-green safaris and a tan belt and her hair was tied back. Where were her oversized lemon-yellow sunglasses? Her eyes were hidden behind pragmatic blacks, even though the sun was not yet over the east horizon. I was ready to step forward to free Mr Summerberg from his seat, but Mr Bin signalled me to stay. Mr Bin and Miss Camlyn came cheerless to the table. I concluded that Mr Summerberg was absent.

'Mozzy ... I have incredibly sad news,' said Miss Camlyn.

What could possibly be?

'Grandad died ... five days ago.'

I crossed my hand to my heart and could not express.

'In his sleep, he never knew.'

Too early, I thought, but it was true: *Death keeps no calendar.* I was stuck in shock. It was hard to comprehend that Mr Summerberg had truly passed away, even though it was most inevitable, was indeed in keeping with the strict and unsentimental order of things.

'He wouldn't have wanted me to cancel. I hope you understand, yeah?' Miss Camlyn teared and I felt her pain deeply. 'He wanted me to record the bird. I'm going to play it at his funeral.'

'We're going to try our damndest,' said Mr Bin.

'*The future shall rise from the past,*' I mumbled.

'Obviously,' said Mr Bin and then twist-lipped as if he regretted speaking.

Miss Camlyn said quietly, 'Did your father say that?'

'I think not, I seem to have found my own way of saying.'

Freddy, the bushbaby, came to Miss Camlyn, jumping onto her shoulder, unaware of the tragic circumstance in which we were positioned.

'Oh Freddy! How I've missed you.' She nuzzled him so that they were one nest of hair.

Her hand held him there and it seemed that she needed a living to hug. Freddy was compliant. Perhaps he was not unaware.

'Would you like to partake of coffee? Ground Arabica of course.'

She nodded, still in a hair and fur mingle with Freddy.

'A quick one please. We mustn't miss the singing hour,' said Mr Bin.

'Mozzy is coming with us, isn't he?' said Miss Camlyn.

'If he can spare us from his pressing duties here,' said Mr Bin in unnecessary and ill-timed jest.

'I'll be serving a most agreeable brunch,' I said.

We drove to the big tree, finding ourselves in and out of respectful silence for Miss Camlyn's loss, held from exuberating by the conventions of a dignified mourning. I indeed was sober-minded to think on Mr Summerberg, a VIP guest to be sure, a man who purposed himself to the very end, a need of all livings, whether birds or persons.

Miss Camlyn and Mr Bin footed into the wilderness together, leaving me to lay a beautiful table. They were gone a long time, but I was not concerned for their safety. Mr Bin would not let any harm come to his guest.

When they returned, Miss Camlyn was in a laughing mood, saying to Mr Bin, 'Do you remember? I asked why hippos don't break their eggs when they sit on them? I asked who puts the straw in the trees for the giraffes?' She put her hands to cover her face.

'And I was a right uptight reclusive—'

'Dipstick.'

'Ja.' Mr Bin was smiling.

'But I'd say definitely not a —what did she say?— yellow jelly. If that's any consolation.'

'It is. A huge relief.'

I thought it unnecessary to helpfully remind Mr Bin of *timid, spineless, useless* and all, as it was no longer true. Mr Bin had reformed, had mended and upturned, just as Mrs Camlyn had enacted the opposite.

They settled down in the Winchester Safari Recliners, even Mr Bin, and the sunlight lapped and splashed prettily on Miss Camlyn's face through the leaves of the great tree. Mr Bin did not restlessly seek out the far horizon or the high sky with his binoculars but stretched himself in the chair, long legs browning after their whitening in the gloomy prison container.

I was minded to excuse myself, to leave the two in cahoots, but there was no gain in adding another RIP by walking away from the safety of Mr Bin's rifle. In any case, I needed to excel myself in service to Miss Camlyn.

I said, 'Did you record my bird?'

'Ding dong merrily on high, we did! It's a proper little song, a genuine carol. It's exactly right for Grandad's funeral.'

'He achieved his dream through his granddaughter.'

'Thanks, Mozzy! Mind you I'm never going to tweet the song, or stream it, or give it to the National History Museum, or out it anywhere. If anyone wants to hear the akalat's song, they absolutely have to come here. They have to book with Akalat Adventures.'

'Akalat Adventures?'

'The new name for Bird Obser … I can never bring myself to say it. It was so naff, so wordy, so unmemorable.'

'She's joining us as marketing director,' said Mr Bin to myself. I was exceeding glad of the information. Mr Bin was taking instruction from me at last. 'We're going to be busy.'

'And we're going to be the best,' said Miss Camlyn. 'It's going to be an awesome, massive, success! If I can double the sale of ball bearings, think what I'll do with thrilling bird hunts … big red gorgeous sunsets … irresistible food.'

'I'm most sincerely satisfied. We're all in concordance.'

'I'll start with the website.'

'Huh? That took me — ages,' said Mr Bin.

'It doesn't show,' said Miss Camlyn.

'It brought you out.'

'Yeah, in a loud scream.'

They were insulting each other already, but were still smiling. Such, surely, were the bantering ways of promising pair-ups.

The brunch was appreciated much; even Mr Bin complimented. Maybe just to be polite but it showed that he was trying.

'What's this, Mozzy?' said Miss Camlyn, picking a snack from the table.

'Sometimes called African polony. Tubers, peppers, peanuts. Ground up and made into a loaf.'

'Mmm, nice. You should serve this sort of thing to our customers. They can get rum and banana ice cream in any Asda back home. We want to blow them away. We want them to experience local tastes.'

Yes, Miss Camlyn was going to shake us up and bring us many VIP diners, for sure.

After, they asked me to sit down, to relax, to be content. 'To hang loose,' said Miss Camlyn. I was uncomfortable to *hang loose* whilst at work but Mr Bin said that Miss Camlyn was no longer a guest and that this was a meeting of the Akalat Adventures company founders and so I should join the meeting. The explanation was to my liking. I sat, even leant back and contemplated the tree like the others. I could indeed find myself appreciating the scarlet and lemon leaves flaring happy in the morning sun, the hum of insects going about their business, achieving important ends like all the livings and personages I respected. This purposing of so-called feral nature I now understood. I no longer wished to muzzle the wild place with fences or wound it with long black scabs of tar. There should be no snaring streetlights. It should be left to be, to please and sustain all livings, whether green whirring bugs, or people.

Miss Camlyn was not silent for long. 'Ben, why can only certain people hear the akalat? I've been dying to know for ages.'

'There's this folklore. I guess it's nonsense really.'

'Yes, it'll be nonsense,' I said. I remembered the scientific document on the akalat that I had found in the Google on the library computer in London. 'Nonsense, spread by a man named Carter.'

'Tell me nonsense then,' said Miss Camlyn.

'It's charming, whether it's nonsense or not,' said Mr Bin.

'Charm me then!'

'The story's very simple ... perhaps there was once a longer version but ... it's this. Those who hear its song together become friends for life.' His face coloured and it started an epidemic because Miss Camlyn rosy faced as well. I had not guessed that she had a bashful heart beneath her upfrontal jawing.

She smiled and said, 'Wow! What do you think of that, Mozzy?'

I shifted myself forward in the Winchester. 'For myself ... I'm not a superstitious man. I'll offer my objective opinion should you find yourself to be friendly with a personage you heard the bird with. If this happens, of course it's to be accepted, even welcomed ... but I think it not magic or sorcery. If you've made the wearisome effort together to hunt the bird and listen for it —through many disturbing circumstances— then that would surely encourage concordance between you. That's the inevitable. The logic.'

'Logic? Yawn!' said Miss Camlyn, 'Let's believe in the magic, yeah?'

'The folklore gives the bird a meaning above its utility and its bird book entry,' said Mr Bin, in scholastic brow. 'It helps us care about defending the natural world.'

'That birdy's so cute,' said Miss Camlyn.

We reposed further, there being no need for haste, Mr Summerberg not pressing us to refrain from sitting about like beach bums and the bird song already in the bag in Mr Summerberg's apparatus.

Miss Camlyn opened her mouth as if hit by a surprise. She gripped the arms of the Winchester. She sat up. 'That's why Grandad so desperately wanted to record the bird ... and wanted it played at his funeral!'

'Because it's ... cute?' I asked.

'He must have read the folklore. He must have known the story.'

She held her hands up to restrain any interruption, to give herself time to think.

'My rellies are all at each other's throats. They've all unfriended each other. My mother won't speak to her sister. My uncle's feuding with my aunt. My cousins are suing each other. But they'll all be together at Grandad's funeral.'

Mr Bin and I held ourselves still.

'Grandad must've been hoping they'd all make it up ... if they all heard the song together.' She lowered her gaze. 'My mother and I are hardly buddies.' She teared. 'I think it upset Grandad.'

Mr Bin and I nodded in slow, thoughtful concurrence.

'I'm going to tell them all at the funeral. I'm going to play the song. Then I'm going to tell them what Grandad wanted.'

Maybe I had been too hasty in my dismissal of the primitive

folklore recorded by Carter. Maybe it had power to move hearts and, in that way, to fulfil its prophesy. I so hoped so, despite my inclination to dismiss superstitions and fabricated yarns.

Miss Camlyn sat silent with a dazed and faraway look. I noted that, unlike her mother, there were no flecks of sulphur, or of black granite, in her eyes. Yes, she had a tender-hearted vision.

After a while, Mr Bin said to me. 'About names … what would you like me to call you? Then spell it for me.'

What would be my name in Akalat Adventures? My birth name was Savalamuratichimimozi, certainly too time consuming to say in a casual discourse even if Mr Bin took time out to study and practice it. Dorothea called me Sava, but it was hers alone for me. In London I had been named Mr Toothy, Mr Tooshy, Jeffman, Man and Tan. All not ideal, indeed all were careless, even unthinking. I saw that for the giver and speaker of a name, the name is the person, as bound to them as their face; and so it is not easy to turn from calling a man Bernard, to calling him Joseph: or Freddy to Caterpillar. Mr Bin had always called me Mozzy. That was the name that he had given me, and it was a name, I believed, which indicated a certain benign, even affectionate, designation.

'I'm happy for Mozzy.'

'Thank God … I can't imagine you as anyone else. I'm called Ben. B E N.'

'I'll practice,' I said. 'Bin.'

'Almost.'

My accent could be misheard. 'But whilst with guests,' I said, 'I insist on professionalism. I'll refer to you as Mr Bin and you'll refer to me as Chef Mlantushi.'

'The guests will love that,' said Miss Camlyn, dropping back in the Winchester again. 'I should know, I was one.'

'I acknowledge the need for deportment at work,' said Ben.

'My friends call me Ella,' said Miss Camlyn. 'I hate Chantella, and only Grandad was allowed to call me El.'

'Ella,' said Ben, practicing to himself.

So Ben, Ella and I raised our glasses brimming with home-made granadilla and mint cordial (a big deal with guests) to Akalat Adventures, to walking with guests on unadulterated ground, to the livings purposing in the wilds, to birds that sing, to superlative culinary creations, to good etiquette and to friendly relations. Yes, I had discerned that it was possible to arrive at my destiny in hand with others.

Why do we dream our dreams, I asked myself. A want for a better life? A changed life? Something more? But for Dorothea and me, our dreams were fantastical thinking. Mr Makata had been correct. We did not know what our dream would be, until it arrived. And Ella? She was the only one whose dream had not been a fantasy. *Not all who ask for the impossible are refused.* Ben? He had been dreamless during that year of my first employment. Even Ella could not find one in him. But now he was free to dream again.

I had been slow to understand my path and I had taken many false turns. I found myself constituting my own saying, which I did not verbalise out loud, to spare Ben's ears.

To become lost is to learn the way.

My phone rang.

Reception was crackling but I heard, 'It's Mr Fairbrother again here Mr Mlantushi. I don't want to press, but have you decided?'

I apologised for not yet ringing him back and drew breath to inform him of my decision to chef for Akalat Adventures, but then my breath stuck, seeing —a startling disclosure— Ben and Ella sitting pretty. We all sat pretty. But what if Ben and Ella quit due to unforeseen circumstances? What if Ella decided after a week of sweaty hottings in the sun and itchy nights from mosquitos, which made red hillocks on her smooth-as-butternut skin, that she did not love the bush enough? That the long and lazy grasses homed too many ticks. That the thorns in the tracks could pierce sandals. That she was at risk of fulminating septicaemia, gas gangrene, tetanic paralysis and pustular putrefaction, warned of by Ben when they first met. What if the poetry of nature became hard prose, as difficult as her heavy book *Purple Hornbill*? She had not shown an inclination to persistence. What if Ben decided he would upgrade to become a Doctor of Philosophy, a campus professor? They could both up those backwaters and pull out. They could hook-up and happy-couple anywhere. They had privileged passports. They could citizen in a place with safety-blanket welfare, high-tech healthcare, roads with white lines for lane keeping assistance. Would that not leave me abandoned in the over-the-horizon village, which the new President had no interest in? I might never escape. I might have to end my days in bicycle logistics for Mr Makata, financed by Pastor Cain, my wife's rapist, until I was apprehended by Mr Bambatiwe —eager to be associated with a successful prosecution— and jailed by the Justice.

True, I had changed. No? Yes, I had learnt. I had been chastised. I had made a good peace and loving relations with Dorothea. I had aided my employer, even been a friend-in-need to him. Had I not even befriended a little bird? But this one thing had not changed: still I was a small-time kitchen cook in the scrub of an African country. I was no further up the path of success than I had been when I left for London. I was square-oned.

And yet. And yet, was I not now content? Even merry and convivial? My ambition altered for the better, my thinking converted? Was I not re-purposed?

'Mr Mlantushi?'

What to say?

'Mr Mlantushi?'

This was surely the last of the three most singular days of my life. Number one: the Knightsbridge kitchen. Number two: the release of my bird. Three: today, this very day.

'Are you coming to help us, Mr Mlantushi? Hello?'

Mr Bin —I found it was brain-hurting me to rethink him as Ben, all sudden like that— had stood up and was trying to move the picnic table out of the sun. I needed to help. Sayings swirled in my mind, from where and from whom I could not tell.

A bird that flies off the earth and lands on an anthill is still on the ground.

What ground? Which anthill?

Birds sing not because they have answers, but because they have songs.

What possible assistance was that?

He who sprints after good fortune and success runs away from peace and love.

But what is good fortune? What is success?

Yes, what is success?

I, Head Chef Mlantushi, would vacillate no further. I would take the blessing.

Acknowledgements

A novel's characters, dialogue, scenarios and locations are invented for the purpose of the fiction, but an author takes tesserae of experience to create the mosaic of the novel. Thank you to both people and places that have gifted me those pieces. Some of the menus that Mozzy creates are to be found in Sarah Lilford's delightful book, *Dusty Road*. Thank you to the editors, book groups and writers who have given precious advice, especially to those who have encouraged me to write with humour.

About the Author

Andrew Sharp's novels include *The Ghosts of Eden*, set in Uganda, and *Fortunate*, set in Zimbabwe. *The Ghosts of Eden* won the 2010 Waverton Good Read Award and was shortlisted for the 2011 Rubery Book Award. He was brought up in East Africa and has worked in several countries in sub-Saharan Africa as a medical doctor. He is based in the East Midlands.

For exclusive discounts on Matador titles,
sign up to our occasional newsletter at
troubador.co.uk/bookshop